Demon's Dare

'What is it you expect of me?' I asked. The bells of the harness I'd been forced to wear shivered as I tried to jerk away from Franklin Harte's probing fingers . . . fingers that were producing a warm, sticky puddle in my chair.

'The woman I saw spreadeagled on her daddy's desk, coupling with her aunt's errand boy, shouldn't have to ask *that* question!' Harte's voice rose with the colour of his face, as though I were thoroughly testing his patience.

'Seduce Damon, for God's sake! Find a way to get his cock out of his pants and into *you*, Vanita! You're the last ace your foolish aunt had up her sleeve, so play yourself well. It's the only way you'll reclaim Wellspring. Desperate women take desparate measures.'

Franklin focused on me again, grasping a tuft of my pubic hair between his thumb and forefinger to emphasise his point. 'And you, dear Vanita, stand to lose it all: the house, the stables, the pastureland – unless you comply. Do I make myself clear?'

I wondered how I'd *prove* it, if Damon ever made love to me, but something warned me not to ask. 'Yes. Quite clear.'

'Yes, what?' Then he drove his finger inside me, making me squirm against the back of my chair.

I scowled and swatted at his hand. 'Yes, sir!'

Author's other Black Lace titles:
Devil's Fire

Readers can contact the author at:

melissa_macneal@hotmail.com
or visit her web site at:
www.melissamacneal.com

Demon's Dare

Melissa MacNeal

BLACK LACE

Black Lace books contain sexual fantasies.
In real life, always practise safe sex.

First published in 2002 by
Black Lace
Thames Wharf Studios
Rainville Road
London W6 9HA

Design by Smith & Gilmour, London
Printed and bound by Mackays of Chatham PLC

ISBN 0 352 33683 8

Contents

1 The Devil Himself

St Louis, Missouri. May 1895

As I entered the red brick building that housed classrooms and the headmistress, the scent of lemon wax enveloped me. I smiled at the girl who now polished the parlour's furniture, recalling my own fledgling days at Miss Purvey's School for Young Ladies. In a few weeks I would graduate! Fully prepared to be the mistress of my own fate, I would return to Wellspring to revive the legacy left me by my parents. Kentucky's finest racing horses would once again be bred in our stables, no matter what Aunt Lillian preferred! In two months, when I turned 21, the estate would be mine.

Meanwhile, Miss Purvey had summoned me, probably to untangle another financial knot. For three years I'd kept her ledgers – and kept her school afloat – because while the dear little woman could charm generous sums from alumni and other benefactors, she couldn't manage money to save her soul. I loved her almost as much as the mother I lost a decade ago. I owed her for educating me in the social graces, and for fostering my academic excellence as well.

Our replica of 'Winged Victory' sat on her pedestal where I turned towards the office. I found it odd that this statue stood as inspiration to us, since the poor thing was reduced to wings and a jutting bust – no arms for doing work, nor head for thinking. And as I strode down the polished hallway, I thought it odder still to hear laboured breathing. When a wail rang out,

I broke into a trot. Clara Purvey was a sturdy woman, not prone to the vapours or other female foolishness.

I stepped through her door and stopped. Miss Purvey sat sideways behind her lamplit desk, with her bottom thrust forward and her head thrown back against the chair. As she writhed, her topknot – which always sat askew, like a bad hat – resembled a rider about to be thrown from an unruly mount. Her shelflike bosom pointed towards the ceiling in twin peaks that strained against her grey dress. She shook all over, yet her moan suggested something other than pain.

Staring, I realised the hand that had flown to my chest was now cupping one of my own modest peaks. It was my duty to investigate Miss Purvey's unusual behaviour without interrupting or embarrassing her. Dozens of times she'd called me in over the years, but I'd never seen such a fit of quivering.

So, to preserve her dignity and mine, I slipped outside, into a courtyard shaded by ancient trees, and stepped between the rhododendron bushes beside her open window. My jaw dropped. Invisible from the doorway, a young man crouched between the headmistress's legs. Miss Purvey's skirts were raised to her waist, revealing pale thighs above her black stockings. With her knees bent over the rogue's shoulders and her sensible shoes swinging rhythmically, she presented a most unladylike picture! Yet her expression bespoke a bliss like I'd never witnessed, on a face turned pink with passion.

Passion! I gripped the windowsill, unable to look away from details made startlingly clear by her lamp's light. The man's head bobbed faster, his dark waves bouncing with each thrust of his tongue. With slender fingers he had parted Miss Purvey's coarse curls to expose rose-coloured lips glistening with dew. His thumb circled the plump nub above her slit, and as he lapped and licked and drove into her, the woman's whimpers rose in a desperate crescendo.

Slick liquid slithered down my thighs. Was it the afternoon heat or was I inflamed by my spying? As the man's movements quickened, his other hand fumbled with his trouser buttons, although he didn't miss a beat with Miss Purvey. I'd seen the stablehands unbutton before, relieving themselves behind the barns, but I wasn't prepared for the long, thick shaft that poked out of this man's pants. The spasms that grabbed me between the legs made me gasp and rock forward.

The man turned, still circling Miss Purvey's privates with one thumb while grasping his impressive erection. I'd seen many a thoroughbred stand at stud, but this fellow rivalled the finest of them – and he was pointing it at me, with a cheeky leer that said he knew exactly how well endowed he was. Like a tom-cat he licked the cream from his black moustache, assessing me. His grin looked downright wicked, framed by a beard trimmed to fit his chin. On any other male, his tousled curls would've seemed childish, but this man, drawn in dark, devilish detail, appeared bold and knowing. Almost sinister.

He'd read my thoughts.

I blushed furiously, but I couldn't pull my gaze from his hypnotic eyes. Nor could I speak and disturb Miss Purvey. Thank goodness she was too caught up in his attentions to notice me gawking through her window! With pudgy fingers, she guided his head between her legs again. He complied as though putting on a show for my benefit, grasping the halves of her backside and burrowing into her inflamed flesh. She shrieked, convulsing until I thought her chair might shatter from hitting the floor so hard, in such a rapid tattoo . . . until I thought I'd fall through the window for want of similar satisfaction.

But he wasn't finished with her. 'Hold yourself open,' he commanded hoarsely, standing so his pants fell about his ankles. 'Farther!'

Miss Purvey's eyes widened to saucer size. He was fondling himself, aiming his plum-coloured head at her dripping sex. 'But Miss Wells will be here any moment!'

'You know my terms, Miss Purvey. The client always comes first, but the Devil demands his due,' he replied slyly. He stood taut, stroking himself with his thumb and forefinger. 'If you want me to keep your secret, you'd better open that hot little hole. You know how you love to watch me come, Clara. See how my cock's throbbing, eager for release? I'm going to shoot like a geyser. Going to gush all over that hungry cunt until –'

'Oh, Pearce, now! Do it *now*, love!'

Just as the headmistress parted her folds, panting, the swain before her cut loose with a cream-coloured stream. Sucking air between his clenched teeth, he pumped again and again, spewing his seed over her sex and on to the fingers flexing around it. Miss Purvey's head fell back and she brought herself to another writhing climax while her lover spent himself.

The headmistress exhaled, her breasts quivering with a final aftershock. Then, smiling primly, she offered him a lace handkerchief from her desk drawer. 'I'll miss you, Mr Truman.'

'You've given me a mission, and I'll return when I've carried it out.'

'Let's hope Vanita cooperates, so you'll ... come again. Sooner, rather than later.' Her coy smile befitted a preacher's wife more than a woman wiping up after a quick tryst. 'She's a dear girl. Contrary at times, but you'll take her best interests to heart, I trust.'

'I'll take her interests and anything else she offers. I'm insatiable that way, you know.'

As Miss Purvey turned to laugh with him, I darted away from the window. Should I believe what I was seeing? My headmistress, that most proper model for young ladies, had taken up with a handsome cad who'd accepted me as some sort of assignment. His ego was as impressive as his privates, I'd grant him that. But forewarned is forearmed. I would *not* be losing my bloomers for him the way Miss Purvey had!

I leaned against the building, hidden in the shade of old oaks, to reign in my wild thoughts while the pair inside pulled themselves together. The headmistress had summoned me for a purpose other than the one I walked in on. Mr Truman had an ulterior motive, too, and I didn't trust him. Not one lick, so to speak.

Yet when I knocked on the office door a few minutes later, all was in order. Miss Purvey, perched on her chair with her hands folded on her desk, was the image of proper decorum when our eyes met. A well-dressed gentleman stood at the window, gazing at her courtyard garden as though visiting Eden before the snake beguiled Eve.

'You asked for me?' I began, searching for signs of their illicit behaviour. Except for a musky undertone, the room and its occupants were keeping the secret.

'Please sit down, dear. This is Mr Truman, and I'm afraid he has distressing news.'

A tremor ran up my spine as I took the seat she gestured towards. A quake of a different sort raced through me when Pearce Truman turned, reaching for my hand. Although his eyes were rimmed in deep green, their large obsidian pupils held me entranced. 'What a pleasure to meet you, Miss Wells,' he crooned in a flowing baritone. 'I only wish it were under happier circumstances.'

They were playing the game beautifully, whatever it was. Still, in his feline eyes I caught the hint: he knew what I'd seen, and I'd pay dearly if Miss Purvey found out about it. His hand closed around mine, and I felt my heart galloping wildly beneath my breasts.

I cleared my throat, holding his gaze. 'And what circumstances are we talking about, Mr Truman? Miss Purvey has taught us to make the best of whatever ... comes before us.'

His hand tightened while his eyes flickered at my turn of phrase. 'Your Aunt Lillian is gravely ill, Miss Wells. She's asked me to escort you home.'

I didn't believe him. But what could I say that wouldn't alert Miss Purvey to my spying? 'What's happened? Why hasn't Clive Reilly come to fetch me?'

Smooth as glass, Miss Purvey produced a letter from her desk. 'Your daddy's attorney is concerned enough that he's staying at the house, watching after Miss Lillian. He's informed me that you won't be returning to school –'

'But I'm to graduate!'

'– because Wellspring will need a mistress,' she insisted, although her voice shook. 'This is your destiny, Vanita. Your dream. A piece of parchment couldn't possibly make you more worthy of assuming the reins at Wellspring. I'll miss you, dear, but I'm so very proud of what you've accomplished with us.'

Her tears attested to this, and I believed what she said – as far as it went. After all, why would she lie about the future and the horse farm that were rightfully mine? Truth be told, I felt worse about leaving Miss Purvey than I did about Aunt Lillian's illness. Mama's younger sister had been my guardian since a lightning bolt orphaned me at eleven, but I'd never liked her. Lillian Gilding had insisted I stay at school for the past several holidays, and had always made me feel inconvenient. Probably because taking charge of me had ended her acting career.

So now she'd sent this disreputable rake to fetch me, knowing her untimely illness would end the education Mama insisted upon with her last breath – the schooling Lillian considered exorbitant, even though it had gotten me out of her way these past six years.

There was no refuting Clive Reilly's inimitable, angular penmanship, however. His letter was concise, explaining to the headmistress that I was needed at home to carry out my duties as a niece and an heiress. My deceased parents would expect such a show of responsibility, in light of the way Aunt Lillian had reared me in their place. He regretted any inconvenience this caused, yet insisted upon my immediate return. The attorney sounded exactly as he had when advising Daddy about legalities of the horse trade: as crisp as new currency and irrefutable as death. No doubt Aunt Lillian would be glad to see the old scarecrow leave, even if it meant tolerating me.

'Well, then,' I sighed, my thoughts in a jumble. 'I suppose I should pack my things.'

'Be quick about it, Miss Wells. We meet our steamer in two hours.'

2 The Serpent Slithers In

'Can you believe that man's arrogance? Demanding that I pack up and leave my life here to accommodate *his* schedule! I'll show that bastard who he's working for now!'

Poor Aggie stood wringing her hands as I flung my underthings into a valise. My roommate had rarely witnessed my wrath – or language befitting a stable-hand – and she was as distressed about my sudden departure as I.

'I – I don't know what to say, Vanita. I'm sorry your aunt's fallen ill before you can finish,' she whimpered. 'And surely Miss Purvey should arrange for a chaper-one, even if this Mr Truman weren't so disagreeable. You'll be travelling with him for three days!'

Bless Agatha Whitmore for reminding me that proper etiquette will see us through the most disagree-able circumstances. I stopped packing to hug her. 'I was too stunned to think of that! Would you be a dear and remind Miss Purvey that a travelling companion is in order? I'd be pleased if *you* could accompany me, Aggie, for who knows when we might see each other again?'

She nodded tearfully, as relieved to have a task as I was to give her one. I needed time alone to digest what I'd seen and heard in the headmistress's office – details I could never shock the proper Miss Whitmore with – and to plan my strategy. A wicked little flame flickered within me at the thought of giving Pearce Truman his comeuppance, but I couldn't think clearly while my cow-eyed companion hovered nearby.

As I went to the attic for my largest trunk, I reconsidered my options. I prided myself on my ability to act rather than to cower and cry; a fortitude learned from Daddy, which allowed me to manoeuvre my cumbersome luggage back to my room without seeking assistance. I could hide, or baulk at Truman's impertinence, but what would that accomplish? I could insist on staying for my diploma, but if Aunt Lillian died, the affairs at Wellspring would become even more entangled than I suspected they already were.

So I would go home, using the journey by steamboat and stagecoach to pry as much information from Mr Truman as I could. Those demanding eyes held secrets I was determined to learn ... secrets he seemed eager to reveal in earthy, personal ways. In my years at finishing school, I'd met the cream of Southern male gentility under the watchful eyes of society, but I'd learned far more about men from their stolen kisses and after-curfew rendezvous than at any formal ball. Jockeys and stablehands had been my unwitting teachers, as well, while I peeked through their keyholes or listened in on conversations about breeding our horses, or our housemaids.

I grinned, leaning over my trunk to pack my loveliest lavender gown. I was by no means a wanton, but I knew how to dangle a carrot in front of a hungry stud and get him to do my bidding.

Two hands grabbed my backside and I gasped. I turned to catch Pearce Truman choking back his laughter. His mirth took ten years from his face and rendered him almost boyish, except for that moustache: closely trimmed, it glistened as black as a raven's wing and clung to the downward curve around his mouth, to meet the narrow beard that followed his jawline to a sinister point at his chin. Noting the direction of my gaze, he smiled, like a snake mesmerising its prey. 'Enjoying the view?' he whispered.

I backed out of his grasp. 'Who do you think you are, Mr Truman? First you accost –'

'Please call me Pearce. It's what I do best.'

'– Miss Purvey, the most *decent* soul on the –'

'It's a point of honour with me, Miss Wells,' he interrupted sternly. He raised his hand as though to grip my chin, but I took another step backwards. 'I never force myself upon anyone. I simply give women what they want, usually because they're begging me for it.'

'Is that so?' I demanded, hoping my bravado compensated for the fact that I'd backed myself against the open armoire. 'Pearce True-Man, are you? Now there's a made-up name if I ever heard one!'

He took a step towards me, his expression pensive. 'I suppose it is. The Sisters at the orphanage had to call me something, after my mother left me at their doorstep.'

'You're an orphan, too? You never knew your mother?'

I should've been smarter than to soften before a serpent in gentlemen's clothing. Pearce closed the space between us, taking the knobs of the armoire doors in either hand. Stepping up and back, I eluded him by slipping between the dresses still hanging there, knowing I was at his mercy ... frightened, yet wildly excited by his predatory expression. The closet's dimness made his eyes shine like a demon's.

'She left me there, saying she had no milk and eleven more at home she couldn't feed,' he continued softly.

He stepped in with me, ducking his head, which put him so close his warm breath tickled my lips. The click of the latch plunged us into total darkness. Crushed among my clothes, all I heard was his even breathing and my own pulse, skittering like a spooked mare. The male scent of him mingled with my sachets as the silence stretched into unbearable anticipation.

'I always felt she did me a favour, giving me to the Sisters of Charity,' he murmured. 'I quickly became the darling of the convent. The nuns loved me too much to let anyone else adopt me, when I showed a penchant for nestling against their pillowy bosoms.'

I sucked in my breath when his hands found my own soft mounds.

'And perhaps it explains my fascination for breasts – a sense of searching for my mother, trying to compensate for what she deprived me of at birth.'

With incredible finesse, Pearce slipped his fingers into my scooped neckline. I barely had time to whimper before his teeth found my front buttons and his warm hands splayed downwards into my camisole.

'No corset?' he whispered, nuzzling my flesh. 'I love a woman who defies society!'

My protest came out as a moan, echoing inside the armoire, as he deftly lifted my breasts out of my unfastened bodice. When I inhaled to scream, he kissed me hard on the mouth. Lush lips took total control of mine, probing in rhythm with the hands that explored my breasts. His thumbs found their two tingling peaks and he flicked his nails across them once, twice, until I squirmed in excruciating pleasure. Pearce leaned into me, pressing me against the back of the armoire with his thigh between my knees and a ramrod erection jabbing my abdomen. Slowly he lowered his lips, scorching my skin with heated kisses as he made his way to my chest.

When he sucked a nipple into his mouth, I cried out. Truman wasn't the first to fondle me, but he threw me into a frenzy like I'd never known. Long and hard he suckled, distending my nipple until I imagined it must be nearly an inch long from the suction his tongue created. I writhed against him like a marionette whose strings were all attached between her legs, from the inside, where a fierce desire set me twitching.

Tonguing my sensitive flesh, he switched to the other breast, still kneading with an exquisite force I didn't want to resist. Deep inside me, the pressure mounted until I thought I'd erupt, like an overfilled tea kettle set to boiling. Pearce must have sensed this, for one hand then snatched up my skirts so he could cup my sex.

'Pearce, we mustn't!' I whimpered, all sense of reason leaving me.

'Mustn't what?' he breathed against my ear. 'You might as well know what sort of man you'll be travelling with. Why should Miss Purvey get all the attention?'

'But when Aggie – She'll hear us banging around in here!'

'And isn't banging a marvellous pastime?' he quipped. Oblivious to the commotion he caused, Pearce kept squeezing my nether lips with a hand that had sprouted a wayward finger. It found the slit of my drawers and then slid along a crevice so wet we created a slippery, sucking sound between us. When he found the hard little nub at the front, he swallowed my scream with a deep kiss. My hips bucked and hot liquid ran in rivulets down my thighs.

The armoire was rocking but I was too desperate to care. Driven by Pearce's masterful kiss, I let his animal passion overtake me; one stroking finger became two, and then they drove up inside me with powerful thrusts that sent me reeling so intensely I nearly blacked out. Gasping for air, I clung to my captor's shoulders as a chain reaction of spasms claimed my body, my sanity. As I gave in to the madness, I cried out and then collapsed against the back wall.

After a few panting moments, the secretive, silken whisper of my gowns reminded me where I was and what I was supposed to be doing. What if Aggie had come back? What if she flung open the doors to see if I'd fallen into the armoire while suffering some sort of seizure?

That's exactly what you did, fool! You've already succumbed, and given Truman the upper hand. 'This is precisely why I sent my roommate to request a chaperone!' I protested, but it sounded weak even to me.

Pearce chuckled and gently disengaged himself. 'You're just as Reilly said you'd be, Vanita. A scrappy little thing who wouldn't give in without a fight. I admire that in a woman.'

In the dark, airless armoire, I couldn't see his expression, but he couldn't be serious! I hadn't fought him at all. I'd simply let down my guard and then let him take advantage of me!

'And what else did Daddy's attorney say?' I muttered. 'I can't believe he's sitting at Aunt Lillian's bedside, putting her welfare ahead of mine! And what position do you hold, that he'd send you to fetch me?'

'A fetching position indeed,' he teased, chuckling at the smacking of my sex lips when he removed his hand. 'He was right again when he said you could fend for yourself, and hold your own with a stranger. Also asserted that you've been an incurable flirt since birth – points in your favour, as I see it. Almost as alluring as the ones sticking out above your dress.'

With an exasperated moan, I fumbled to make myself presentable again, which was nearly impossible with a ravenous panther still breathing down my neck. I could only hope the buttons of my bodice found their correct holes and that my hair wasn't too badly mussed from rubbing the wall behind me. My drawers were soaked, filling the closet with the telltale aroma of my climax.

'Your secret's safe with me,' Pearce whispered as he fumbled for the catch in the doors. He caught my hand and placed it against the hard shaft hidden in his pants. 'I can't wait until we're alone in the steamer cabin. I know you'll repay this favour, even though you firmly believe you'll never succumb to me again.'

How had he read my thoughts? When the two doors opened out, allowing light and fresh air to find us, my first instinct was to move away from this presumptuous – yet dangerously perceptive – man. Then I'd snatch fresh drawers from my valise and cleanse myself in the water closet, before anyone else saw me in this dishevelled state. Aggie would faint dead away if she had any idea what I'd been doing in her absence!

A little gasp froze me in place as Truman backed out of the armoire. And when he stepped down, my heart thudded heavily in my chest: both Agatha and Miss Purvey stood gaping at us, not eight feet away. The headmistress's bosom and topknot shook, but I didn't think it was indignation causing her to stare. My roommate, however, appeared completely aghast, as though the devilish man before her were a magician emerging from his cabinet after performing unthinkable tricks upon me. Her cheeks were flooded with the shame I should've felt, and for the first time I couldn't think of a thing to say to her.

As though nothing felt awkward or unseemly, Mr Truman bowed slightly to the two onlookers and then reached back to assist me. My face was flushed from my exertions, and as I stepped out of the armoire, feigning propriety, I realised my dress was still hiked up on one side. Pearce grinned. He was enjoying this little drama at Miss Purvey's School for Young Ladies, just as he'd gratified his early urges among the Sisters of Charity.

'Although I respect your intentions, I think you ladies can see Miss Wells is in capable hands, with no need of a chaperone,' he said with a debonair smile.

I bit my lip against a retort. He'd been eavesdropping! He'd known where Aggie was going and had used her errand as a chance to insinuate himself, thinking I'd be unable to speak against him! I had, after all, spied upon him first, and then allowed him to take liberties. I'd trapped myself with my own devious behaviour, as surely as Mr Truman had allowed me to.

Yet when Miss Purvey opened her mouth to speak, he deftly used the same tactic upon her, the woman he'd pleasured so thoroughly not an hour ago. 'Forgive me if I sound insensitive or impertinent,' he crooned, 'but we've a boat to catch and a gravely ill woman to attend to. If you'll excuse us, we'll be on our way as soon as we complete Vanita's packing.'

What could Miss Purvey say? This was partly her doing – and I vowed to grill Pearce every waking moment of our journey home, until I knew *exactly* what was going on. With a tight smile, the headmistress guided Agatha Whitmore into the hallway, leaving me no chance for an explanation or a proper goodbye. It stung that my dear friend's final impression of me would be as scarlet as my face.

But we'd all learned first-hand that Pearce Truman would have his way.

As though divining my thoughts once again, the rogue beside me chuckled. 'Discovering the lay of the land these next few days will be quite exciting. Don't you agree, Vanita?'

3 The Deception Unfolds

I'd barely caught my breath when Pearce pounded on the door adjoining our two steamship cabins. After my humiliation at school and the hurried hackney ride to the pier on the Mississippi, the last thing I wanted was another conversation barbed with double-talk. Truman was the randiest braggart I'd ever met! So why was I surprised when I opened the door to find him stark raving naked?

And *raving* was the only word for that pole he stroked. I'd been impressed by its size when it poked out of his pants in Miss Purvey's office, but full daylight gave me a new appreciation for the appendage jutting between his room and mine.

'Penny for your thoughts,' he murmured.

I could've slammed the door on that pecker he was so proud of. 'I think you're the most outrageous, underhanded bastard I've ever met, and I want no part of you!'

'Now there's a lie if ever I heard one.' Pearce stepped through the doorway, giving me no choice but to retreat further into my room. 'At least you can't accuse me of slipping an ace up my sleeve or keeping my feelings for you to myself. Perhaps –'

'Feelings for *me*? Let's ask Miss Purvey about that!'

'– you're too young to realise it, but most men are notorious for cheating and secrets, Vanita,' he continued earnestly. 'I'm showing myself freely and without reserve. Every inch of me, open for your inspection.'

'You think I'm going to drop my drawers, just because you've got a prick like a percheron?'

'Only a matter of time, my sweet. You swagger when you talk – and your quick wit made your daddy proud, didn't it? But you're a filly in heat, Vanita. I'll wager my pay that *you'll* be mounting *me* before I get you back to Wellspring.'

Damn the man, he knew how I loved a challenge! But he was also opening the door to the discussion we needed to have. 'Who are you?' I demanded again. 'No funny stuff or sidestepping.'

He raised his arms in feigned exasperation. 'I've told you, Miss Wells. My name's Pearce Truman, and I've been sent to fetch you home.'

The gesture tightened his entire body, making him the finest example of masculinity I'd ever seen – although his stricken expression parodied Christ's on the cross. While he didn't flex the hardened muscles of a field hand, the dusky planes of his chest and abdomen, accented by well-placed patches of black hair, attested to a strength as primitive as a panther's. A drop of cream topped his plum-coloured head, so I felt it best to look him in the eye. 'And how do you know my Aunt Lillian?'

'I was summoned to the mansion to meet her. I'm no doctor, but her skin was a ghastly yellow – jaundiced, perhaps – and she could barely raise her head from the pillow.' He paused, his intense gaze swallowing me whole. 'If I believed Lillian Gilding would survive until you graduated, I would've insisted you receive your diploma. I admire the way you've trained yourself in account-keeping and the skills needed to maintain Wellspring, Vanita.'

I blinked, sensing a sincere compliment. 'Thank you. It's rare for a man to applaud my success – except for Daddy, of course. He taught me to believe I could accomplish anything I set out to. All my life, I've wanted nothing except to carry on his fine tradition of breeding and racing Kentucky thoroughbreds.'

With a slight bow, Pearce reached for my hand. It was quite unsettling, standing so close to a naked man that I could feel the heat radiating from his body. His erection swayed, as though sniffing out a hot, wet hiding place, but I reminded myself not to think of such things. If I were to glean the information I needed, I had to focus on words rather than deeds. The image of Miss Purvey writhing in her chair, at the mercy of this man's tongue, made me quiver in spite of my best efforts to maintain control.

'So why did Aunt Lill send *you*? Even if Mr Reilly is playing caretaker, one of the hands could've come for me.'

Truman shifted. 'I'm not yet privy to the details, but I suspect the hired men have left.'

Such awful thoughts had occurred to me, when Aunt Lillian kept finding reasons for me not to go home, but I'd tried to deny them. Was Pearce lying? As he awaited my reply, he ran long fingers through that cap of overgrown curls, his hunger growing more apparent.

'You're saying Mr Reilly's the only one there with her?'

'I recall mention of a Lorena, but I never saw her.'

'Mama's maid. Puts up with Aunt Lill only because her brother managed our stables for years. But if Will's gone . . .'

Pearce rubbed my hand between both of his – such long, dextrous fingers he had – yet he'd once again slipped my harness. 'You still haven't told me why my aunt chose *you* to bring her exiled niece home, Mr Truman. I'm going to keep asking, you know.'

'Persistence is another of your strengths,' he observed, fixing those mystical eyes on mine. 'All right, then, it was Clive who suggested I come. I've assisted with his casework before.'

'So you're an attorney?'

'Not exactly.'

His tone brooked no argument as he wrapped my hand around his erection. I gasped, more from the sensation of touching him there than from the blatant way he was again diverting my attention. His skin, a thin velvet sheath, radiated a heat that throbbed as he tightened his grip around mine. Slowly up and then slowly down he moved, until I was either nudging his slick pink tip or nestling against the downy set of testicles that bulged between his thighs. I licked my lips. My pulse was accelerating with his, as it had when he'd backed me into the armoire.

'Do you like to humiliate your clients, Mr Truman?' I demanded, although the quaver in my voice belied my interest in him.

'Only if they enjoy it. But I've assured your daddy's attorney – and your headmistress – that I'll deliver you safely home with your virtue intact.'

I fought a snicker. What sort of man says *that* after he's groped a woman's body, and then entered her room undressed? Yet Pearce had set aside his arrogance now, calmly folding his arms at his chest. 'I'm confused,' I mumbled. 'What exactly are you trying to prove?'

'I'm a man of my word, Vanita. A man of restraint, who honours his employer's wishes,' he explained quietly. 'I'm also the sort who protects a woman's reputation and remains in control, despite great temptation and desire. Because you're to inherit a grand estate, it's in my best interests to prove my trustworthiness without taking undue advantage of you.'

'*That's* why you came naked?' His erection showed no sign of ebbing. If anything, Pearce's throbbing grew so pronounced I wondered if he was about to erupt again.

'Have I taken my own pleasure, Vanita? My intentions may have seemed less than honourable when I fondled you in the armoire, but I've proven my ability to give without receiving. I've been aroused ever since we met, but I'm walking away. Unsatisfied.'

He kissed me, removing his member from my grasp. I felt like a little girl in a candy store who's had a peppermint stick snatched away, supposedly for her own good. 'But *why*?'

Truman turned at the door, his smile an enigma. 'I want you to believe in me, Vanita. I want your trust. Unexpected circumstances often surface when an estate passes from one generation to the next, and I want you to turn to me when all else fails you.'

When the door closed behind him, I shivered with a powerful foreboding. Pearce Truman had visited Wellspring recently, and had no reason to misrepresent what he'd seen. He had indeed displayed monumental control – he'd been bone-hard all the way across town to the pier – yet he was still the randy wolf who'd lapped at Miss Purvey and then put me in a compromising position for the fun of it.

My drawers were sticking to me again, while my nipples shoved painfully against my taut bodice. I was not as untutored as he assumed: I knew quite well that Pearce Truman was a cat toying with a mouse. I had grown up at a girls' school, because my parents suspected my wayward inclinations even when I was young, and had tried to preserve my reputation until I was old enough to become the mistress of Wellspring.

But that didn't mean I'd followed their rules. Or Miss Purvey's.

I stood in the middle of my room, feeling the tilt and sway of the steamer as it plied the Mississippi, hearing the sailors' voices above, while the constant thrum of the steam engines underscored my every thought. For the next two days, I'd be on my own: I was no longer a student at the School for Young Ladies, nor had I yet taken the reins of my estate. In the adjoining room sat a fascinating man, far superior to the young swains who'd fawned for my favours between partners on my dance cards. He radiated lust yet talked restraint; he deftly drove me to the shattering point and then turned away unsated.

He wanted my trust.

Nipping my lip, I glanced towards the door between our rooms. My fingers, of their own accord, fumbled with the buttons of my dress. As it puddled around my ankles, I cupped my swollen breasts and breathed his name. I was quite aware that he'd set this alluring trap with one purpose. I was equally aware that I should allow him his honour and his best intentions, to prove myself as upstanding as he.

But who was I fooling? His heat still warmed my palm, driving my fingers between my legs in imitation of his own. It wasn't the same, however, without his lush lips pressing into mine and the tickle of his wicked moustache. And once we arrived at Wellspring, I might not have the opportunity to answer the question that smouldered in my soul: how would it feel to have Pearce Truman buried inside me? He was huge and smooth and hot, so eager to please it seemed selfish not to repay the favour – just as he'd predicted I would.

Oh, he knew me well, that man. And as I pictured him sitting in his room, facing the door, naked and stroking himself in anticipation, I finished undressing. Never had I so brazenly approached a man, for when had there been such a temptation as Truman? He was a far cry from the stablehands and trainers who'd eyed me at home, and he knew things about women ...

things that drove them insane with pleasure. He'd insisted on protecting my reputation, but I knew his ruse. Two could play this game!

I crossed the small room, liquid silk slickening my thighs, and threw open our common door. He would thank me for relieving him of his burden – my virtue. He'd be delighted that I saw through his better intentions and was so ready to mount him!

But the room stood empty.

I looked around, sensing another trick. I checked beneath the bunk and inside the small armoire. 'Damn you, Pearce, show yourself!'

No answer. Only the slap-slapping of the sternwheeler's paddle, and the braying laugh of a sailor from the deck. Or was it?

How he'd eluded me, I hadn't a clue. To spite him, I snatched the pillow from his neatly made bunk and folded it between my legs. Kneeling on his mattress, I humped and rubbed myself into enough of a frenzy to come all over his pillowcase – and then, so I couldn't miss him, I took a nap in his bed, swayed to sleep by the steamer's rocking. I took up residence in his room, in fact, feeling angrier and more frustrated with each hour of his absence. My tour of the ship's nooks and crannies the next morning yielded nothing, either, as though he'd evaporated like the spray churned up behind the boat. I couldn't even find his luggage.

I despised being made a fool of. Pearce would pay dearly for this.

He awaited me at the end of the gangplank when we docked in Louisville. 'Good afternoon, Miss Wells,' he said with a sly smile. 'I've hired us a driver, and we'll be on our way as soon as he loads your luggage. I trust you've had a pleasant, restful trip so far?'

I strode past him without a word. And when Truman

slipped on to the carriage seat beside me, thumping on the ceiling to signal our driver, I moved to the opposite side. Why should I open myself to further ridicule? Or anything he might conjure up with those magician's hands?

After the initial lurch of the carriage, we settled into a silence punctuated only by the clip-clopping of hooves and the singing of the wheels against the street. I gazed out the window so intently my neck went stiff, but I refused to look at him or to speak first. Instead, I focused on the rolling green countryside I loved and had missed while away at school. Fine, sleek horses grazed this pastureland, which extended as far as I could see, into a horizon of heavenly blue. The air smelled sweet, like grass and recent rain, as the sun's rays warmed my face.

'Your hair fascinates me,' he began in a low voice. 'Like spun sunshine, with streaks of starlight and gold. I can't wait to see it spread over my pillow. Or cascading like a silk curtain, closing out the rest of the world when you make love to me.'

I crossed my arms, intent on the passing scenery.

'I bet it's the same lovely shade between your legs. Isn't it, Vanita?' he whispered. 'Soft as the down of a baby chick when I stroke it ... then part it with my fingertips, to tongue your honey when you open yourself to me. It won't be long now.'

'Forget it. You had your chance.' I shifted, wishing my pulse would behave itself.

'I apologise for leaving you with only my pillow for a friend. I was helping you keep my promise, you know,' Pearce crooned. 'Once I deliver you to Wellspring, we'll indulge in all the pleasure you can handle. I'll fuck you night and day until you beg me to stop.'

Much as I tried to ignore him, he was the first man to ever direct that deliciously forbidden word at me.

Heat surged through all those places I was hoping not to notice.

'How do you like it best, my sweet?' the man across the carriage went on. His voice had settled into a mesmerising timbre I tried to shut out, even as my hips twitched against the leather seat. 'Lying back with your legs spread, perhaps? Or straddling my lap, to ride me?'

'If it's my virtue you're protecting, why would I know the answer to that?' I snapped. 'You're very rude, Mr Truman. If this is how you treat Mr Reilly's clients, how do you keep your position with him?'

'Clive would assume any position I told him to.'

I choked, startled by the image of the skinny-limbed lawyer getting it from *anyone*. 'I'll pass that sentiment along when I see him. I'm sure it'll endear you to him further.'

'He's not my type.' Pearce shrugged, smiling as though he discussed such subjects with women every day. 'I'd much rather speculate about the fireworks you and I will create, Vanita. In my fantasies, I enter you from behind, easing my cock into your hot, wet pussy, and then pumping you until we both scream for release. When you knelt on my bed with your backside pointed at the window, I had to bite my fist so no one would hear me panting.'

'You watched! Have you no decency at all?'

'Damn little, I'm afraid.'

'And you were ... handling yourself? Out there on the deck? While you *spied* on me?'

'So you're aware of such things,' he murmured, scooting forwards on his seat. 'I thought so, considering the nature of horse breeding. You'll soon learn, however, that even if you've had several men, you've not made love until you've coupled with me.'

I laughed at his arrogance, but his expression made me suck in my breath. His gaze locked into mine with eyes so darkly dubious, so ominously promising, I couldn't talk. The corner of his mouth twitched, rippling his beard and moustache, drawing my attention to full lips that parted so he could lick them with the pink tip of his tongue. His ebony curls dared me to spear my fingers through them as I pressed my mouth to his. Dressed all in black, Pearce Truman defied social convention – defied decency – by looking so blatantly carnal. He gripped his thighs, his fingers tight and white against his black pants, and then drew his hands upwards so I couldn't miss the bulge behind his fly. It moved, as though an animal in there wanted out.

'Ask and you shall receive, Vanita.'

I was beyond being embarrassed that he could read me so easily. Fact was, I was squirming to relieve the ache between my legs, despite my determination not to humour this decadent devil.

'You realise, of course, that you'll arrive home uncompromised if I merely pay you ... lip service. Miss Purvey would approve, don't you think?'

His silken voice, and the subtle rubbing of his splayed hands, and those images of the headmistress, proved my undoing. After all, men staunchly believed sex hadn't happened unless they'd dipped their sticks into the honey pot. Licking and sucking were permissible, so long as everyone came away sated. It seemed a philosophy worth adopting, since we had several hours before we reached Wellspring.

Uncrossing my ankles, I reached for my hem with both hands. Slowly I raised the layers of green serge and the ivory silk petticoats beneath my suit, revealing my ankles and then my calves. Just above my knees, my dark stockings stopped – and so did I, when a hint of pink thigh showed. Pearce watched as though entranced, which I found gratifying. Lord knows how many women he'd coaxed down this path, after all.

'Enjoying the view?' I mimicked in a hoarse whisper.

'God, yes. Slide forward and I'll remove your bloomers. Let's keep them dry this time.'

'Sorry, but I can't do that.'

Pearce glanced up. 'But I've assured you –'

I thrust my bottom to the edge of the leather seat yanking up my skirts as I spread my legs. The man across from me laughed and sprang forwards to crouch in front of me. 'Vanita, you wicked girl! What would Miss Purvey say if she knew you'd left off your drawers?'

My laughter rose into a moan with the first touch of his tongue. Pearce was all over me, exploring my warm skin and the secret, wet folds we both wanted him to lick. I hooked the heel of one shoe against the window frame and placed my other leg over his shoulder. In and out he plunged, like a cat lapping a saucer of warm, sweet cream. He followed the edge of my hairline with his tongue's tip, tickling mercilessly before settling on the hot little nub above my slit.

Sucking it into his mouth, he then rubbed my clit with a friction that drove me delirious. I writhed, slipping my fingers around his head. Up and down I coaxed him, and he accelerated with my need, anticipating the liquor that oozed from inside me. His fingertips were parting my folds, opening me wider to receive the full brunt of his tongue.

'Pearce ... Pearce, *please*, I want you inside me. NOW.'

A stealthy thumb slipped into me and I heard him unfastening his pants. 'You can see it and touch it, but that's all.'

I smiled, having other ideas. 'Deeper,' I wheezed,

gasping with the force of the two, then three fingers he inserted.

Still rocking me against the back of the seat, he stood to let his trousers fall free of his cock. It pointed at me like a pistol, shiny and reddish-purple and already bubbling with cream. 'Do you want to suck it?' he rasped.

'I want you to slip it inside me first. I've never tasted ... myself.'

'Next time,' he breathed, wagging his eyebrows devilishly. Then he ran his slick middle finger over my pussy lips before sliding it suggestively into my mouth. 'How's this?'

I closed my eyes as I tongued his finger, mainly to distract him while I grasped his swollen shaft. It felt hot in my palm, with his lifeblood throbbing in the vein along its underside. Through my slitted eyelids I watched Pearce rocking, eyes closed in the ecstasy of my massage, and then I arched upwards to catch my prize. When the tip of him slid across the wet flesh of my sex, he jerked to attention.

'Little feist!' he murmured. 'I adore your spunk, but this time we play by my rules.'

He grasped the outsides of my thighs, laying me lengthwise along the carriage seat, and then raised me higher to pump between my pressed-together legs. Each stroke brought his engorged tip into view, while rubbing my sex relentlessly, yet prevented penetration. Faster he thrust, stroking my clitoris until the spirals of desire rose to dizzying heights. I climaxed with a howl, shuddering so hard I thought we might knock the seat loose. Then Pearce braced himself, gripping me harder as he grimaced. Pale cream spewed above me, splattering the upholstery.

Apparently the driver was accustomed to such behaviour in his coach, for he never called towards the window or slackened his pace. That we'd gone to such lengths to avoid coupling made me giggle uncontrollably. Our clothes were askew and the carriage reeked of sex. We now shared a delicious little secret, however, and Pearce Truman no longer seemed as distant or imposing. Diabolical, yes, but in a more playful way.

He lowered my legs and helped me sit up. 'It's good to see you laughing, Vanita. A sense of humour will help you through the trials ahead, I'm sure.'

He was referring to Aunt Lill's illness and death, of course, but I set that situation aside. 'Who *are* you?' I breathed, stroking his clipped beard. 'And why do you have such an effect on me? Others have toyed with my affections, but *you*, Pearce –'

He silenced me with a deep green gaze that seared my very soul. 'I'm your knight in tarnished armour, Vanita. A fallen angel you can't resist,' he murmured in a mystical voice. 'Just as my darkness yearns for your light, your unsullied soul resonates to the beat of my carnal heart. My magic's black, and it's best not to question it.'

His reply filled me with the thrill of the forbidden, with promises a proper lady should never keep.

Yet when we rolled through the arched gateway to Wellspring, Mr Truman's words took on a different meaning. The spring grass looked scraggly, and the white plank fences stretching in every direction desperately needed paint. I stared out the window, dismayed at the disrepair of the stables and barns, with their missing windowpanes and clumps of overgrown weeds.

Shabby, that's how it looked. Like squatters had taken over in my absence. Like the very heart of Wellspring had stopped beating.

I should've ignored Aunt Lillian's instructions. Should've hired a ride home long before this, I chided myself. Sensing I needed time to take it all in, Pearce helped me to the ground without comment. An eerie silence enveloped us. No nickering of curious horses trotting to the fence, nor clanging from the farrier's forge, nor trainers speaking above the squeal of the iron carousel used to exercise the foals.

And the house ... the house where I'd been born and orphaned seemed to have settled in upon itself, despairing the grandeur of its past. Mama's prize azaleas huddled in spindly bunches around the verandah, where the railing resembled a mouth with missing teeth. A shutter dangled from the second-storey window of my bedroom. The semicircular brick drive bristled with grass, and as I stepped hesitantly towards the stairs, I noted large white splotches dotted with purple on the dusty ground-level windows. The birds still ate our mulberries and let fly against the house. At least that hadn't changed.

Tears trickled down my cheeks and then anger kicked in. There was no excuse for such decay! Aunt Lillian had the funds to maintain *five* estates, and if it took her dying breath I would hear her reasons for allowing my inheritance – my home – to go to ruin! My heels thundered on the verandah and I was in the house before Pearce could open the door.

'You should remember, Vanita, that your aunt's a very ill –'

Cries from the dining room stopped us in the front hall. Such grunting and moaning bespoke anything but a deathbed scene, and although my companion grabbed my hand, I strode forwards to confront the woman who belonged to that theatrical voice.

I wasn't ready for what I saw. Aunt Lill hung suspended from the crystal chandelier, naked, while a skinny, balding man knelt before her on the table. He was so intent on spooning some sort of sauce between her splayed legs, and she was making so much commotion, neither realised we were watching.

'How thoughtful of you to have lunch ready,' I blurted. 'Your warmth and hospitality have always overwhelmed me, Aunt Lill, but this time you've outdone yourself.'

The pair stared, but only for a moment. At least Clive Reilly had the decency to appear appalled, enough that he slunk into the butler's pantry. This left my red-haired guardian fully displayed, grinning like a hoyden.

'Well, well, well. Our little princess has returned, so *eager* to hear of her aunt's passing she got here in record time. You've performed admirably, as usual, Pearce. You'll be receiving your bank draft from Mr Reilly shortly.'

I jerked my hand from his, stepping warily away as I eyed these two traitors. No doubt in my mind that I was a pawn in some unthinkable deceit, in which even Daddy's long-time friend and attorney had conspired against me. I was too angry to cry, so I shot the demon beside me a venomous look. 'You may go, Mr Truman. I've no further need of your services.'

'Vanita, I can't –' He had the nerve to look enraged himself, the weasel! 'I swear to you, this woman was at death's door, yellow and barely breathing!'

'Things aren't always what they seem,' I muttered. His duplicity sickened me, but not as much as my own willingness to fall for it. 'See yourself out, and don't ever show your hideous face here again.'

His mouth tightened grimly, that sinister black moustache accenting the downward lines of his frown. With an ominous glare at my aunt, he stalked out.

Lillian Gilding made no effort to unfasten her hands; the crystal prisms of the chandelier whispered illicitly as she began to laugh. Her breasts and belly, firm for a woman her age – and showing no sign of infirmity whatsoever – shimmied with her mirth, and I had no trouble imagining Pearce Truman in the place Clive Reilly occupied moments ago.

'You disgust me,' I muttered, though I could've been addressing my own reflection in the dining-room mirror. I bolted from the room, her nasty laughter nipping at my heels.

4 A Brazen Betrayal

As I looked out the large window of my musty, unused room, tears slithered down my cheeks. The stables stood empty. Without horses to keep it eaten, the rolling green pastureland had grown unkempt and ragged. Everything around me felt sadly distant and sealed away, as though I'd entered the home of a dear friend who'd died months ago without my knowing it.

Who was on my side? Clive Reilly, Daddy's attorney since I was a child, had defected. Aunt Lill had apparently donned her stage paint and done a stunning performance of her deathbed scene for Pearce, but I couldn't trust him, either. His duplicity hurt, because I'd so willingly thrown myself at him. I'd lapped up his attention, and all his mystical mumbo-jumbo about being my knight in tarnished armour, my angel in black.

Black, indeed! Like a sinuous snake who'd slithered into my life – with Miss Purvey's assistance and encouragement – and sweet-talked me into this untenable position. Like the demon serpent who'd beguiled Eve in the garden and then left her to make her own excuses to God.

How I despised being the last one to learn this horrid secret! Wellspring had fallen into total ruin, and everyone I'd loved and trusted had betrayed me.

I wished desperately for Daddy, who would know how to take charge of this impossible situation. I longed for Mama's tender touch, for the soft voice that could ease my hurts and encourage me to go on. But I had no one. No one except myself.

Swiping at the tears on my cheek, I gazed out at what was otherwise a glorious spring day. It wasn't my nature to mope or to feel sorry for myself. Daddy had taught me to get up and immediately remount the horses that threw me, to prove to myself and those unruly creatures that I was in charge – that I would prevail over whatever mischief or vengeance they tried to wreak in my life.

And as I envisioned Jared Wells standing tall and proud in his fine suit, ever smiling at me as though I were the centre of his universe, I felt a flicker of hope. I could almost hear him saying, '*All is not lost, dear Vanita. You have the land. You have your intelligence and your integrity, and the Wells family name and reputation to stand upon. Use what you have, and you cannot fail.*'

I took a shuddery breath, drawing myself to my full height. This was a test – nothing more than a flock of imposters trying to steal what was mine! Banding together like thieves to rob me of my rightful estate! I could get to the bottom of this, for I'd been Miss Purvey's prize student in accounting and economics. Unless Aunt Lillian had destroyed the ledgers in Daddy's desk, I could find out just how grave my situation was and dig my way out from there. No sense crying and snivelling: the figures, in bold black on white, would give me the explanation I needed to confront those who circled me like vultures. Then I'd shoot them down.

As I turned from the window, however, I was greeted by my actress aunt. Lillian Gilding stood in the doorway, her lissome figure draped in a silk robe of an Oriental pattern in peacock blue, which became her colouring. She was a comely woman, nearly 50 years old but looking more like 35 ... which explained why Pearce was *her* lover, too. With her peaches-and-cream complexion and her aqua eyes, she bore a haunting resemblance to my mother – except for the audacity with which she smiled at me, as though we were to become fast friends.

'Just the person I need to see,' I began, my ire rising. 'You have a lot of explaining to do, dear aunt. Mama would be appalled – not only at your behaviour on the dining-room table, but at the state of affairs you've called me home to.'

She smirked. 'I don't owe you a damn thing, Vanita. Least of all an explanation. After all, it was your dear, deluded mother who insisted you attend the finest of finishing schools until you reached your majority. Can I help it if your blessed education has drained the estate?'

'That's a lie and you know it!'

'What do *you* know, really?' she shot back. As she stepped into my room, her dressing gown whispered seductively while her eyes remained on mine. 'You've been a student for six years, little girl. You have no right to condemn me, nor what I've done to carry out your parents' wishes, for you've grown into a fine-looking woman who's perfectly able to make her own way. Matter of fact, I've done my sister one better. I've arranged the perfect match for you.'

It was all I could do not to cross the room and slap her. 'If you think for one minute I'll agree to *your* arrangements –'

'I think you'll do exactly as I say. You have no choice, sweet niece, for Mr Reilly has already drawn up the papers to finalise the union. And you have no choice if you ever want to be the mistress of Wellspring, either.'

This smacked of yet another betrayal. My aunt's expression remained unruffled, as though she'd planned and schemed and connived the whole time I'd been away, working things to her own advantage as only a woman of her persuasion could.

'What do you mean, "If I ever want to be the mistress of Wellspring", dear aunt?' I mocked. 'I *am* this estate's mistress. It was my birthright, passed down from my mother – and her mother before her.'

'Only because Olivia was born before I was.'

This was an attitude I'd never before heard her express. When she'd taken over as my guardian, Aunt Lillian made sure I knew I was an imposition, but she'd never shown the least inclination towards being a landowner herself. Mama had regaled me with stories – carefully edited, I'm sure – of her red-haired sister's days on stage as she travelled from town to town with a small troupe. Lillian was ever the free-spirited wanderer, defying society to go wherever excitement and drama called. No house full of brats or responsibilities for her.

'So why have you taken it upon yourself to arrange my marriage?' I demanded. 'I can have any man I want. I've entertained proposals from several eligible bachelors – most of whose ambitions towards Wellspring now seem pale, compared to yours.'

Her smile was thin and wicked. 'You'll marry Damon Harte because it's in your best interests, Vanita. It's the only chance you have to regain your estate.'

I choked on my laughter. 'Damon *Harte* has asked for my hand? We all know –'

'Damon has graciously agreed to accommodate our plan.'

My mouth fell shut. The gentleman we spoke of was the son of Franklin Harte, who owned coal mines and vast tobacco plantations to the south and east of us. We'd met at holiday gatherings during our childhood, when he and his twin sister, Desiree, had been herded into my nursery quarters while the adults dined downstairs. The Harte children had the distinction of being albino, with translucent skin and the palest of pink eyes that squinted at the first hint of sunlight. Last time I saw Damon, he hadn't seemed the least bit interested in me, or in anything other than designing odd clockwork contraptions to amuse himself. He was the last sort of man to run his father's empire, let alone take an interest in a horse-breeding estate like Wellspring.

'Spell it out,' I said, crossing my arms to keep from strangling her. Again she had that cat-that-ate-the-canary look about her, and was obviously enjoying this little game.

Aunt Lillian smoothed the front of her silk gown, making the fabric sing as she caressed herself. 'Surely you realise all the breeding stock is gone, along with the hands. And a complete idiot could see that this house needs attention – a total refurbishing only money can buy. Figure it out, Vanita. It's what we sent you to school for.'

My heart kicked at my chest. The niggling insinuations of the past few years, and those Pearce had hinted at, all came crashing down upon me. Somehow my aunt had run through all the money earned by previous generations, which Daddy had increased a thousandfold by raising Wellspring's reputation and breeding quality after he married into my mother's legacy.

And somehow she'd dragged Franklin Harte and his colourless son into it, implying that they offered my only hope of salvation. I shuddered. Franklin was a burly, boisterous man, full of himself – and full of bourbon most of the time – who was notorious among Kentucky breeders for mistreating the fine stock he bought. Tales of cruel trainers and skimping upon rations and his chicanery at the race tracks ran rampant. That Lillian thought I'd have anything to do with this family disgusted me.

'Spell it out,' I repeated, too frightened to say more, or to second-guess this villainous woman who dared look me in the eye as though she'd done the right thing on my behalf.

Aunt Lillian chuckled, shaking her head as though reasoning with a small child. 'We all have our little habits ... our pastimes. That inalienable right to life, liberty, and the pursuit of happiness our country's forebears fought so diligently to attain for –'

'Oh, cut the rot!' I cried. 'You've swindled me out of Wellspring, so stop acting the coy, beguiling lady of the manor and tell the truth for once. You owe my parents *that* much!'

'No, your parents will forever be indebted to *me*, Vanita – and don't you forget it! You'll thank me for what I've done to preserve your – But no! You couldn't show gratitude if your life depended on it. Which it well might.'

It seemed my aunt the actress was not about to relinquish her role. Nor was she going to allow me out of this room until she was damn good and ready. But she wasn't the only woman in this family who knew how to get what she wanted.

'Fine, Aunt Lillian. I admit that I've not gushed out my gratitude over the years – nor would I have done so even if you'd allowed me to come home. But you've had your fun now, and you've obviously shared yourself and your wealth with Clive Reilly and Pearce – and Lord knows who else. And you've come to the end of your tether, haven't you? Spent your last – *my* last – dollar, so now you've fetched me home to get you out of your bind. What sort of deal did you make with Franklin Harte?'

She licked her lips, and the faintest hint of remorse tinted her cheeks. 'He's covered my debts at the track.'

'*What?* My parents' assets totalled more than three million dollars! Not counting the income from breedings and the races we should've won since their death.'

'Your mother would've expected me to entertain in a manner befitting the Wells name,' she replied petulantly.

There was no sense in pointing out each and every way she could've avoided whatever sin she was about to confess. I just kept glaring at her, my arms crossed so hard I could barely breathe. 'And?'

'And everyone in the horse business has suffered setbacks – extra expenses – these last few years of so little rain.'

'And?'

'And those damn trainers and grooms kept insisting on new equipment! Nearly ate us out of house and home, too, the ingrates!'

'And?'

'Well – the upkeep of this place is no little matter!' she blustered.

As if she'd done any of that. 'We seem to be straying from your debts at the track. If you knew or cared a damn thing about horses, I'd be tempted to think you *gambled* away my estate. Betting on awful jockeys and poor horses.'

'You'd think those little bantam roosters would be better in bed, the way they ride those thoroughbreds! And you'd think they'd show some consideration for the favours I allowed them, by *winning* more often!'

This time Aunt Lillian didn't try to appear contrite. The losses this vile woman had incurred came at me now with hurricane force.

'You're telling me you've gambled away Wellspring

– and all the hands and the horses – and that Franklin Harte has floated you?'

She nodded, smiling slyly. 'In more ways than you can imagine.'

'And now you're getting *me* involved? How *dare* you –'

'You're all I have left,' she stated with childlike audacity. 'You were my ace in the hole, Vanita, and I've played you to Franklin because he wants his son to marry and produce an heir. He's agreed to leave Wellspring intact and pay off the liens and taxes – while providing you a suitable husband!'

Before I could protest, she rhapsodised about her accomplishment, clasping her hands at her ample bosom and looking raptly to the heavens. 'It'll be a glorious wedding, Vanita! Now we can afford a voluminous gown with Belgian lace and beadwork! We'll hold it in the rose garden – like your mother would've wanted! And we'll invite the governor and all your daddy's fine friends, for he would've boasted of this fine match between two of Kentucky's oldest families –'

This time I did slap her. 'Don't you *ever* gush at me about what my parents would've wanted! Get out of my house, you – you whore! You've defiled my family's name! My daddy would've *died* – would've shot *me*! – before he let me marry a Harte. And you know it!'

Gingerly touching the cheek I'd smacked, my aunt showed the flip side of her coin so fast a casual observer would've been spinning. 'Call me what you want, little bitch, but I'm still your guardian. And I have control over Wellspring until your birthday in July,' she said tersely. 'You're damn lucky Franklin Harte would agree to these terms. Damn lucky I found a way for you to marry someone who has no designs on your fortune!'

'What fortune?' I railed. 'You've taken care of that! You've sold me down the river like a slave – and you're proud of it!'

Before she could lay out any more lies, I shoved past her, my footfalls echoing loudly in the second-floor hall ... because the Persian carpet no longer covered the plank floorboards. Damned if that woman hadn't started selling off the furnishings! Or had she traded them away to stall Franklin Harte?

I was too angry to care. I ran down the grand staircase and then clattered across the verandah and into the yard. If it was the last thing I never did, I wouldn't marry Damon Harte! I refused to believe that taking such an odious vow was my only hope of saving my legacy. I doubted, deep down, that the watery-eyed albino was any more interested in the match than I was – which might be the best leverage I had to work with.

At that moment, however, I needed a chance to think – a long, hard ride on the horse Daddy gave me right before he died. Pegasus was too old to withstand the hellbent gallops across open pastures that saw me through many a lonely, tormented heartache as I grappled with the horrendous loss of my parents, but the surge of his powerful legs beneath me, and the force of the wind in my face, and the warm, horsey scent of him would give me strength to face yet another betrayal. Aunt Lillian's voice and little affectations taunted me as I slipped into the stable farthest from the house.

The scents of dry hay and old tack, mixed with the sweet hint of horse rations and the musk of manure teased at my nose. Yet even these sensual memories fell short: the front stalls were empty, as I expected, and the stale air was split only by shafts of sunlight coming through broken-out windows. But I wasn't ready to discover that the large stall with PEGASUS on the gate was deserted as well.

Why hadn't I been told he'd died? It was like the last vestige of my childhood – the final reminder of my beloved parents – had been stolen from me. This, on top of the odious news that Wellspring had been gambled away, and my future along with it.

I plopped on to a hay bale, heedless of my suit. And when my seat crumpled beneath me, I gave in to the realities of my situation. Everything I'd educated myself for – all that I'd been born to and had dreamed of carrying on – now rested in the hands of a man Daddy and I detested.

I had to plan my strategy very carefully. Rather than an heiress, I was now a pawn in a game my foolish aunt had played, with a robber baron who made up the rules as he went along. I had little to work with, and no one I could trust. The sand was racing down the hourglass, too, because Franklin Harte would waste no time claiming me for Damon once he heard I was home.

I placed my head in my hands, breathing deeply to invoke the beloved scents and sights of my childhood, the feelings of security and pride Daddy had imbued me with. If I could summon the fortitude he'd passed on to me – figure out how *he* would've handled this situation – I could survive my aunt's treachery.

But this time, I couldn't recall Daddy's face.

5 My Deal With a Demon

I awoke with a start to find night had fallen. My fitful nap, brought on by exhaustion and the heat of late afternoon, left me muzzy and disoriented, with fragments of nonsensical dreams dancing in my head. I'd revisited my childhood, riding my roan gelding, Pegasus, and I'd seen Mama and Daddy as clearly as if they'd bent over me to brush the hay from my hair. As I did this for myself, I also recalled seeing Lorena, Mama's faithful maid, her eyes filled with sadness.

'I'm so sorry you came home to this mess, child. I just couldn't stand no more of it.'

Had Lorena died or met with foul play? Or had she left with her brother, Will, knowing her days under Aunt Lillian's rule were numbered? Either way, I had the distinct impression Lorena was gone from Wellspring – along with everything else I'd cherished. I stood up to brush off my clothing, weighted down with a sadness I'd never known.

But sentiment would get me nowhere. I had some sleuthing to do if I were to escape the nasty game my aunt had played with Franklin Harte.

As I slipped across the lawn between the stable and the house, I wondered what I'd find in Daddy's study. He'd kept meticulous records in a firm, slanted hand, records Clive Reilly might have taken over, since it was no secret Aunt Lill wasn't financially inclined. I hoped to find receipts crammed into boxes, or at least dated notes concerning amounts she owed, for I suspected no one but Lillian Gilding and the man who'd bilked her knew where the Wellspring fortune had gone.

If I could slip into Lexington, perhaps I could convince Daddy's banker, Beale Cornelius, to cover me until my birthday, when I could legally sweep Mama's shiftless sister out the door. Perhaps others – Judge Cavendish, or yes, even the governor, Sterling Banks – would assist me, for they'd all respected my father both as a man and as a breeder of Kentucky's finest racing stock, which they themselves had invested in. If they learned of my aunt's skullduggery, surely they'd come to my defence.

But I had more immediate fish to fry. The house stood dark and still from the outside entry to Daddy's study. It matched the other tall windows at the back of the main level, but was actually a section of wall that opened out to increase the room's air circulation in the summer. More than once when I was a child, I'd jimmied the latch to get inside after a midnight visit to a newborn foal. I slipped a hairpin into the vertical crack, grinning when the panel opened.

Daddy's study had always fascinated me, perhaps because even after his death I could savour the aroma of his pipe tobacco and look at his imposing portrait when I sat in his leather chair. At least Aunt Lillian hadn't visibly changed his sanctum. I opened the top centre drawer of his desk to find matches, but held my breath before lighting the lamp.

From above me came secretive footsteps, and voices.

'... know she'll come back in ... Can't expect her to –'

'She's made her bed and she'll lie in it. Just as you've made your bed with me, Clive. And here you are.'

I swallowed, my temples pounding. Never in my wildest imagination had I pictured the oh-so-proper Mr Reilly cavorting with my aunt, let alone being in cahoots with her. The bed creaked as he climbed on to it, and a sultry laugh floated above me. I had a good idea what they'd be doing, and no desire to listen. But at least it gave me time to study the ledgers without their interruption. I would have to sneak around the house like a thief to gather my evidence for Judge Cavendish, so I had to use my stolen moments to best advantage.

'Oh, Lillian, God ... God, they're so soft and full.'

'Lick my nipples. Come to Mama and suck your supper.'

Wincing, seeing their bare bodies in my mind, I carefully opened the bottom drawer of the mahogany desk where Daddy had managed his empire. The slightest squeak of dry wood would bring them down here, and I wanted to see them naked again even less than I wanted them to catch me. I'd hoped for a glance at the leather-bound ledger on my last visit, a few years ago, but Lillian prowled the house like a barnyard cat whenever I was home. Now I knew why.

'Sit on my face, lovey. I can't get enough of your dripping hot pussy.'

Closing my eyes against that image, too – for my aunt, although trim, outweighed the attorney by a good 40lbs – I gingerly set the ledger's spine on the desk and opened the covers. It smelled of must and neglect. It didn't help that as I struck a match, the floor above me groaned in a telltale rhythm as the fourposter bed began to rock ... the bed where my parents had conceived me, which Lill had commandeered for herself. I didn't want to think about how many lovers she'd shared it with. I'd been too naive on previous visits to suspect such a thing went on under Daddy's roof, in Mama's beautiful bedroom.

I set the lamp above the ledger's top edge. The page open to me revealed notations about the payroll that month, and disbursements for white paint – probably the last paint those miles of plank fences ever saw – and a barrel of whisky from a nearby distillery. The entries, in Daddy's hand, saddened me, so I pushed on. It would be my luck that the lovers came downstairs to satisfy the other hunger they'd worked up with all their carousing. That fourposter was now dancing a jig.

I turned the page, covering my ears when Lillian's ecstatic cries rang out. 'Oh, Clive! Stick it in me – harder! Pump my cunt and –'

Just as my palms pressed the sides of my head, two other hands covered mine – and then one quickly moved over my mouth.

'Shhhh,' my visitor whispered. 'Let them have their fun while you and I straighten things out. I'd love to be fucking you, too, but that'll have to wait.'

Pearce! I was at once livid and overjoyed that he hadn't left Wellspring, because we did indeed have a lot to talk about. And dammit, his musky body heat excited me more than I cared to admit. He kissed my temple, his breath tickling my neck.

'Promise not to scream?'

I nodded emphatically.

He released me, but then ran his tongue along the sensitive rim of my ear.

'Stop this!' I hissed. 'I threw you out, and you're not going to kiss your way back!'

'We'll see about that.'

I detested his cocksureness as he sat against the edge of the desk, looking down at me from an advantageous angle. 'You've got hay down your front. Let me pluck it –'

I slapped his hand. 'I'll let you explain yourself in thirty seconds or less, mister! You've lied as blatantly as everyone else in this house. I fell for you once, but it won't happen again.'

Pearce folded his hands in his lap, which made a sensual sight. He sat close enough that his thigh touched mine; I caught the scent of our sex still lingering on his skin. His dark face appeared demonic in the lamplight, his eyes lit like embers as he studied me. 'I'm sorry about all this, Vanita. When I was last here, I didn't think your aunt would make it through the night.'

'Now you know why she was so popular on stage. But that doesn't explain your connection to her, when you claimed to be Reilly's assistant.'

'Now you know why she was so popular on stage,' he mimicked softly. 'I'll admit I'm a knave of the highest order – the randiest bastard you'll ever meet. But I'm a man of my word, sweetheart. I'm not working for your aunt.'

'You said you promised them you'd fetch me home intact and in good time, and *then* you said you were a man of your word. Where's there any loyalty to *me* in that sequence, Pearce?'

He studied me silently. 'I suppose my actions, in Miss Purvey's office and then in the armoire and the carriage, speak louder than my words. And I didn't misrepresent myself as a man of passion and unquenchable desire, Vanita. But I've also told you I was your knight, your angel. I've asked you to believe in me.'

Pearce reached for my hand, which I reluctantly surrendered to him before he continued. 'Couldn't you tell, by the way your aunt ordered me around, that she didn't want me getting a word in edgeways? I swear to you – I thought she was dying! I suspected she'd connived you out of most of your estate, but I played no part in that. I was simply doing what Clive asked of me.'

Above us, Reilly yowled like an alley cat. The racket

from the shifting bed filled the study, until we had to stop talking. Pearce grinned mischievously, which made that nasty moustache glisten, and sharpened the line of his jaw with a satanic edge that cut through the last of my sensibilities.

Dammit, I couldn't take my eyes off him. What if he was telling the truth? My aunt *had* run the show, from the moment she found us gaping at her and her tabletop lover. Clive had left the room, apparently shamed by his own duplicity – not to mention being caught in such a compromising position by his client's daughter.

But I couldn't be too hasty. If I knew anything about the man beside me, it was that he could change like a chameleon, working on me with those probing eyes and that lush mouth and that come-hither look for as long as it served his purpose.

'So why are you here? You did your job. You were free to go, even without Lillian dismissing you, or me pitching you out.'

'I thought you could use a friend about now.'

I nearly choked on that one. 'A friend? Is that what you call a man who backs you into an armoire, and then teases you with his naked body before making a fool of you in his empty stateroom?'

'And the choice is still yours, isn't it? I've excited you, and pleasured you, and made you laugh –'

'And swear. And blush. And cry.'

'– but you're still the virtuous girl I fetched from finishing school, just like I promised.' He leaned closer, cupping my jaw with his tender hand. 'Please, Vanita, have a little faith in me. I can be your best confederate, as long as no one else suspects I'm around. Your aunt would just as soon shoot me as look at me.'

'Oh, really? She sounded like you'd been on intimate terms.'

He threw up his hands. 'Of course she did! Lillian *wants* you to despise me, and to think I betrayed you! What will it take to make you believe in me, Vanita?'

His bottomless black eyes pierced mine, filled with an arcane desire I couldn't deny; forcing me to seriously consider the turn our conversation had taken. My pulse was pounding and I could taste the kiss I suddenly wanted. But Pearce Truman should have no illusions about what I expected as proof of his allegiance. 'I want Wellspring back –'

'And so you shall have it.'

'– and I won't marry Damon Harte to get it.'

His eyes widened, shining like marbles in the lamp-light. 'Those are the terms? What in God's name has she done to bring it to that?'

How much should I reveal to this man of the shadows? Of course, for all I knew, other local landowners had already heard of Lillian Gilding's deal with that other demon, Franklin Harte. Could be she'd slept with most of *them*, as well. So telling Pearce the sordid details couldn't drag the Wells name through any deeper mud.

After the next round of outcries above us, I replied, 'It seems my illustrious aunt gambled away everything that's not nailed down – and she's turned that over, in promissory notes, to Franklin Harte. He wants his son to marry and produce an heir, so guess which part I'm to play if I want my estate intact.'

Pearce scowled. 'What's wrong with a wealthy sort like Damon that he can't catch his own wife?'

'An astute question,' I replied ruefully. 'I haven't seen him for years, but he's an albino who seldom leaves home. And he has a much greater desire to design mechanised toys than to chase after women.'

'Ah, that.'

'He has a twin sister, too,' I teased, punching his

knee. 'She's just as pale and just as pretty – and I've never heard that she's married, either. Perhaps you should look into her.'

'Perhaps I should. I rather like blondes, you know.'

When he slipped his fingers into my hair, I didn't shake him away. Something made me want to trust him, despite my doubts about his slippery nature. 'Desiree's hair is white,' I corrected. 'Pale pink eyes. Pallid skin. In a deathly sort of way, I suppose one could consider her exotic.'

'I'll decide for myself. But right now we've things to accomplish – the first being a pact.'

I drew away from his caress. 'Excuse me, Pearce, but I'm hardly in a position to form any binding alliances.'

'I can change that in a heartbeat,' he breathed, shifting closer. 'But first let's review the facts. You've lost your home, your entire inheritance. Your aunt has gambled it all away and thrown you in as the last bargaining chip. And I, dear lady, have promised to restore your fortune. As long as I'm drawing breath, you won't have to marry Damon Harte.'

I gazed at his dark, handsome face, desperately wanting to trust what he said. 'Why are you doing this, Pearce?'

'To prove I can. To show you I can indeed work magic, as long as you believe in me.'

I felt like the heroine in a fairy tale, where the bold prince saves the lady from some ghastly dragon. But a man doesn't make such a promise without expecting a prize in return. 'And what do *you* stand to gain from all this chivalry, Pearce?'

'You.'

His whispered response made me shiver. 'So far, you don't seem inclined to stick with one woman, Mr Truman. I –'

'So far, I haven't had to. Haven't wanted to.'

'– can't think you really want *me*. Unless you're referring to those nether regions men get so obsessed with.'

'Your prime little pussy? Your beautiful breasts? Your skin like silk, and the rest of a body that's turned my cock into a rock?' He grinned lecherously, yet I'd never seen him look more endearing. 'Those are reasons for any man to want you, Vanita. But I want *you*. All of you.'

I raised a doubtful eyebrow. 'Such talk comes easily to a man who knows I'm just as . . . inclined towards pleasure as he is. Are we calling this an alliance of convenience? Just until Wellspring is mine again? We're talking about millions of dollars in –'

Pearce's slim finger closed my lips. 'We're talking about the magic between a man and the woman he wants, heart and soul. Especially soul, Vanita.'

I swallowed, for the ante had suddenly been upped. His face appeared utterly serious in the lamplight, and the house had grown so still, it was as if the walls themselves were standing as witness to his vow. 'So this isn't a fairy tale, where the handsome prince rescues the fair maiden and pledges his undying love? It's *Faust* with a twist, where the maiden makes a deal with the devil.'

He smiled, looking more potently mysterious than any man had a right to. 'Something like that. Only because such a deal is irrevocable, and because the danger of it – the highest of stakes for both of us – is the very thing that draws us together. You want something that's irretrievably lost, and I've promised to get it for you. In return, I'm asking for your mind and body, your heart and soul – the sum total of *you*, given solely to *me*. Promise me that, and Wellspring will be yours again. Free and clear.'

'That's absurd, Pearce! You can't –'

'Only those who attempt the absurd can attain the impossible.'

With that he kissed me, claiming my mouth with lips of velvet that became more impassioned by the moment. His tongue sparred playfully with mine, conjuring up images of his cock delving into my wet sex. When his hands closed over my breasts, hot and possessive, I thought my dress would go up in smoke.

'Say yes, Vanita. I dare you.'

When those hooded eyes probed mine, I couldn't look away. Like a mystical magician, an illusionist of the highest calibre, Pearce Truman penetrated my very core, reading my doubts and fears along with my desperation. I felt mesmerised, helpless against the tug of his spirit fighting to capture mine – yet fighting to free it, as well.

But who was I fooling? I didn't know a thing about this man! He'd told me nothing, yet he expected me to pledge myself to him – a leap of faith no woman in dire straits should take. If I were dealing only with Aunt Lillian and Clive Reilly, I could find enough weak links to break the chains they'd bound me in.

But with Pearce, it was just too soon.

He sighed, blending the gesture into a soft kiss that made me ache to have such tenderness in my life every day, every hour. His hands massaged my breasts until my nipples poked against my camisole, begging for more. Shameless, such a brazen response to a man who couldn't possibly deliver what he'd promised. His talk of magic was so far-fetched, only hearts of last resort would dare believe him.

And why should I trust him, after what I'd witnessed with my headmistress? And if he was so concerned about my welfare, why had he abandoned me aboard the steamer, yet pressed for every sort of contact short of claiming me, in the carriage? He was wicked. Up to no good.

The liquid pooling between my sex lips dribbled down my thigh. I had no choice but to submit to his powerful kiss, to the hands that brought my body to life. Lord knows I *wanted* to believe in Pearce! Something in his manner, something in his expression and tone, begged me to find the faith I'd never had in a man. With a thrust of his tongue, he pushed me further into submission, knowing I had little resistance left.

Who else could I trust, after all? And who else was offering to give me back the estate – the very life – that was rightfully mine?

I nodded before I lost my nerve.

'You believe I can follow through? That I can restore Wellspring to you?'

I kissed him back, pushing up hard against his hungry mouth until it was Pearce groaning instead of me. Our tongues duelled like velvet sabres unsheathed, wet and hot and eager, until his chuckle reverberated from his chest into mine. Then he pulled back.

'Is this a yes, Vanita?' he whispered. 'I want you to be very sure. There's no room whatsoever for doubt.'

Again I nodded, my heart filling with a blind faith, a hope that flashed like the lightning between us.

'And in return – no matter what happens between now and then – you'll be mine? Completely and for ever?'

A sob escaped me as I nodded my final assent. I was making a promise I couldn't possibly keep – I sensed this as surely as I felt Pearce's erection prodding my midsection. Yet this man's magnetism had pulled me out of myself, into his mystical sphere. 'Take me now. Seal the bargain for both of us before you go.'

'You think I'm leaving?' he replied with a sly smile.

His fingers had found the hem of my dress and were working up my inner thigh.

'It's not safe for you to stay – at least not in sight. And besides,' I added saucily, 'if you're to settle things with Franklin Harte, you've got your work cut out for you. My aunt's made a horrendous mess of things.'

'So I noticed. Not a single ledger entry the past few years, and they're sparse before that. Which means if anyone's keeping a record of what she's lost to Harte, it's Harte himself. Not a position you want him to be in.'

Why was I not surprised that Pearce had read the ledger? The man had powers I had yet to ascertain, and was already at work on his part of our deal. It was my turn to show my intention to carry through ... my faith in what this man with the wicked grin could truly do. After all, who had ever made me feel so beautiful – so desirable – as Pearce Truman? And now that Daddy was gone, who else had applauded my business skills the way this mysterious stranger had?

I unbuttoned my cuffs, smiling up at him with all the courage I could muster. 'I hope you're ready, Pearce. We're going to get this right the first time, and every time, you know.'

His eyes widened. 'You want to do it here? On your father's desk?'

I glanced behind him, to the stately portrait of Jared Wells that dominated the office. 'Seems the perfect place to consummate a deal of such magnitude. It's Daddy's desk, and it's Mama's legacy we're out to reclaim. Somehow, I think they'd approve.'

6 Caught in the Act

The chuckle rumbling in Pearce's chest was the purr of a predatory cat – a cat ready to play with his prey. Would I be strong enough, plucky enough, not to be consumed? When aroused, the power of his eyes and his presence – the very essence of sorcery – rose before me. He reached for my clothes, but then stopped. Blew out the lamp. Let the silence seep in, to reveal the study's shadows as places where we could hide and seek as only new lovers know how.

'So beautiful, you are. Let me undress you.'

Together we rose beside the desk. Pearce deftly unfastened my bodice and then my skirt, and when I shimmied to make them fall, he grinned. 'Quite the playmate, aren't you? It's good you're not the vestal virgin one assumes Miss Purvey's girls to be. Much more fun that way. Much less awkward.'

'You couldn't be awkward if you tried,' I breathed. My camisole and drawers slithered down at his silent command, as though his gaze alone made them disappear. 'How do you do this, Pearce? How do you mesmerise me into believing I'll have my happily-ever-after?'

'Believing is seeing,' he replied quietly. 'A man's power reflects the woman he's with. When she throws herself into pleasing him – *believing* with him – they can work miracles.' He drank in my body, draped only in pale finery spun by a minimal moon. 'Your turn,' he breathed.

I felt childishly clumsy as I undid his shirt buttons.

His chest rose and fell more quickly now, and I suddenly realised I, too, possessed heightened powers – the power to drive this man to insanity, just as he did me. The power to motivate him to reclaim my estate, even though I wasn't sure why he wanted to.

But that didn't matter. When my fingertips found his bare skin, he pulled me hard against his hips. 'Vanita ... Vanita,' he whispered, and in his low melodious voice my name sounded like an entreaty. A prayer for salvation.

I kissed the column of his neck, sliding my mouth in a moist path along the silky skin beneath his ear. My tongue teased at his close-cropped beard, delighting in the differences of texture: the incredible softness of the hair, and then the skin, like fine sandpaper where he shaved.

He groaned, impatient. Ravenously he kissed me, his mouth rampant upon mine, with a desperation bordering on brutality, yet so very controlled. Power, indeed. He opened my mouth with a tongue that delved inside to explore relentlessly.

Pearce then shucked his boots and shed his pants with the minimal efforts of a man who lived on the edge, a man who took action at a moment's notice. He splayed one hand over my hips to hold them against his pelvis, while the other sent my hairpins spinning around the room. Then he speared both hands into my hair.

Such a surge of arousal! Such contrasts, of a man's bare body rubbing mine: a downy thigh rustling against my smooth ones, his narrow pelvis pushing into my softer midsection, the muscled chest scraping my breasts, making music with the coarse hair that concealed nipples as hard as my own. The muscles of his butt bunched as I parted the halves of it with my hands, in awe of their virile conformation. He took my mouth again, with a ruthless abandon that sent my pulse into full gallop.

Pearce slipped his hands under my hips and lifted me on to the desk. In one fluid movement he coaxed me flat, opening my legs. With his mouth still working mine, he kneaded my body beneath his. I wrapped my legs around his waist, already dripping with need. My slit pulsed with heat and an itch that had to be scratched.

I canted my hips beneath him, feeling for his cock. He angled it between the petals of my sex, to rub me in a most exquisite way. My liquid heat spread between us, wet and welcoming, while my clit thrust upwards in search of relief.

'Patience is a virtue,' Pearce whispered – although I felt him laughing.

'What good is virtue, when I can have you?' I quipped. 'You've invited me into your darkness and I've accepted, Pearce. She who hesitates is lost.'

'Lost,' his breath echoed. Still rocking against me, he ran the slick length of his erection against my sex.

I picked up his rhythm, and at the next opportunity I impaled myself. Pearce let out a fierce breath, raising up to look at me. 'This is where push comes to shove, Vanita. The point of no return. Are you ready for surrender?'

I rammed against him, filled with the extraordinary length and girth of the cock I'd admired earlier. 'Too late. I'm already yours.'

His raven gaze lingered upon our joined bodies, which glistened with heat and reeked of our lust. Keeping himself completely still within me, he claimed another brazen kiss. 'Squeeze me,' he breathed.

I did, astounded at the way my cunt pulsed to match the throbbing of his cock. We were one in the most amazing of ways, yet Pearce implicitly promised more.

Slowly he stood up, fully extended inside me as our taut bodies formed a right angle. 'Look at me.'

I quivered when our eyes locked. Was that a streak of lightning in his gaze?

'Don't move. And don't close your eyes,' he commanded. 'Don't even blink.'

I saw a lion with a tousled mane, drawn in the colours of the night; a hunter with utmost control. I couldn't have looked away if I'd tried, for his face glowed like a demon's; a man possessed. Yet it was I who'd been taken. I who stared unblinking at an untamed beast about to unleash himself.

He began slowly, rocking so his blunt head nudged the sensitive spot deep within me. My legs were spread to their fullest, my sex stretched wide by the slow-moving instrument he tortured me with. I wanted to writhe and cry out, bucking against him to relieve the ache that threatened to swallow me whole.

But Pearce had commanded it, so I lay still. Mesmerised yet again.

His eyes burned with a more ominous fire. His breathing became laboured with his efforts at control. His cock pulsed and flexed within me, sparking starbursts all along my inner passage. A rich squelching sound now accompanied us, and we panted like animals.

Neither of us blinked. My muscles shuddered and I stilled them, fighting the force that wanted to explode within me. Pearce's fingers drifted over my skin, inciting little riots of gooseflesh around my breasts and navel; still he nailed me to the desktop with his unwavering gaze. Above us, the fourposter thumped to life again, and his beard flickered with a grin.

'Seems it's a fine night for fucking.'

I couldn't answer, for fear I'd howl with my need. My cunt wanted to grip and suck him in. It took all my effort not to thrash when his thumbs found my clit, working up the wetness from below.

Pearce tensed, his ebony eyes drawing me further into his spell. 'Let me plumb the depths of you,' he murmured. 'Let me delve far beneath your surface. And when we find the very base of our souls, and meld them together, we will indeed become one. Inseparable.'

My eyes widened, entranced, while my body caught fire. Still he moved inside me with that slow control, watching my every flicker, playing upon each internal outburst to produce the next. He arched, rubbing that same nub he'd crazed with his thumbs, until a jolt of heat raced between us. I moaned and then cried my release – which Pearce quickly swallowed with a kiss.

He pumped into me then, his hypnotic eyes shining only an inch from mine. I answered every thrust, for I no longer owned my body. Pearce possessed it, driving me into a quivering madness of wet skin and hard heat and elemental surrender. He controlled me with his gaze, which sought out my secrets before I could hide them. Then, with a jaw-clenching groan, he convulsed. Liquid heat shot into me time and again, as Pearce finally squeezed his eyes shut to release himself.

He collapsed, his forearms braced on either side of me. Together we caught our breath. My eyes closed at last, yet images of our joining were indelibly tattooed inside my eyelids. I would see no one else but Pearce Truman, even in my sleep.

His kisses lit like butterflies, around my hairline and beneath my ears and then across the bridge of my nose. I giggled, smacking his backside. As I shifted to adjust his weight, so pleasantly heavy, I had to laugh. 'Pearce, we've made love on the ledger. You've truly taken me into account.'

'We've left our mark upon the annals of Wellspring,

to be sure.' He teased my lips with his wicked moustache. 'I intend to be a diligent bookkeeper, making notations every day. More, when I can.'

I reminded myself that such pretty talk came from a lot of practice. And when our pledge was met, I still had no hold over him – for Pearce would always cast the deciding vote. He would always control the part of me I'd vowed never to relinquish.

'You're mine, sweet Vanita,' he declared. 'I'll keep my promise, and whatever you ask of me, I'll never refuse you. As long as you believe this, it'll be true.'

Laughter from the doorway made us stiffen, and Pearce covered my body with his.

'You have such a lovely tongue in your head, my dearest Pearce,' Aunt Lillian's voice accosted us. She paused, to let the meaning of that thumping bed above us sink in. 'But I've just made you a liar, because Franklin's here to claim his boy's bride. And if either of us sees you sniffing around Vanita again, you'll be fed to the dogs like horsemeat. Right, Mr Harte?'

'You said it, sugah.'

I cringed with the effort it took not to scream. Without a word, or so much as a glance, Pearce slowly rose out of my embrace. It cut like a knife when he shook off the hands I tried to hold him with. I squeezed my eyes against tears, listening to him gather his clothes from the floor.

Take me with you! I cried inside, but I knew what his answer would be. Between heartbeats, between his final tender promise and Aunt Lill's first cutting word, he'd abandoned me. On noiseless feet, he left through Daddy's back exit.

He hadn't protested. He hadn't set them straight about how things would be – about how I was no longer the pawn in their dreadful game. Pearce Truman had simply walked away.

So I was left, sprawling naked on Daddy's desk, like a maiden about to be sacrificed in some ancient ceremony. Behind me, a match spat fire and the lamp cast an incriminating light on my situation. I struggled up, desperate to cover myself with a piece of clothing from the floor, but Franklin's bark halted me.

'Stay right there. I want to inspect my prize.'

With that, the burly tobacco master moved into my view. His dark hair was slicked back with pomade and he reeked of Aunt Lillian's perfume. Swarthy cheeks puffed around piggy eyes that glittered at the sight of me. He wore a white linen suit over a snowy silk shirt, as did many southern gentlemen, but a beast lurked beneath his finery. His hands were encased in tight white gloves, like a second skin – gloves that had made those attending my parents' funeral murmur in fresh speculation. But this was no time to ask him what they hid.

'Well, well, well,' he murmured, his eyes lingering on my breasts before travelling to that thatch between my legs, now matted with the wet remains of sex. 'You've grown into quite the lady, Vanita. And wouldn't your daddy be *so* proud of you right now?'

'Damn you to –'

'And a feisty one, too!' he jeered, grabbing the hand I slapped him with. 'None of my other girls struck Damon's fancy, but I think you'll do. You just might do. Now spread those legs!'

I clamped them shut, of course, kicking his shin. After hearing of this man's cruelty to his animals and his help, I should've realised I was only digging myself a deeper hole – and that Franklin Harte loved it that way.

'Lillian, you must teach your niece to *obey* when a man commands her,' he drawled. 'That finishing school put some silly ideas into her head, and we'll have to change them. *Won't* we, Vanita?'

I was about to retort, when my aunt pinned my arms behind me. This pulled me into an awkward half-sitting position, which allowed Harte to spread my thighs for a full view of my wet assets.

'Like a perfect rose after a rain,' he murmured, flicking my sex lips with his kid fingertip. When I flinched, he laughed. 'And so responsive – as Mr Truman proved admirably. But you can forget him, Vanita. Where you're going, he won't come within squirting distance – even with that big prick of his. But I assure you Damon – you remember my boy Damon, don't you, darlin'? – will be eternally grateful that Daddy got him a good one this time.'

With the dew on his fingertip, he drew a cross between my bare breasts. 'And you, little lady, will do well to seduce him as soon as possible. Because if you can't bring him around, it'll be *me* ploughing your pretty furrow. Do we understand each other?'

7 Prodded Into Submission

With every jolt of the carriage, I cringed. That bastard Franklin had twisted my wrists behind me and marched me naked across the yard. Then he'd shoved me into his carriage's leather seat and fastened my arms above my head with black satin straps. My skin was sticking to the ebony upholstery, and my legs, held open by ankle bindings on the floor, felt sticky from the ooze of Pearce's juice. In this position, my hips were thrust forward, poised on the edge of the seat. Franklin sat facing me, enjoying every bob of my breasts as we bounced down the county road.

'The Lord had the right idea when he created moonlight,' the planter crooned in his leisurely drawl. 'Sheds such loveliness on us all. Makes the ladies flutter and want to bed their men, and makes the men –'

'Into beasts,' I muttered. As though taking offence at this remark, a wheel hit a hole in the road, making me yelp from the pain in my tailbone.

'Your pretty little backside must be sore, from getting pressed into your daddy's desk. Should've thought about that before batting those big brown eyes at Truman, sugah.' Franklin held a gold-headed cane between his knees. He gripped it in his gloved hands, resting his chin on them to study me. 'Left a stain on the pages of his estate, that's for sure. Good thing old Jared isn't around to see that.'

'And we all know how much *you* have to be proud of,' I shot back. 'How many women have you presented to your illustrious son? Why doesn't he respond to your ... gifts?'

'Because his mama ruined him.' Harte locked his gaze into mine, to drive home another important warning. 'Alice was lifting her skirts for some pathetic, colourless lover, because it's obvious the twins can't be mine. She spent the rest of her life pandering to their weaknesses, to spite me. Not a smart thing to do.'

His words chilled me. From what I recalled about Alice Harte, her gracious ways hadn't rubbed off on either Damon or Desiree – and certainly not on her husband. I wanted to ask what had happened to the fiancées who came before me, as well as to his wife: shortly before my parents died, Alice had mysteriously disappeared into a thick mist of rumours. Ladies had whispered behind their hands that she'd met an unthinkable end, and this tyrant's leer warned me to watch my mouth.

'Part of my reasoning is that Harte's Haven has been too long without a mistress,' he continued. 'So, not only am I removing you from the embarrassment of Wellspring – from the blight of its impoverished state – but I'm providing you a whole new life, Vanita. Harte's Haven, along with the status that comes with being the lady of such a fine estate, will now be yours. And all you have to do is spread your legs. We both know how you love to do *that*, now don't we, darlin'?'

I bucked against my bindings, and then felt foolish for lashing out at him from such a position. His raucous laughter filled the carriage. Franklin tapped his cane on the floor with each guffaw, and then he suddenly shoved its carved gold tip against my exposed privates.

I sucked air, holding absolutely still.

Damn the man, he leaned forward, staring blatantly. 'I like your big tits, Vanita.'

I bit my lip until I thought it might bleed.

'I *said*, I like your big tits, Vanita. Didn't they teach you the proper response to a gentleman's compliment at that school?' He scooted forward by a few more inches, insinuating the cane between the lips of my slit. Expecting a response I refused to give him.

'You've chosen the wrong time to keep your mouth shut, sugah. Let's try this again.' Franklin twisted the stick, pressing its carved tip on to my poor little clit. The rough, irregular texture made my sensitive flesh pull back in pain, but I had no way to retreat – no way to shift out of Franklin's reach. 'I'm guessing Truman rammed it into you so hard, you're sore now, aren't you? You'd like me to quit this, wouldn't you?'

'Yes,' I rasped.

'Yes, what? For a young lady of your station, your manners are sadly lacking. Your mama would be appalled.'

'Yes, Mr Harte. Sir.'

He chuckled, probing my sex petals until I grimaced and had to open farther. 'Your mama, Olivia, she was a fine woman. Had the decency to refuse my propositions for most of her life. Not that it did her much good.'

My eyes flew open and he laughed. 'Her sister, now – *there's* a pussy in heat! I'll miss keeping company with Miss Lillian while we work on my son, but she knows I'll be back. If she doesn't come sneaking over, wanting it, before then. And what do you say to that, Vanita?'

The cane head gained entry, stretching my sore passageway. 'Yessir,' I hissed, hating myself for not being able to fend him off. Despising my body for not wanting to, in some secret, wayward way.

'Call me Daddy. We're going to be family, after all.'

I scooted back to avoid his probing, but it was futile.

Franklin twisted his instrument, subtly, lightly, so I could feel its raised texture as the bulb stroked my clit.

'They're going to smell you from a mile away,' he teased, increasing the speed of his torment. 'By God, Miss Wells, I think I've finally found the perfect woman for my son! Once he gets a snootful of your pussy's perfume, he'll be buried to the root.'

I fought my trembling, clenching my eyes shut against such degradation. I tried very hard not to respond – tried to picture that rabbitlike boy of his, with his watery pink eyes and white-pink skin – but I was still partly aroused when this beast had taken me away from Wellspring, and my body was betraying me. Ironic that my most private parts had joined everyone else who'd given me over to this insidious man.

'You're about to come, aren't you, Vanita?'

I gritted my teeth, but my body's spasms belied my arousal. And I'd only make things worse by not responding. 'Yes. Sir.'

'I told you to call me Daddy. And when you do come, it better be my name you're crying out. And what name would that be, Vanita?'

'Daddy, sir.'

'Louder!'

The cane head was spinning quickly against my clit, until I couldn't sit still any longer. The bonds bit into my wrists as I began to writhe, tugging against my ankle tethers to spread my legs even farther. 'Daddy,' I choked.

'Can't hear you.'

'Daddy!' I croaked, on the edge of the very wet leather seat, and about to explode. A rhythmic, slippery sound was coming from between my legs, which throbbed with a pain that burned dangerously close to pleasure . . . a degrading pleasure I tried to deny myself. I had a hint then about why Aunt Lillian had loved to strut upon the stage.

'Lord, but you're a stubborn one,' he jeered. 'Scream it like you mean it! Let the world know who owns you now!'

His sudden thrust buried the cane head inside me and placed the smooth, cooler shaft against my aching clit. The difference in its temperature sent me over. I flailed in the seat as though caught up in a seizure, spewing my juice as I cried, 'Daddy! Daddy! Oh, God – *Daddeeeeeeeey*!'

Damn the man, he refused to leave me with a shred of dignity. The moment I collapsed, he cast his cane aside and knelt between my legs, lapping at me like a dog. With his gloved hands cupping my butt and his mouth devouring me, I became an even more powerless prisoner to his rampant attack. In and out and around his tongue plunged, taking full advantage of the shockwaves he'd created earlier, to drive me mercilessly towards another climax.

It was several moments before I again became aware of the bumping carriage and the slick seat beneath me. The man in the impeccable white suit sat serenely across from me, wiping his face with a silk handkerchief. Then he folded his white-gloved hands over his cane.

'Almost home,' he remarked benignly. 'And I sincerely hope you'll find Harte's Haven a fitting love nest, darlin'. Despite what you must think of me, I only want the best for my son – and for his lovely, delicious little bride.'

He leaned forwards, his beefy cheeks glistening with my honey and the first light of day. 'Just in case you've wondered, Vanita – you will *not* be released from the deal if Damon doesn't co-operate. You will simply be sleeping in my bed instead.'

Time had done Harte's Haven no favours. I'd visited this sprawling plantation home in its prime, as a child – only because Mama felt compelled by social necessity to attend Alice's holiday gatherings – and it seemed the exterior had succumbed to the same fate that had befallen Wellspring. While it was true our beloved South still reeled from the effects of the War Between the States, even 30 years later, Franklin's extensive tobacco empire had prospered despite the end of slavery. He owned coal mines as well, so he was supplying Northern industry and hauling in a handsome profit.

But his house gave me the shivers. In the half-light of morning, it rose like a beckoning spectre, with a spiked iron rail around its roof and lightning rods between its brick chimneys. White columns alluded to a grandeur of a more gracious day, but I saw beneath this genteel facade: just as Franklin's snowy-white clothing didn't make him a saint, Harte's Haven could never be rendered homey with a coat of fresh paint. Groundskeepers had manicured the lawns and rose gardens, and azaleas lined the sides of the semicircular drive to the front entry. With great trepidation, I watched it loom larger as we approached. The shuttered windows looked like closed, soulless eyes.

'I'd like my clothes, please,' I stated quietly.

'Folks in hell want lemonade, too,' Franklin replied, and then the carriage rang with his laughter. 'You're the bride, Vanita! Certainly no stranger to a state of undress. I find it highly symbolic that you're coming to your new life in the same state you entered the world – naked and complaining.'

The carriage lurched to a halt, and for a moment my

host simply sat gazing at me. My extended arms had gone bloodless. My head drooped from lack of sleep. My entire body ached from my coupling with Pearce, and then from struggling to resist this ogre's torment while still bound hand and foot. Yet this demonic man apparently couldn't take his eyes off me. Or else he was waiting for the morning light to brighten, so all who peered curiously from the house would see my degradation more clearly.

But no one came out. Why wasn't a butler greeting us? Why hadn't the driver hopped down from his seat to open our door? Indeed, the estate seemed eerily silent.

As though anticipating my question, Franklin remarked, 'I prefer to come and go without my staff hovering to meet my every need. They know better than to get in my way.'

I wasn't sure how this would affect my welfare, so I didn't respond. I was weary of all my remarks inspiring his sarcasm – or ridicule – and I simply wished for a bath and a bed. Surely Franklin would allow me those simple amenities before he presented me to his son.

But no, this man's world didn't revolve around the social niceties. He swung the carriage door out, allowing the morning chill to creep in, knowing the effect it would have on my unclothed body. He grinned when my nipples rose to attention – taut little berries bursting with flavour, the way he undoubtedly saw them – and assessed my parted thighs with equal interest.

'You may thank me for cleansing your cunt and your legs, Vanita. By now they'd have been so sticky you couldn't leave the carriage without some skin staying behind.'

He brayed like a jackass, but then stopped abruptly. 'I *said*, you may thank me for thinking of your comfort. Not every man would, you know.'

'Thank you, Mr Harte,' I muttered, my pulse pounding out my hatred.

'Lord, but you're dense! Whatever that finishing school charged for tuition was totally wasted on you!' He stood, ducking his head to avoid the carriage ceiling, and leaned over me with an ominous look. 'What do I want to be called, Vanita? You're far from stupid, and acting ignorant only enrages me more. Consider yourself warned!'

My cheeks prickled with red heat as I swallowed a scathing retort. 'Yes, Daddy. Thank you, Daddy,' I whispered tersely.

The humiliation of this little lesson was nothing, however, compared to his next suggestion. 'Roger,' he called out the open door, 'tell Damon and Desiree they have a guest! She's awaiting them with open arms!'

'Yessiree, Mr Harte.' The carriage shifted with the driver's weight as he hopped from his seat. Roger – a barrel-chested servant with sprigs of white in his bristling hair – leered at my nakedness, chuckled, and then hurried towards the house.

Blood rushed to my face and I glared at the middle-aged monster confronting me. 'What are you trying to prove? Why do you think Damon's any more likely to want me when he sees me trussed up this way? Perhaps that's why the others didn't suit him.'

'The others knuckled under long before I brought them this far.' His smile would've made him almost handsome if he weren't such a beast. 'At least you have spirit, Vanita. Even if you can't win him over, I'll enjoy watching you try. A man my age still loves the chase, you know. Your daddy was no different. He liked the younger fillies, too.'

Once again I bridled at the allusion to my parents' sexual secrets, but approaching footsteps warned me not to lash out. Far better to sit composed, as Miss

Purvey had taught me, than to greet whoever approached as though I were an animal escaping a cage. I sat straighter, replacing the exhaustion in my face with a forced smile – as if this would keep anyone from staring at a young woman who sat bound and naked in a carriage!

The face that poked through the doorway was pale as porcelain, with voluminous white hair pulled into a topknot; her brows and lashes disappeared into skin the same shade of ivory. I had expected Desiree Harte to be an expert with cosmetics by now, but she seemed no more troubled by her colourless state than by my nudity.

'Vanita, it's been years,' she said in a low, eloquent voice. 'Damon and I were *so* pleased to hear Daddy was bringing you to live with us! Life gets deadly dull when it's passed in darkness.'

As she stepped into the dim interior of the carriage, I recalled how the Harte twins had avoided exposure to light because their lack of pigmentation made them susceptible to sunburn in only seconds. Desiree had matured, just as I had, but I noted her boyish figure with secret glee.

I did not expect it, however, when she leaned over me to fondle both my breasts, pressing them between her cool, pale palms. I lurched backwards in shock, but of course I had nowhere to go. With my hands still bound above me and my ankles fastened at the floor, I was wide open for her inspection.

Desiree laughed softly, but the edge in it sent knives up my spine. 'Damon doesn't know how lucky he is. Why is it, Daddy, that you bring *him* such lovely gifts, instead of me?'

Franklin, who'd watched her with jaded fascination, made a rude sound that passed for a laugh. 'You, my daughter, have always taken what you wanted before

I could give it to you. While I admire your ambition, it makes surprising you – or pleasing you – very difficult.'

He rose from the carriage seat, tapping his cane as he grinned at me. 'Desiree will show you to your room and help you settle in. I doubt my son will appear until dinner, so rest and prepare yourself for the occasion. I expect nothing short of a stunning appearance and the most beguiling behaviour when you greet him. You owe me for this favour, after all.'

He stepped to the ground with a grunt, and then headed briskly towards the house. This left me in his daughter's clutches, in every sense of the word, and I felt extremely uncomfortable as her gaze continued.

'What in God's name are you doing? Get me out of these damn straps!' I spat.

Desiree backed away, feigning shock. 'My, my, but we've come a long way since our childhood! I can remember you hovering behind your mama's skirts, too shy to even speak, and now you swear like a stevedore! I missed a great deal, not being able to go away to school.'

I had the impression this woman had lacked for nothing, and she was the last person I'd ever feel sorry for. 'And how would *you* like to be trussed up like a plucked turkey, with your private parts hanging out?'

'Very well, I thank you. But obviously mine don't hang out as far as yours.' When she unfastened the satin bands hooked above my head, the circulation returned to my arms with a shooting of sharp pains that made me cry out. Then she knelt to free my feet, sniffing brazenly between my spread legs. 'What's this I smell on you, sweet Vanita? Did Daddy come on you – or come at you with that nasty cane? Or is it another man's juices I smell?'

Her left eyebrow quirked, giving her a regally wicked smile. 'This is too, too delicious, Vanita! Did he catch you fucking somebody? It wasn't that skinny little Clive Reilly, *was* it? You'll have to tell me all about him while I run your bath! Things will be *much* more exciting around here now!'

Thank goodness she kept her hands off me on the way to the house. Indeed, Desiree Harte escorted me through the door as though I were dressed in appropriate attire for calling on her – even though we both knew this would never have happened without the insidious arrangement between her greedy father and my despicable aunt.

Once inside I got the chills all over again. It was as though all light and air had been sucked from the house, leaving only a gloomy coolness that hung like a shroud throughout. The rooms off the entry hall seemed to hold their collective breath, like children who feared some horrible monster might spring up and grab them. As I pondered the vestibule's pea-green walls, an imposing grandfather clock whirred to life, bonging like a funeral knell, six solemn strikes. Another clock immediately took up the toll, its lugubrious tones still echoing as timepieces in all the nearby parlours chimed in – a cacophonous welcome to this dungeon Miss Harte called home.

From the room at my right, a figure in a white suit came out of the shadows. I thought it was Franklin until I heard the surreptitious catching of cogs and noted the hesitating gait of a wind-up clockwork toy.

The young woman beside me snickered at my widened eyes – and then again at the approaching mechanical man, who suddenly wound down. His face froze so he appeared to be leering at my naked breasts, with his arms outstretched. This creature didn't wear white kid gloves, but its hands had stopped in a curved position, as though preparing to caress my assets.

'Damon's sent his favourite creation to greet you,'

she explained, knocking on its painted face to produce a hollow, metallic sound. 'Frankie's rather a fine likeness, don't you think? Even Daddy says so – and it's rare for him to compliment anything Damon does.'

I nipped my lip. This creature's human counterpart had brought me here, to this claustrophobic lair, to breed me as though I were a mare to be favoured with his fine stallion's seed. Yet I was far more frightened by my potential groom's hobby, and the fact that Damon had sent this mechanical ambassador instead of showing himself.

Had Alice's absence all these years driven her family to their nasty habits? She would never have condoned such behaviour, to have a guest fondled by her daughter, and then greeted by a metallic mockery of her husband. Even its glass eyes glowed with Franklin Harte's insatiable desire to subdue and humiliate.

'Sorry,' I wheezed, sounding more scared than I cared to. 'Damon's talent for toy-making has risen to new heights since I last saw him. I'm very tired, Desiree. I'd be forever indebted for a hot bath and a soft bed, and some time alone until dinner.'

'Indebted indeed,' she replied with an imperious lifting of her chin. 'Your wish is my command, Miss Wells, but I take full payment for every wish granted. Sooner or later.'

I was certain she meant what she said, but too drained to consider what might come of it.

8 Illicit Whisperings

Exhausted as I was, in this house of shuttered windows and drawn velvet draperies, sleep overtook me the moment I stretched out on the bed. Normally I would've studied my room's decor – the shadows camouflaged various oddities and interesting clocks – but my need for rest, for an escape from the unthinkable things that had turned my life upside down, overruled my curiosity. I awoke several hours later, when a succession of cuckoo birds and striking, chiming clocks brought me out of my disturbing dreams into my new reality. It was time to prepare myself for the man I'd vowed never to marry.

Hoping to avoid the Hartes, I padded into a bathroom that must've once been a dressing room – Alice's, perhaps – and stopped short. I'd planned to run my water as quietly as possible, but the claw-footed tub stood full, with wisps of steam rising in the dimness. Who had anticipated me? Or, more to the issue, who had watched me closely enough to know when I awoke? Crawling with fresh gooseflesh, I stepped in and shut the door behind me. There was no lock, nor was there a keyhole cover.

As I submerged myself in the tub of steaming, lemon-scented water, my thoughts were anything but serene. So much had happened to me since yesterday – since Pearce Truman had fetched me from school, actually – that I needed time to consider my circumstances. Never in my life had I been confronted with so many villains and traitors! I'd been taken captive by a man my family had detested for decades, and until I found a way to escape, I was stuck in his mausoleum of a mansion. I had no one to help me.

I rested my head on the back rim of the tub with a sigh. Everything around me bespoke a grim frame of mind – dark colours, a spartan atmosphere – probably because Alice disappeared so long ago, and Desiree was under her daddy's thumb, as far as how the place would be decorated. Recalling the way this white-haired siren had fondled my breasts – while Franklin watched! – made me shiver despite the hot water. I'd always thought her odd, those times we'd attended the same functions while growing up, but I hadn't anticipated her taste for females. A few of the girls at Miss Purvey's school went for that sort of thing, but they'd never approached *me*.

Vanita ... Vanita, my lovely ... wash your breasts, so I can pretend the hands that soap them are mine.

I blinked. The indistinct whisper seemed to come from everywhere at once. Or had this random, randy thought been one of my own – just lewd enough to startle me from my wool-gathering? Gripping the tub's slippery rim, I sat absolutely still, listening for another illicit command. But only the soft lapping of my bath water replied.

My imagination was playing tricks – even my own mind betrayed me now! Small wonder I wasn't already insane, after the way Franklin Harte had bound me naked in his carriage and degraded me with his cane. He'd taken the most obscene delight not only from insulting my mother's reputation but from humiliating me and then watching my body betray my passionate nature. Even now, the folds of my sex ached from the rubbing of that damned gold-headed cane – the ridges he'd pressed into my sensitive flesh to make me beg for mercy, which he had no intention of showing.

That was nothing, however, compared to the way Pearce had humiliated me! My thighs trembled at the memory of his weight between them, and my slit quivered again as I recalled the sweet deepness of his thrusts, his rampant cock pushing against the very core of me. My God, what a lover he was! Bad enough that he'd been right: now that he'd claimed me, I'd be forever branded and would never find another man acceptable.

But I'd been too much a sucker. It pierced my heart to recall the way he'd left me on Daddy's desk without a backward glance, after vowing to reclaim my estate. The bastard! He'd gotten paid to bring me home, and he was probably laughing aloud at the naive schoolgirl who'd fallen for his talk about magic and how we'd achieve it. He'd known how Harte would hold me captive in this cave of snakes, and had been part of their plan all along. A hard lesson learned.

Vanita ... rub yourself with the sponge ... there between your lovely legs, where the blonde thatch curls around your cunt.

My eyes flew open again and I searched the dim room. I could've sworn someone had slipped into the shadows behind me: in this small lavatory without windows, it was impossible to distinguish between the grey shadows cast by a cabinet and the top tank of the toilet. Had someone been hiding behind that cabinet before I came in? Damon, perhaps? This time the voice was deeper, more male, and more insistent.

Come on, sweetheart, don't be shy. You're a woman of insatiable desires, and we all know it ... and we all want a piece of you. Pleeeeeeeeeeease let us show you an ecstasy only we can bestow.

I swallowed hard as my pulse began to pound. Damn that Desiree for leaving me without a lamp! I gripped the tub again as I gazed about, aware that someone might be spying – ogling my breasts, which bobbed on the water's surface, where the soapsuds gathered like admiring lovers ... like those who now tormented me with their whispered intentions!

As several moments of heart-pounding silence went by, my breathing returned to normal. But the wariness remained. So did the memory of Pearce's face as he'd walked out on me – without a word of reassurance, after the vow I'd made to be *his*, nor a word of warning or rebuke for Franklin or my aunt. Never had I felt more alone, or more foolish. I'd trusted his pretty lies and look where they'd gotten me! It was one thing to detest Aunt Lillian, because she'd caused the lifelong struggle between us. It was another thing to give myself to a man, heart and soul, and moments later have him act as though we'd never met.

But it was over. Believing *was* seeing, as Pearce had said – and now I believed Vanita Wells was the only person I could trust if I were to see Wellspring reclaimed.

Prop your heels on the rim of the tub, Vanita. Spread your pussy lips with your fingers and then rub that sensitive flesh ... I can see you quivering, straining to find the sweet spot ... going after it – God, but you're beautiful, and I can't wait to taste you!

'Stop it!' I cried. I would've stood up and grabbed for a towel, but I imagined the hand of my voyeur materialising to grab it from me. Shaking, I felt the gooseflesh overtake my body again as I stared into every corner of the small bathroom. Now it was the sound of breathing, deep and erotic, that surrounded me, like a thousand ghosts sighing at the sight of my wet, bare body.

'Ahhhhhhhhh. I see you now!' I murmured. Because the floral wallpaper tricked the eye, I hadn't noticed the row of holes located directly behind and above the tub, with a small sliding cover. Whispering tubes.

Many large homes had such a system of pipes built into the walls, like the ones aboard a ship, so the captain could send orders to his sailors. In this case, the mistress of the house could communicate with servants in certain rooms, or the other family and staff could relay messages as well.

I let out my breath. Chances were good that no one was spying on me as I bathed. Desiree was just the type to toy with me, to catch me off guard, and perhaps the other voice belonged to her brother, a man with a marked warp.

After all, I'd met Frankie. And as I was escorted upstairs, Desiree had pointed out more of Damon's creations: large clocks with elaborate systems of cogs and weights and pendulums, as well as table-top playthings with winding keys in their backs. Clockwork toys – but not the sort one would show a child! Most of them were designed to shock the curious observer, like the frog that stuck out a huge tongue resembling a cock. My bath water felt suddenly chilly, and I thought it best to return to my room. I stood up and covered myself with a towel.

The door opened to admit Franklin Harte. In the steamy dimness he appeared almost ghostly in his white linen attire, but his expression bespoke a very earthy, tactile purpose. 'Feeling better now, Vanita?' he whispered, his gaze slithering along the length of my body.

'Yes. Thank you.' I detested the way he ogled me, making plans no woman would ever consider desirable.

'You're as lovely as your mother, sugah. What a fine surprise, to find her double! Yet her daughter is *far* more adventurous and wanton,' he clarified slyly. 'After all these years of pining, thinking a lightning strike had forever deprived me of Olivia's charms, it's so nice to –'

'Shut up! My mother wouldn't have given you a second glance.'

'You're right. She closed her eyes,' he murmured. 'Especially when her climax became so violent that her juices shot out in a torrent. I affected her that way, you see.'

'Liar! Get out of here – *now*, before I –'

'Before you what? Scream?' Harte chuckled, tapping that damn cane on the floor. 'I think you realise that would only bring Desiree running to your rescue, no doubt with her brother in tow. They're eager to welcome you to Harte's Haven, Vanita, like the proper neighbours we are!'

His smile looked as bogus as a carny barker's when he gave me a final once-over. 'I was merely being the proper host, seeing that your needs were met. Your dinner dress has been pressed to perfection, and we look forward to your presence at our table. Seven o'clock sharp.'

His two-fingered salute made me clench my jaw against another retort. Again I wondered what his white gloves concealed, because no matter how much the gentleman he considered himself, a tobacco planter and owner of coal mines didn't cover the leathery skin manual labour caused, or worry about exposure to the elements.

I sighed with relief as the door closed behind him. As I began to rub my body dry, however, soft, suggestive laughter drifted from the wall.

My, my but you've certainly tickled Daddy's fancy, Vanita. Keep him laughing and smiling that way – we all benefit. Dare to defy him – inspire his wicked wrath – and you'll owe us a lot more than an apology with those lush, kissable lips ... God, my cunt's quivering already ... the honey's running down my leg ...

I clutched the towel around my head to block the laughter that drifted around me like the steam from my bath. Not a day in this house, and already they were eating away at my composure and sanity.

I had to get out of here. Harte's Haven and all within it seemed determined to destroy me, even before I could make good on Franklin's mating mission – not that I intended to. Not only would I lose my estate, but my very self as well.

I let out a long breath and began to rethink my strategy.

It wasn't my way to cave in so quickly – nor to admit defeat before I'd even begun to fight! How long had I known these Hartes, after all? And for that entire time – ever since my childhood visits, with a mother who was leary of them, too – I'd realised the whole family was infected with something noxious and unearthly. It went far beyond Franklin's mistreatment of the fine animals we sold him, and the fearful tone I recalled in Alice Harte's voice before she mysteriously disappeared. It was reflected in the translucent pink eyes of their twin offspring: a rabbit-like wariness and vulnerability. A madness so innate it must've hidden in their genes.

But that was the least of my problems at the moment. I had to make my appearance at dinner. I had to act as though I intended to go through with this farcical marriage proposition – to get the lay of the playing field, so to speak, so I could win this game despite opponents who would constantly change the rules.

Why was I not surprised that Franklin Harte awaited me in my room? And why was I even less surprised that instead of the freshly pressed gown he'd promised, two other objects lay across the bed? I clutched my towel around me and tried to make them out. The dark wallpaper and velvet draperies allowed so little light it took me a while to distinguish things.

Because my white-suited host was grinning, I didn't delay. Best to get on with this sick little subterfuge and be done with it. I walked to the bed and slowly picked up the closest object, made of leather straps with jingling bells, metal rings at the junctures, and a buckle. 'Why have you given me a harness? Apparently a dog harness?' I ventured, my stomach already tightening.

Harte barked a laugh, his cane thumping with mirth. 'How astute, Vanita! But let's not forget what I've asked you to call me. Rephrase your question, if you expect an answer.'

I glared at him, gripping the stiff leather to keep from throwing the damn thing at him. 'Why have you provided me a harness, *Daddy*?' I spat.

'You don't recognise it?'

My temples began to throb with my anger. He was standing beside the room's only window, but I refused to walk near him for a closer look at the harness in the thin strips of daylight around the draperies. Then, however, I realised that the other object on the bed was a blanket, like one placed under a horse's saddle. This one looked worn, but the faded green and gold pattern, with the letter W woven into its stripes, could only have come from one place.

My stomach bottomed out. The bastard had somehow gotten hold of the saddle blanket I'd used with my favourite pony, Josh, and then again when I became a more accomplished rider and competed for awards on Pegasus. Snatching it up, I bit back tears. 'Who gave you these things? What right do you have to –'

'Your Aunt Lillian wanted you to have familiar things here at Harte's Haven,' he replied in an oily voice. 'And since the circumstances of our departure prevented you from packing, I thought these might comfort you. You'll look fetching in them at dinner.'

The bells on the red harness jangled angrily as I gripped it – far from the merry sound it made when Samson, Daddy's huge black mastiff, had worn it to pull me in a little red wagon. The dog was my constant companion when I was a toddler, and he'd lived until I was nearly ten. That Lill had taken this harness from the tack box where I'd stored my best memories – and that this warped jackal now expected me to wear it – was beyond any cruelty I could ever imagine.

'Ah, so you do remember,' Harte remarked, his eyes glittering. 'Your daddy was so damn proud of you, riding in that cart with your frilly dresses and your golden ringlets. Like a little doll, you were. I can see you don't appreciate this token of my welcome, but you'll thank me if my son takes notice of it at the table. Trust me, Vanita, I'm trying to make another prospective bride attractive to a ... reluctant bridegroom. I'll see you at seven. Do us both proud.'

I threw the damn harness after him, but it struck the back of the door. Franklin's laughter echoed in the hall. Then I was alone in that sepulchre of a room, with my hatred and humiliation, and the ticking of those onerous clocks. This room had three of them, and as I tried to think of a way out of my intolerable situation, they began to strike, one after another.

The first was a regulator wall clock, bonging nicely enough until I noticed its pendulum was a crouched brass monkey, fondling his oversized cock. Then came the cuckoo clock near the bathroom door, which had weights shaped like phalluses and a face that formed the opening between carved female legs. The bird gave a suggestive little moan when it popped out where the clitoris would be. At least the anniversary clock on the tallboy simply spun beneath its glass dome, clockwise ... then counter-clockwise ... with prisms that would've glistened beautifully in a room where there was light. All this to tell me it was half past six.

If I stayed in this horrid room, I'd be seething and unable to eat – and I was famished. Better to appear on top of my game, unruffled, than to let these people know they could make me grovel before the first day was out. So I pulled the red harness over my head with a last, sad thought of Samson, and buckled it at my waist. It was stiff with age, but the centre strap bisected my chest and joined the collar ring and the waistband, which fitted me snugly. I tried not to wince at the way my bare breasts hung out from this contraption.

Next I draped the saddle blanket around my waist, trying to cover myself – and then had a better thought. If I had to provoke Damon into taking notice, I might was well *do* it. By knotting the blanket at my waist in the front, I could display my sex with every step I took. It was a far cry from a dinner gown, but Mama had always told me if I smiled and carried myself with poise, grace and dignity, even rags would pass for evening attire. How could she have known I might need that shot of confidence to reclaim her estate?

I stepped out of my room, peering along the upstairs hall. It seemed a good time to get my bearings in this behemoth of a house, for I might need to beat a quick retreat or find a hiding place sometime. Here, the wall-paper was the colour of dried blood, with black flocking. I couldn't think Alice Harte had chosen such ghastly decor – just as I couldn't imagine her placing pewter lamps fashioned like nudes on her fine walnut tables.

The other bedroom doors were closed, and an expectant hush enveloped the hall, as though the very house were drinking in my lewd costume. With bells on, I had to walk very carefully so as not to alert anyone of my presence. When I came to the grand staircase, inspiration struck: I flipped the blanket up over my hips and muffled that damned jingling by pulling the wool tightly across my back. Mama would be rolling in her grave. What if someone saw me this way, exposing everything from my waist down?

But no one awaited me downstairs, nor did anyone come down the opposite staircase which, with the one I descended, wrapped gracious, carpeted arms around the front hall. Again, if it weren't for walls the colour of pond scum and the heavy ebony furnishings, Harte's Haven would've looked as grand as Wellspring had when my parents were alive.

Past massive credenzas and display cases I padded, not pausing to study their mechanical toys. Tables seemed to have been placed solely for the purpose of holding timepieces, and the front hall boasted two ornately carved grandfather clocks as well. Why were these people so enamoured of *time*? There had to be a servant whose main occupation was keeping all these instruments wound and clean. And what sort of racket must they make at the striking of each hour?

I didn't want to know. I used these moments to peek into the downstairs rooms where Alice would've entertained: a drawing room with a lovely grand piano, a front parlour with furniture so overstuffed it might swallow whoever sat in it, a study with an inlaid desk and bookcases, which must have been where Mrs. Harte dispatched her social correspondence. All the rooms had been designed with floor-to-ceiling windows – and all were cloaked in heavy velvet draperies, as though the household were in perpetual mourning . . . or sought to conceal some hideous secrets.

I came upon the dining room, and was met by the assessing gazes of all three Hartes. In the light from two massive candelabra they sat, as though seated for a wake. Perhaps mine. I tugged at the horse blanket to cover myself, now sorry I'd been so bold as to leave the gap in the front. Franklin rose from his chair, leering as he brandished his goblet at me.

'A toast to the bride!' he called out, his gaze fastened on my bobbing breasts. Desiree snickered, but otherwise the twins did nothing to acknowledge their father's salute. Dressed in a crisp black evening coat with a snowy-white shirt and cravat, Damon sat across from his sister, facing the door but not looking at me. He stared instead at his wine, as though wishing he could jump into it and drown.

It was going to be a lovely evening.

9 My Humiliation Continues

In that awkward moment, as I gripped the moulding around the doorway, I studied the man who represented my salvation. I hadn't seen Damon Harte for years, and I was pleasantly surprised at the gentleman he'd become. He'd attained a continental air, a confidence born of expressing his own personal style. He wore his snowy hair cut shorter than was the fashion for men, hugging his head like a neat cap. His features were so pale that on first glance I thought he had no eyebrows or lashes, and the hands holding his goblet were nearly the colour of his shirt.

Yet when he looked up at me, and actually smiled, Damon Harte was breathtakingly beautiful. His bearing bespoke better manners and disposition than his twin's. He stood up then, with the grace of a well-practised dancer, and pulled out the empty chair beside him.

'How nice to see you again, Vanita,' he murmured, and with a debonair bow he gestured for me to join them. 'Please excuse us for pouring our wine before you arrived. Father's excited about your visit and couldn't wait to begin the festivities.'

I noted not a hint of condescension or sarcasm. Indeed, this striking man had spoken the first civil words I'd heard all day, and continued to smile as though I were as properly attired as he and his sister. If this was another nasty trick the Harte family had in store for me – leading me on again with pretty lies – at least Damon was gracious enough to sugar-coat it.

As I sat down, however, and sipped at the sherry he poured for me, I sensed my intended was behaving so kindly because he didn't like this scenario any better than I did. Franklin watched the two of us closely while downing another glass of wine. Although he was arrayed in white, he reminded me of a vulture; a scavenger waiting to feast upon me after his children had eaten their share.

It took mere moments to exhaust the usual conversational pleasantries, because we had so few of them. What did a lady say as she sat with her bare breasts protruding through a red dog harness? Every time I moved, I jingled like Santa's sleigh. The scratchy old horse blanket gaped open, exposing my bare thighs and everything between them; the fact that the table covered this part of me gave little comfort. I noticed Franklin's gold-headed cane resting against the arm of his chair, and I didn't like it one bit.

As Roger brought our soup, Harte flipped open my napkin and leaned close enough to place it in my lap. I stiffened, praying those gloved fingers wouldn't stray to my slit while the twins and the driver-turned-butler watched. The pudgy servant eyed my bare breasts and gaping blanket as though he longed to spill soup down my front, as an excuse to clean it up. As though reading my thoughts, Franklin laughed lasciviously.

'Ah, Vanita, it does my heart good to converse with a young lady who can still blush – even after I've seen that man fucking you on your daddy's desk,' he said in a sinuous voice. 'You're just the sort of woman my son needs. Experienced, yet a social equal. Your aunt should be very proud of such a match, as well.'

My eyes flared. He was glossing over a situation I wasn't sure the twins knew about – and by God, they would hear my side of it! 'And how ... *decent* of you to assume her gambling debts, and then force her hand with foreclosure! The two of *you* would make a fine match, I'd say!'

Franklin laughed aloud, and with a squeeze of my thigh he addressed his soup. 'No, Miss Lillian has her heart set on that bandy-legged attorney. I'm too autocratic, she says. And I wouldn't allow her to play her little games and go through *my* money the way she has yours!'

My cheeks flamed with his rebuff. Damon was sipping his soup as though trying to ignore his father's crudeness, while Desiree, across from us, stole teasing glances at me. Mostly at my breasts. There was no fire in the grate, and the dining room felt chilly – which meant my nipples had puckered out like hard little berries for someone in this devious trio to pick.

'Lovely soup, Roger,' Desiree said to the butler. 'Please pass my compliments to Magnolia.'

'Yes, she's done a superb job. Don't you agree, Vanita?'

My host was becoming more brazen by the moment, now rubbing my knee with his. I was famished, so I ignored him to take a spoonful of the pale broth. It tasted wonderfully rich, and I dipped up slivers of the meat and vegetables, savouring the warmth of it going down my throat. At least I'd eat well while I was here. And since it was impolite to speak with food in my mouth, I downed the entire bowl in short order, as an excuse not to answer him.

'Excellent. A woman with an appetite,' Franklin said, waving away the empty bowls. 'I've asked Magnolia to prepare a special meal in honour of your coming to live with us. I hope the food and your room meet your highest expectations, sugah. You were raised to expect the best, after all.'

His arrogance turned my stomach: he was baiting

me, of course. But I replied, so he wouldn't think he was winning. 'Yes, Aunt Lillian has told me you have plans for a splendid wedding ceremony! A proper young lady can't ask for more than that.'

Franklin smirked. 'She told you there'd be a festive event? With garlands of flowers, and guests enjoying dinner out on the lawn while an orchestra plays?'

'She didn't get specific.'

'Good. Because the notion of a showy wedding is absurd! Just another of her actress fantasies,' he replied with a nasty laugh. 'You think I'd lavish that sort of luxury on a girl who's here to fulfil a debt?'

It wasn't a scene I intended to see anyway, that wedding, but I could've found things about the day to enjoy at his expense. As he mocked me with those gleeful, piggy eyes, I knew he meant what he'd said. Another belief betrayed, that ceremony my aunt had gushed about. Yet another way Lillian Gilding had sold me down the river to atone for her own sins.

'It's none of my doing,' I reminded him, meeting that gaze with an unwavering one of my own. 'You know damn well my parents would never have condoned Aunt Lill's gambling, or –'

'But your parents have nothing to say about this!' he hissed, insinuating his hand between my legs. 'Do you like what I'm doing to you now?'

'No!'

'Then why's the honey dripping from your cunt?' he demanded with a malicious laugh. 'In all fairness, I'll tell you my son won't pay you this much attention. You're not the first woman I've tempted him with, Vanita – to the point that I don't give a damn about a wedding! I don't even care about him producing an heir! I'd just like to hold my head up among my friends and call my son a *man*.'

I swallowed hard. He was discussing these matters

as though Damon weren't sitting on the other side of me, and I wanted no part of this enmity between father and son. I simply sought answers to questions that seemed to change with each conversation.

'What is it you expect of me, then?' The harness bells shivered as I tried to jerk away from his probing fingers ... fingers that were producing a warm, sticky puddle in my chair.

'The woman I saw spread-eagled on her daddy's desk, fucking her aunt's errand boy, shouldn't have to ask *that* question!' Harte's voice rose with the colour of his face, as though I were thoroughly testing his patience. 'Seduce him, for God's sake! Find a way to get his cock out of his pants and into *you*, Vanita! You're the last ace your foolish aunt had up her sleeve, so play yourself well. It's the only way you'll reclaim Wellspring.'

'*That's* how she came to be here?' Damon demanded. He gripped the edge of the table so tightly his hands shook. 'Of all the despicable –'

'It was Lillian's idea, boy. Desperate women take desperate measures.' Franklin focused on me again, grasping a tuft of my pubic hair between his thumb and forefinger to emphasise his point. 'And you, dear Vanita, stand to lose it all – the house, the stables, the pastureland – unless you comply. Do I make myself clear?'

I wondered how I'd *prove* it, if Damon ever made love to me, but something warned me not to ask. 'Yes. Quite clear.'

'Yes, what?'

I scowled and swatted at his hand. 'Yes, sir.'

'Yes, *what*?' he repeated. Then he drove his finger up inside me, making me squirm against the back of my chair.

What sort of ogre did this to a woman, in front of

his own family? This onerous moment had to pass, so I closed my eyes and muttered, 'Yes, Daddy.'

'Oh, Jesus. I refuse to –' Damon threw down his napkin, scraping his chair back from the huge table.

'Sit down!' his father thundered, jumping to his feet. His face now matched the scarlet flocking on the wallpaper, and the room went airless, leaving the rest of us holding our breath. 'You will behave as a proper gentleman and entertain our guest – *your* hope for salvation, my boy! I'm doing you a favour! I've told you before that if you continue to disgrace the Harte name, cavorting with your queer friends, your sister inherits the entire estate and you'll be out on your pretty little ass with nothing! Understand me?'

Desiree shifted in her chair, the anger in her eyes suggesting they'd weathered this hurricane many times. Damon resumed his seat, sighing his disgust.

'What's your answer?' Franklin demanded, his voice making the prisms of the chandelier quake. 'Do you understand me, Damon?'

'Yes, you've made yourself quite clear.'

'Yes, what?'

Together the twins focused their curious pink eyes at the man standing to my left, as though they could shatter his stony heart with their gazes. 'Yes, Daddy,' Damon spat.

'You're a disgrace,' the older Harte muttered. 'I wish your mother were here to see how she ruined you.'

For several moments we sat in an awkward silence broken only by the ticking of the clocks on the mantel. Roger peered from behind the screen at the kitchen door, deciding the end of Franklin's tirade was his cue to serve the main course nobody was hungry for. With a flourish, he presented the platter to the master of Harte's Haven, holding it while Franklin chose the best slices of roast nestled among boiled potatoes, carrots and cabbage wedges.

'Thank you, Roger. Smells delectable,' the man in white crooned.

'Yessir, she does.' The butler cast me a knowing glance as he offered Desiree the platter. In profile, his erection formed an obvious peak beneath his apron. 'Plenty here for you, Miss Vanita. The finest meat you're ever going to find.'

'I can wait until you've served the others, thank you,' I replied tightly. 'Dark meat, cut from the hind quarters, has never been my preference.'

Franklin's eyes closed in deliberate ecstasy over the bite of roast he was chewing. Beside me, Damon cleared his throat to cover a chuckle as he forked food on to his plate.

Carefully, so as not to touch the leering butler, I helped myself to some roast and a cabbage wedge. I had to lean harder than I'd expected on my knife, but I was so hungry – and so eager not to draw further attention to myself – that I sawed vigorously at the meat before popping the first bite into my mouth.

My white-suited host was watching me as though he couldn't get enough of my working jaws. I cut more of my roast. It was chewier than I preferred, and had an odd taste and texture compared to most beef, but I said nothing. If the cook had taken special pains, I didn't want to get on her bad side my first night.

'What do you think – in a word?' Franklin murmured.

'In a word? Delicious,' I fibbed. 'Miss Purvey economised by serving a lot of poultry, so a roast is indeed a treat.'

I was taking another bite, thinking I'd had about enough, when the head of Harte's cane found its mark under the table. I sat up with a gasp, instinctively closing my legs, but Franklin had the element of surprise in his favour.

'We must thank your aunt for so graciously providing us this delicacy. She insisted, again, on sending along a token of her goodwill while you carry out her part of our bargain. Which is why I chose your attire the way I did.'

My fork paused in mid-air. 'I wasn't aware she sent any food, so I don't know what you're talking about.'

'But you recognised the saddle blanket immediately. And an equestrienne like yourself has surely visited the Wellspring stables and found something ... missing.' Without a flicker on his swarthy face, he prodded my slit with the head of the cane, twisting it against my clitoris.

Bile rose up my throat. Pegasus's absence had shocked me, but I'd never dreamed ...

'Daddy, you didn't!' Desiree's hand flew to her mouth as she spat out its contents. 'How could you do this to me? You should've told us, dammit!'

The young woman grew even paler than I thought possible. She stood suddenly, sending her chair clattering on to the floor as she ran from the room. Franklin laughed, his eyes never leaving my bloodless face as he tormented my sex with his cane.

Damon rose, too, bristling with indignation as he pulled my chair back. 'This is inexcusable! Of all the crude – Vanita, I assure you that had I known about this, I –'

'Oh, save it,' his father snapped. But this time he didn't order his son to sit down, nor did he stop me from leaving. He'd once again established himself as master of everyone around him while sickening and humiliating us, too. I held my hand to my mouth as Damon steered me quickly through the kitchen, past the cook stirring a sauce, and out to the little back stoop. Despite my attempts at appearing unruffled, I retched behind the nearest bush.

A few moments later, Desiree straightened from doing the same, visible in the velvety night because her white face shone like the moon. She brushed her skirts, looking ready to cry – until she saw her brother steadying me, making a valiant effort not to vomit himself.

'Bitch!' she whispered. 'Now you've got Daddy all riled up and –'

'Vanita had no more to do with this than we did!' her twin replied in a matching voice. 'Now shut up! He's probably listening – or has Roger posted by the door. Let's go. The least we can do is get her out of this ridiculous costume.'

'Hah! She was eating it up – flirting with Roger, no less! Didn't you see the way she shook herself to make her tits shimmy?'

Damon was guiding me along the rear wall of the house, and I was close enough to his sister to grab her dress. 'Would *you* like it if some madman forced you to wear a harness that belonged to the dog you loved as a child? And the blanket you'd saved from your first pony – while serving your favourite gelding for dinner?' I demanded. 'First chance I get, I'm ramming that cane up his backside!'

Desiree shrugged out of my grasp, yet I discerned a smile on her milky lips. 'You'll have to stand in line, missy! But don't get any ideas about us *wanting* you here! Things are fine just as they are, you know.'

'Fine for *you*, maybe!' I retorted. 'Believe me, this was the last place I'd intended to come! Did you realise your dear daddy was in thick with my Aunt Lillian?'

'How do you mean, in thick?' Her expression went wary. No matter what I said, this young woman – her daddy's girl, just as I had been – would believe Franklin before she believed me.

'Up to his hilt, I'm guessing. I thought that bed upstairs might come through the ceiling.'

This gave her pause, and then her face lit up with a wicked grin. 'And it's true he caught you fucking somebody on your daddy's desk?'

'That's why I don't have any clothes. He and my aunt were lying in wait like a couple of wolves, to pounce on me and seal their deal.'

Desiree relaxed then, giving her brother a knowing look. 'Well, then. It seems the blonde doll baby from Wellspring has acquired an education she didn't get at finishing school! Do you think she's ready to play, Damon? I know I am.'

10 An Intimate Initiation

Damon ran his slender fingers through his hair, glancing from his sister to me. 'Get her something to wear, Dez. I'll show her downstairs.'

This seemed a topic ripe with innuendo, which charged the air around us like an electrical storm. Was it my imagination, or did Desiree pull her shoulders back and wink at her brother? Damon, too, grew taut, as though anticipating a much nicer time than we'd had at dinner. My stomach had settled, and as the striking albino beside me opened a door at the back of the mansion, I sensed I was being let in on a delicious secret ... something these mysterious siblings didn't reveal to their father. I'd somehow passed a trial by fire, and was now accepted into that tight inner circle twins were said to share.

Down a dark, carpeted set of stairs we went, like a service access to a wine cellar. And indeed, we came out in a catacomb of racks, where jars of preserved foods filled shadowy shelves. I was thinking how glad I'd be to get rid of the dog harness, which chafed the skin between my breasts with every step I took. The wool blanket rubbed me wrong, as well, and I couldn't wait to stop itching and jingling.

'Let me light a lamp.' Damon cautiously turned the knob of the darkened door we'd reached, as though an intruder might await us. He then struck a match. 'None of the other women my father's chosen have seen my private domain, Vanita. If anything offends or upsets you, just say so. Desiree and I often escape to this room, because here we can truly be ourselves.'

I squinted, adjusting my eyes to the circle of light and what lay beyond it. 'What happened to those other girls, Damon?'

'Father sent them to Devil's Dungeon, to shovel coal. Not a pretty fate.'

Devil's Dungeon was the region's most extensive network of coal mines, and Franklin Harte had made a large part of his fortune from those black bowels of the earth. Stories of explosions and cave-ins had been enough, when I was a child, to make me glad none of the Wells family had such holdings. 'But why –'

'Dearest Vanita.' Damon took my hands in his soft, pale ones, appearing luminous in the lamplight. 'I'm sorry your Aunt Lill and my father have treated you so horribly. But I'll tell you up front that I have no interest in marriage or mating. It would be a *relief* if Desiree inherited Harte's Haven, and the stables and the mines! I *want* her to have them!'

He leaned over me so his crystalline eyes caught mine, continuing in a low, earnest tone. 'What good are fields of tobacco I can't oversee? My skin sizzles after only moments of exposure to sunlight! And if my sister managed the estate, I'd be free to create my clocks, and the clockworks we play with down here, because that's what I do best. I'll gladly help you get Wellspring back, Vanita, but I won't be bedding you!'

Call me Pearce. It's what I do best.

My heart stumbled over these words, for Damon had just pierced me as surely as that demon who'd dared me to believe in him. How cruel, that two men should invite me into their private worlds – their areas of expertise – and then deny me what I needed! Pearce, so dark and virile, had walked away after challenging me to be his, while this pale fellow wanted nothing to do with me as a woman. I looked into eyes so colourless in the light, it was like seeing through a clear stream to its bed.

'Can't you just *pretend* to want me, long enough to convince your father?' I pleaded. 'I'm losing everything I've ever loved! Surely I can't be so unattractive as to repel –'

'Oh, Vanita, you're lovely! Make no mistake!' he gushed, his gaze roving over my bare, harnessed body with true appreciation. But it was an artist's view he was taking, rather than a lover's. 'I'm simply not made that way. I was born to bring enjoyment and beauty to those who share my world. I've known it all my life – and quite frankly, I love rubbing my father's nose in it. It causes Franklin Harte the ultimate anguish, because he can't control my inclinations. So he can't control me.'

I wished I could hate Damon for spelling things out. Considering my misadventures of the past few days, however, his honesty refreshed me. If I didn't want to end up breaking my back in his father's mines, I would have to come up with another ploy, because – despite Pearce's high-and-mighty promises – I might still be saving myself from this despicable situation. The landmarks had changed, but I was the only one who could plot my path out of this hell where Franklin held me.

When Desiree showed up with a dressing gown, I reconsidered my concerns for the future. Perhaps these twins, now that they seemed to befriend me, would help me *escape*. If I played along – discovered an ace I didn't know I had up my sleeve – I might convince them my cause was worth their efforts.

'Thank you,' I murmured as I took the lovely gown from my hostess. It shimmered in the lamplight, whispering promises as only crimson silk could.

Desiree's smile seemed speculative, as though she

were playing out an ulterior motive. But then she turned to her brother, all interest in me evaporating. 'Come and play with me, Damon. Forget about Daddy! What does he know? I'm yours and you're mine, and that's all that matters.'

I wasted no time unbuckling the harness and letting it drop to the floor with the saddle blanket. The dressing gown was generously cut – far too large for the woman who'd brought it – but I didn't dare second-guess where she'd gotten it. As I wrapped the delicious fabric around my body, knotting the sash at my waist, I took my first good look at this place. Something illicit crackled in the atmosphere, making more of this cellar than had first met my eye.

As Damon and his sister lit sconces on the walls, the cavernous room came to life in an unexpected way. This was no mere workshop for a man who spent his best hours tinkering with springs and cogs and pulleys; it looked like a carnival after dark, enclosed, yet endless in its possibilities. I felt like Gulliver, landing in a strange world where size and perspective and everyday objects took on startling proportions.

Clocks were everywhere! Ornately carved cuckoo clocks lined the walls, bracketed by more sombre pendulum models. Some of the floor clocks were encased in glass, showing elaborate displays of brass and coils and cogs that turned with the click of each movement. The room resounded with these tickings, at various pitches – and then Damon opened the lid of a cabinet beside me, and wound the crank on its side.

Music tinkled out, like the liquid notes of a waterfall transformed into delicate sound. His face took on an ethereal joy as he turned towards his twin, his arm extended gracefully. Desiree clasped his hand and they circled each other with a rapt happiness I felt awkward witnessing.

Yet I couldn't look away. With fluid movements they removed each other's clothes, their faces shining in the candlelight. His suit and shirt fell away to reveal a firm, sleek body more beautiful than any Greek statue, with the understated strength of a dancer. He quickly stripped his sister, running agile hands over her creamy skin to peel off the layers of black serge and white silk underthings. They had forgotten all about me by the time they scurried to the room's other side, laughing like lovers.

The flickering light revealed a large anniversary clock – the kind of timepiece that ran by the rotation of a silver pole pendulum in its centre, which curved into four tips topped with silver balls, by spinning first in a clockwise direction and then going counter-clockwise. Most unusual, however, was the sheer size of this creation: Damon slid the glass dome in its track, and then he and his sister stepped inside, on to the flat slats of the spinning pendulum, like children mounting a merry-go-round platform. Laughing, they grasped the centre pole, which shone with spiralling meshwork all along its spinning shaft. They then stood on two of the silver balls, facing each other, to ride inside the phenomenal clock.

I could only stare from the shadows. Enraptured by the delicate strains from the music box, I gazed at the twin figures: Desiree with her elegant, upswept hair of platinum, her small breasts bobbing on a body that vibrated with her excitement. As the light caught her in a spin, her hair sparkled – even the patch of curls between her thighs shone diamond-white. She grasped the column, and then swung up like an acrobat to wrap her legs around it.

Damon urged her on with his smile, his expression transcending any joy I'd ever seen. Gone was the humiliation his father had laid upon him. Long gone was any concern about the future of Harte's Haven or my own predicament. He was living a fantasy, dancing with his twin as though performing an intricate ballet. Their laughter was low, mingling intimately, as he grasped the spinning silver shaft so his knuckles brushed his sister's slit.

I nipped my lip. This taboo activity was almost too exquisite to think about, let alone watch, and I found my own sex quivering with every flex of Desiree's slim hips. She rubbed herself against her brother's hands as they spun on the clock's pole. Damon, too, was thrusting in time, against the soles of his sister's feet, with his erection nestled between them.

The clock spun in its elegance while the delicate tune tinkled around us, and it was nothing short of magic. White magic; illicit, forbidden magic that had me slipping my hand beneath the crimson robe as I watched it play out. I knew then that Damon and Desiree had eyes only for each other as they bobbed and thrust in this elemental dance they'd shared since they began in Alice's womb. They were not two people, they were halves of a spinning, magnificent whole. And one could not – did not wish to – exist without the other.

Desiree pumped more fervently against her brother's knuckles, and when she threw her head back, I gasped at her sheer beauty – and at the quiverings in my own body. Slipping my fingers between my sex lips, I spread the slickness around my hot skin, undulating in the rhythm I beheld in front of me. Damon thrust at alternate beats with his partner, so that after he surged upwards between Desiree's feet, she slid down the backs of his hands. Her thighs splayed farther, and in moments when her back spun towards me, she appeared to be making love to a very tall silver cock. Likewise Damon, when he spun to face away from me, seemed to stand between his twin's spread thighs.

Their breathy exclamations sped me on. Words not meant for my ears drifted around me, resounding beneath the clocks' ticking and the innocent tinklings of the music box.

'Damon ... lover ... you're so hard and hot.'

'Yessssss, my darling ... grip me tighter. Spread yourself, so I can watch you flex ...'

'You feel close ... ready to explode.'

'And I will ... when I feel your juice spewing over my hands ...'

I moaned, leaning against the wall to keep from falling. Canting my hips towards them, trying not to call attention to myself, I flicked my fingers more rapidly around a pulsing hole that responded to their every nuance. As Desiree began to rub in earnest, I saw rivulets of her honey running down the clock's shaft, and then felt my own juices mimic them. Her pale feet clenched delicately around Damon's erection, making him grimace with an ecstasy that lit his entire body. It was luminous poetry, set to the music of spheres that had spun forever between male and female, scented by my own heady essence as I rubbed my desperate clit.

'Yes, Damon, yessssssss,' she hissed, as the sibilance filled the room with a tightening I felt in every pore.

The two of them were spinning like figures atop a music box, thrusting in time, driving each other to a completion they could find nowhere else – bodies so beautifully alike, so stunning in the lamplight as they glistened with the sweat of their efforts.

With a grimace, Damon thrust rapidly, spurting his cream up the pole. Some of it splashed against Desiree's rippling belly and she wailed like a banshee. Arching back until her arms were fully extended and her head was level with her hips, she bucked frantically against the shaft. On and on her cries went, covering my own low groans as my body convulsed.

For a moment we were enveloped by the continuous tickings and our expectant silence, the aftermath of a passing hurricane that still possessed great power. Hoping to remain inconspicuous, I slipped my hand out of the dressing gown and tried to compose my face. Damon steadied his sister as she slid down the pole. As one, they tilted to the side and kissed languorously, their bodies pressed against the pendulum made slick by their juices.

With a sigh that relieved the entire room, they relaxed. Desiree shook her head, as though clearing her vision. Then she glanced at me. 'I think Vanita's ready.'

'Let's find out.'

I moved away from the wall, but they were advancing like sleek white cats, their bodies graceful in a furtive, feline way. 'Perhaps I should've left you to your –'

The cuckoo clock nearest my head whirred to life, its little yellow bird popping out of the trap door to proudly crow the hour – which seemed to signal the other clocks around us. One by one they struck, the large floor clocks bonging sonorously while the ones on the wall chimed ten times and went silent. The cacophony was deafening, yet exhilarating; I'd never seen such a collection of timepieces, nor heard such a sounding-off.

Damon watched me closely while his sister came over to my other side. They had an ulterior motive, so I quickly gathered my thoughts: admiring Damon's handiwork would get me into their better graces, while stalling for time from whatever they planned to do to me now.

As the chimings and little music boxes subsided, I

was still held spellbound by the cuckoo clock that had started it all. It was a beautifully carved piece, German in detail, and after its little bird went back to his nest, a small platform revolved with pairs of dancers – the men in hats and lederhosen and the women wearing full, embroidered skirts and vests. Around and around they whirled in place as the carousel carried them inside the clock and back out again.

'What marvellous detail,' I whispered, sincerely impressed with the expressions on their little wooden faces, and the shadings of their colours. 'Did you make this one, too, Damon?'

He bowed slightly. 'One of my early projects, modelled after a clock Mama brought back from Europe. Desiree and I could hardly wait for the hour to strike, when we were children, so we could watch the dancers spin to the music. As cloistered as we were, any signs of life relieved our dark drudgery back then.'

'Damon was inspired by this piece to move on to ... bigger and better things,' his sister added, questioning her sibling with an arched brow. 'It's another way he and I pass these long evenings ... a clockwork creation we've shown to none of his other prospective brides, because they simply wouldn't have understood the beauty of it. Would you like to see it, Vanita? I think you'll be ... quite impressed.'

The undertone of her contralto voice warned me that my decision would have its consequences, for nothing Desiree offered came without its price. Yet I was genuinely curious, and I thought the twins might be distracted from their carnal designs on me.

'I'd be honoured,' I replied. What other options did I have? Going upstairs, where lewd voices came through the whispering tubes and Franklin might be awaiting me, was something I could put off as long as possible.

With an albino on either side, I was escorted through

the room, past the larger-than-life anniversary clock that now whirled silently beneath its glass dome. Desiree walked ahead to light more sconces, which illuminated the farther corners of this huge room. 'If you like my cuckoo clock – and merry-go-rounds,' Damon said, 'you'll find this toy's a carnival in itself.'

We stopped near an oversized replica of the cuckoo clock's dancer platform, identical except that the wooden dancers stood alone, awaiting partners. Had I come upon this contraption by myself, I'd have been scared witless, as the six-foot figures had frozen in odd positions after their last dance. One of the men was stooped, his jointed wooden arms reaching towards me – which made the leer on his painted face seem eerily sinister. The other man stood with his arms outstretched, bent at the knees, apparently inviting the woman across the platform into his embrace. She cast him a coyly painted come-on in return, and her body was tilted to one side as though she had a bad back. The fourth figure, another female, was bent forwards at the waist and caught in the act of throwing her skirts over her shoulders.

I realised, of course, that these were merely statues – carousel horses in human form – but their facial expressions and fabric clothing made them extremely lifelike in the dimness. I nipped my lip. As a child, I'd been frightened of the mannequins at Mama's dressmaker – headless forms which stood beside each seamstress, proportioned like her clients – because I feared these models were dead people that might spring to life or grab at me when my back was turned.

My stomach knotted as I thought about the lewd entertainment Damon and Desiree had designed this contraption for. Mechanical lovers, were they? Clockworks to replace the friends these sheltered twins couldn't visit – or perhaps didn't even want? As my pearl-skinned escort stepped over the wooden platform to the belt-driven machinery in its centre, I was wishing I'd found a reason to go back upstairs.

When Desiree read my apprehension, she slipped her arm around my shoulders. 'For your first ride, Hugo here is probably the best bet,' she said playfully, pointing towards the stooping figure. 'Come and meet him. He's really quite friendly.'

'I'm not the only one going for a ride, I hope?' I stammered. 'I'd hate to deprive you of your favourite partner.'

'Oh, Dezzy loves them all,' her brother said with a snicker. He was cranking a handle on the side of the gearbox, while the large coil inside tightened with a whine. 'Once the music starts, it's like having our own carnival ball –'

'– but the dancers never miss a beat or step on your toes,' his sister added gleefully. 'I'm in the mood for Horace, I think. Unless *you* want him, dear.'

'Harriet's calling my name, thanks. Hop on, ladies. Ecstasy awaits us.'

There was no escaping the surprisingly strong arm Desiree had placed around me, and as she ushered me on to the platform, I couldn't deny my fascination for what might happen next. Again, the painted detail on the platform was startling and colourful, and the figure she guided me towards was fashioned of a fine pine polished to a gloss. Almost the colour of my skin, he was, with his features a rakish caricature drawn in black – piercing eyes with arched, dark brows, a bulbous nose, beneath which parted a lush moustache. Hugo was smooth-shaven yet I couldn't miss the resemblance to Pearce Truman, which made me laugh in spite of my misgivings.

'So you like him?' Desiree queried. 'Place your feet on those footprints in front of him, and this fellow will give you a ride like no other. This time, let him lead, Vanita. When you've become accustomed to the tilt and rhythm of his movements, I'm sure you'll conjure up all sorts of variations. Let's go, Damon!'

The platform lurched beneath us as the mechanisms sprang into motion. Calliope music began to play, and Desiree hurried over to stand in front of Horace, across the platform from me, while her brother hopped nimbly aboard to approach the wooden woman bent to one side.

I was suddenly scooped up by two solid hands cupping my butt, and I let out a delighted shriek. Hugo, head and shoulders taller than I, had come to life, his head tilting to and fro as he studied me with a roguish grin. His fingers flexed, singing against the silk of my robe when he plied my backside, and as he tipped me towards him I grabbed his broad shoulders.

Then he began to spin slowly in place, and as the music grew louder he stuck out his tongue ... a very phallic tongue of curved, red wax. The sight of it made my sex clench in anticipation – until I saw the rod coming up from the front of his short pants. Its bulbous tip was sheathed in kidskin, with lacings that tapered to fit the shaft. The entire apparatus appeared about eight inches long, and incredibly ... tantalisingly thick.

'Oh my Lord! What do I – ?'

Desiree's laughter rang out across from me. 'Give him his head, Vanita! You'll never find a finer cock than Hugo's, because I designed it myself!'

'Follow his lead,' Damon urged from a few feet away. He'd hopped on to Harriet's bloomered backside, and was tilting like a bronco rider, buried to the hilt inside her.

When my partner's erection parted my legs, I let him have his way. The tip spun slowly, while the entire phallus vibrated with its own inner mechanism. Meanwhile, I was being gently lowered on to it by those firm, unerring hands. My fears evaporated, changed into a rush of inner sensations, like those brought on by a spinning, dipping carnival ride. Hugo kept turning, and all the while his head bobbed to the music and his arms moved me up and down. On one revolution, I saw Desiree vault up to straddle her dancer's face, squealing with the delight of a child. Damon was being rocked in a rhythm as old as creation itself, his colour rising with his excitement.

With another burst of coils and gears, the platform sped up and the dancers did, too. Giddy with dizziness, I began to laugh and couldn't stop. The tilting and whirling created a high-flying madness within me, spurred on by the ribbed piston inside my pussy. I gasped for air, aware of the heat spiralling outwards from my core, higher and tighter, from the friction of the kidskin lacings, until I thought I might burst from the need of release.

With a final cry I gave in, holding tightly as Hugo dipped and swayed, penetrating my sex as the swift, squishing sound of my juices echoed around me. Then he clutched me against his wooden hips and probed deeper, vibrating against my clitoris with the perfect pressure. On and on I rode a wave of sublime pleasure, until finally, when I thought I'd lose consciousness, the machinery spun slowly to a halt.

I leaned limply against the wooden figure, trying to catch my breath. What had just happened? Honey was running down my legs and the crimson robe clung like a second skin, holding in the heat of my wild exertions. I was afraid to move, for fear I'd topple off, yet afraid to stay put, thinking the twins might crank up the mechanism again. I heard their laughter as they regaled their own rides, but their voices came from a distant, foggier place.

Then I felt hands – flesh and blood ones – and Damon was steadying me. 'Didn't Desiree do a fine job with Hugo?' he asked with a husky chuckle. 'She does my painting, as well as challenging me with ideas for new clockworks and all manner of sexual delights.'

I opened my eyes to see Hugo's immobile smile, rather garish in the flickering light. Yes, Desiree had designed him as only a white witch could, and yes, he bore an unsettling resemblance to the lover I'd had last night. But all I could think of was retreating to my room for a rest ... and how sore I'd be when my inner muscles, stretched and challenged to their limits, reminded me how I'd spent this unusual evening.

Then it was the female twin soothing me, brushing the sweaty tendrils of hair from my forehead. 'My, my,' she crooned in that low singer's voice, 'you certainly threw yourself into this, body and soul. There's more to you than meets the eye – or my childhood memories of you – sweet Vanita.'

I drew a shuddery breath and stood upright. 'I think I'll go to my room now. Probably should've stayed upstairs and let you have your fun, the way you're accustomed to,' I said in a wobbly voice. The room had stopped spinning, but I was still unsure of my balance. Powerful indeed, this experience had been.

'Oh no, sweetheart, we *wanted* you to come and play,' Damon replied, and before I knew what was happening he stepped behind me while his twin took my hand and guided me forwards, off the dancer platform.

'We wanted to see your reaction. Which, by the smell of you, was very, very intense,' Desiree continued in her husky voice. 'Open your robe, Vanita. Share your sex with *us* now.'

'I don't think –'

'You won't need to think,' the man behind me whispered. His hands slid down my sides, and then he deftly slipped a foot along the inside of mine and scooted it sideways. I lost my balance, dropping back against him as his other foot made the same move. He was holding me with my hips resting on his thighs and my legs apart, as though this were a position in a dance routine. 'You look absolutely gorgeous in Mama's crimson dressing gown.'

'As I knew you would,' Desiree joined in, grinning lasciviously. She was untying my sash, watching me quiver in my uncertainty. 'You understand that we're doing this to help you. If Daddy catches a whiff of you, he'll punish you for pleasuring yourself – or he'll tell Roger to take what *he* wants. He's a possessive man, but he believes in keeping the help happy.'

Before I could protest, she'd flung the sides of the gown apart and was eyeing me hungrily. I tried to break loose, but Damon held me fast. His chuckle rumbled against my back.

'You can't tell me this repels you,' he breathed against my ear. 'I saw the way you watched us, and you had as much interest in my sister as you did in me. She's splendid, isn't she? And she's got a wicked tongue in her head, too.'

A little gasp escaped me as Desiree knelt between my spread legs. Damon's tongue was teasing the shell of my ear as his hands drifted upwards to catch the underside of my breasts.

'Oh, there's a sight!' his sister replied, and she fluttered her fingertips up the insides of my thighs. 'Luscious they are, but I've fondled them once, so I'll save them for another time. Right now I want to get to the heart of the matter. We *Hartes* are like that, you know.'

I giggled in spite of myself, for she was tickling me with that touch that hovered just above my skin and made me wriggle against her brother. They both chuckled with me, enjoying the play of the candlelight upon my scarlet robe and its contrast to our ivory skin.

'But what I really adore is the way her hair curls along the edge of her wet pussy,' the lissome woman sighed. She was gazing overtly at my sex, and then her fingertips drifted upwards to explore what she'd commented upon. With the lightest touch of her fingernails she played with my coarse curls, swirling them in the slickness from my climax, cooing to create a breeze upon the still-inflamed skin. She brought her face closer, and I could only stare, apprehensive yet fascinated about what might come next.

'Yes, Vanita, you have a cunning little cunt,' she breathed, allowing her warm breath to ruffle the curls she was playing with. 'Like a brilliant pink rose it is, with its outer petals falling loose around a slick, firm bud. And that endearing little opening, just waiting to be stroked.'

I groaned with the first touch of her warm skin on mine. With a single fingertip she explored the sensitive, wet tissues, spreading my juice as she watched my muscles flutter. Where had this come from? Though I'd gone to a girls' school, I'd never imagined this intimate touch from a classmate. Yet the way Desiree looked at me, I thought she was enamoured beyond my wildest beliefs. She inserted her finger just an inch, and wiggled it.

'Ah!' I bucked backwards against Damon, who nuzzled my neck as he chuckled. 'You're warming up to this, aren't you, sweetheart? I knew you would. And I'm glad, since my mission is to make my sister happy. Shall we open you wider?'

Again he inched his feet outwards, displaying my slit fully spread, only inches above his twin's adoring face. Her fingers were busy, inciting little riots along the folds of my sex, rubbing in the wetness that escaped me as I began to writhe.

'Yes, flex yourself – open that hole and let me probe it,' she whispered. 'Let me watch you explode again. Then I'll lap you up, so Daddy won't know what we've been doing.'

The mention of Franklin – the danger he represented – revved my pulse, and Damon's caress of my breasts had me jutting against his palms. I was vaguely aware that I couldn't fight all these fires at once – the way the male held me while the female enticed; the way my mind rebelled yet wanted to comply; the warning that I couldn't let on about any of this when I got back upstairs, even though I knew I'd be reliving this moment of madness for weeks, in my dreams.

Again Desiree played with my pussy hair, pulling it gently into clumps between her fingers so she could tug it – and pull apart the seeping folds of that flower she was sniffing. She closed her eyes and breathed deeply of my essence. Then she licked her lips, parted my slit until it ached, and stuck out her tongue. The sight of that pink, pointed tip, like a tender arrow going towards its target, made me quiver all over with anticipation.

Damon tilted up my chin, claiming me in a kiss at the very moment his sister plunged inside me. My body became a mass of itching little twitches that made me spasm uncontrollably. While a tongue slipped inside my mouth to explore, an identical tongue circled the rim of my pussy again and again, before thrusting inside me. Desiree sat taller, pressing her mouth against my aching clit as she intensified her tongue strokes.

Utterly helpless, I was. My feet left the floor, while my hips wriggled against taut thighs and I was held by a slender arm beneath my breasts. Damon moaned as he kissed me deeply, and it was echoed down below as Desiree drank her fill. Her lips plied mine with increasing pressure, goading me towards a climax that both appalled and amazed me.

Never had I felt so totally aroused, overtaken by sensations I was unable to fend off! I gave myself over to the spirallings inside me, crying out into the brother's mouth as I oozed juice into his sister's. They drove me relentlessly, until I clenched in one huge body knot. As though from a distance, the clocks in the huge room began to strike the hour, one after another, as though proclaiming my climax in all their various pitches and tempos.

I went limp as a rag doll. With a final kiss, Damon released my lips and supported me against his warm body. When I could open my eyes, it was to watch in fascination as Desiree lapped the liquid from between my splayed legs, like a regal cat delicately sipping her cream. Every inch of my engorged flesh was lovingly laved until I stopped seeping. She then stroked my folds into place and once more arranged the hair around its edge.

Sitting back on her haunches, she wiped her face with the hem of my dressing gown, grinning. Her nipples rode high and rosy on her chest; her body flexed fluidly as she stood up to smooth her sparkling white hair into place.

'Far better soup than we were served at dinner,' she quipped. She gazed at Damon, and on her silent command, he released me. 'Now give me my dessert, and we'll call it a night.'

For a brief moment I wondered what was expected of me next, but I had no part in the rest of their ritual. The two of them embraced warmly, their pale, naked bodies entwined as they kissed like the dearest of lovers. Again I was confronted by all I'd been told was taboo and unthinkable, while drawn in by their closed eyes, vibrant white flesh and soft sighs.

When they broke apart and dressed, I was aware that I'd been included in their circle yet would remain forever outside it in a very important way. And as we three went upstairs to the main part of the house, it occurred to me that if I were ever to make good on Franklin Harte's condition – if I were ever to convince his son to make love to me – I would have to imitate his twin.

I would have to become Desiree.

11 A Surprise in the Night

With my door shut and a chair propped beneath its knob, I studied myself in the mirror. The lamp on the vanity gave off a low glow, and for a moment I could pretend my honey-blonde hair was white and my eyebrows didn't arch in a slightly darker shade than my brown eyes. I could make my face thinner by sucking in my cheeks – and if Magnolia kept cooking what was implied as horsemeat, I'd soon be as slender as the woman I wanted to match.

But when I let the deep-red dressing gown drift over my shoulders, I knew it was hopeless. Where Desiree was boyishly small, I blossomed with undeniably ample breasts. I sighed, my head spinning with images and my spirits sinking. Silly me, thinking Damon Harte wouldn't sense immediately that I was not his twin.

'If I didn't know better, I'd think you were giving up, Vanita.'

As that low voice came at me from behind, a hand slipped around to catch my gasp. I stared wide-eyed as a face appeared behind mine in the mirror, framed by a dark, distinct beard and a mane of tousled hair that blended into the shadows.

Pearce smiled, loving the fact that he'd caught me by surprise. 'You thought I'd abandoned you. Thought I'd just walked away, cold and callous, to leave you to Franklin Harte's dubious devices. If I let go, will you stay quiet? The house has ears, you know.'

His eyes flickered towards that row of holes in the wall nearby, the whispering tubes that would carry our conversation to others as clearly as they'd conveyed those earlier, illicit messages into the bathroom. I nodded, for despite my rising anger, Truman was right.

He released my mouth, then folded his arms around mine, below my chest. 'Feels good, holding you here while the light plays upon your breasts and this silk whispers all sorts of suggestions.'

'Too bad I won't be falling for any of them,' I retorted in a whisper, loosening his embrace. 'Why would I want to, after the way you *left* me there, sprawling on that desk? Open for those vultures to attack me!'

'I knew they wouldn't hurt you. Lillian had to keep you flawless and intact, and Franklin was too fascinated by his prize to paw at you just yet.'

My mouth dropped open. 'Never mind that he prodded me across the yard – naked! – with his gold-tipped cane! And where were *you* when he cuffed my wrists and ankles in that damn carriage?'

Pearce cleared his throat as though trying not to laugh. 'Wish I could've seen that, my sweet,' he replied, 'but by that time I was halfway to Harte's Haven. I watched the carriage arrive at dawn. Saw Miss Desiree escort you into the house.'

'You've been here the whole time? And you didn't help –'

He clapped his hand over my rising tirade, gazing purposefully at me. 'It's part of my plan, Vanita. You'll have to trust me. Until you arrived, I wasn't sure what Harte had in mind for you, so I couldn't put my counteractions into play. Checkmate him, as such.'

'So I'm just a game piece to you, too? Bad enough that Aunt Lillian –'

He silenced me with a hard kiss. His bold move caught me off guard, and his mouth made itself quite welcome. But I was too upset for such shenanigans.

When I tried to free myself, he released my lips but kept our faces a mere heartbeat apart.

'Vanita,' he breathed, his dark eyes probing mine. 'Can you really think I extracted such a pledge without committing myself to you in return? I may look like the devil and behave as a fiend, but inside this chest beats the heart of a man who would never, ever betray you. For our plan to work, however, Franklin has to think I've forsaken you completely.'

I desperately wanted to believe that. With all my heart – without further doubts – I wanted to know Pearce Truman would carry through on his promise to restore Wellspring ... and possibly carry on with me, as well. 'If you've been eavesdropping all this time, you know the horns of my dilemma. I've promised myself to you, but if I'm to get my estate back, I have to seduce Damon Harte beyond a shadow of his daddy's doubt. Now how am I supposed to do that?'

His eyelids lowered and his lips brushed mine. 'I believe you'll find a way, Vanita – just as I believe I'll triumph over Harte. Because you're already mine. You always will be.'

His words sent a shiver up my spine. With only the fingers of one hand in my hair he held me. I could've stepped free of him and left the room, to show him exactly how he exasperated me, yet the magician had returned; the illusionist was at work with those piercing green eyes that refused to let go of mine. I was his, all right. Possessed, as though the demon from deep within him had been passed through to me during our coupling – the demon that would own my soul and never let me go.

Somehow this dark angel had materialised from out of nowhere, just as he had last night in Daddy's study. Once again he was declaring me his mission, renewing our vow. And yet another time, I felt myself falling under his spell, despite my better judgment and all my daddy had taught me about walking proud and thinking for myself.

I let out the breath I'd been holding. 'So how are we going to do this, Pearce? I can't help you if you keep me in the dark.'

'And I can't help *you*, if you know too much,' he replied with his maddening logic. 'Best to keep playing along with Franklin, and to ingratiate yourself with the twins – as you did so very fetchingly downstairs tonight.'

'But, Pearce, they're insane! They make those clockwork toys instead of making friends!' I protested in a strident whisper. 'You've got to get me *out* of here before this horrid house – and everyone in it – eats me alive! Damon told me straight out he'll never –'

He lifted my flushed face with his finger. 'While I admit the Harte siblings have a most unusual kinship, their cavortings did inspire my deepest . . . interest.'

'Interest, hell,' I muttered, for my hand had brushed between us to find his impressive erection. 'You're hornier than a two-peckered goat! And pretty damn proud of yourself for watching all this without crying out and getting caught.'

Pearce sighed, chuckling. 'You know me too well, Vanita.'

'There's no crime in that, is there?' I whispered, suddenly realising how the power of this secret meeting was now shifting towards my favour. He was nudging my hand with his hardness, rubbing blatantly against my palm as he held my gaze. I grasped him through the fabric of his pants, amazed at how my own sex was aching again, after so many encounters today. 'By the time this ordeal's behind us, I'll know you inside and out. In ways neither of us anticipated.'

'Let's start with this way – with you taking me in hand. You can lead me wherever you choose, Vanita.'

Was he relinquishing control so easily? I doubted it. His expression sharpened, accentuated by that rakish beard and the moustache that framed his wanton grin. Yet a part of Pearce Truman would always remain focused and aloof. I couldn't imagine him ever giving in to total surrender, the way I had when the twins took me between them.

I smiled, letting the crimson silk slip the rest of the way off my body. Here in the lamplight we seemed softer around the edges, more mellow and less brazen – and of course we knew better than to make any noise. And frankly, after a long day of one unexpected turn following another, I was in no mood to howl like an alley cat in heat. I wrapped my hand around his hard cock, squeezing it. 'Let's get you naked. And into my bed. It's been a long time since I rode a really fine mount.'

His eyes alight with anticipation and desire, Pearce shed his clothing quickly. For good measure, I stuffed two of the black lace doilies from the vanity table into the whispering tubes, knowing that any wild vibrations from the bed would alert the Harte household to our trysting. On inspiration, I took the third piece of lacework and fastened it to my chest by sticking my taut nipples through crocheted holes on either side of the diamond-shaped doily.

Pearce chuckled, yanking back the deep green coverlet. I'd been given a room of average size, ruled by a high bed on an iron frame, with a spindled headboard patterned in cherubs' faces. The dark metalwork rendered their expressions downright jaded, as they watched our shadows dance upon the dark walls. My lover's skin made a fine, olive contrast to the ivory sheets as he stretched out, taunting me with his rampant erection. It rose like a pole, straight up from his abdomen, and when he'd plumped a pillow beneath his head, he reached up to grasp the spindles of the decadent headboard.

He made a fetching sight, lying as though tied to the bed, watching my every move – and the patch of black lace bobbing on my chest. I approached him slowly, wondering what I should do, for I'd never sat like a jockey except while mounted on an actual horse. Pearce flexed and raised his hips, like a stallion eager to mount his mare, and I was hooked.

I hopped on to the bed and swung my leg over him, positioning myself just behind his proud cock. It nuzzled my mound, seeking its pleasure outright, but I eluded it by rocking, as though I actually sat on a horse. I listened carefully to the bed's reply, gauging how feverishly I could ride him without being heard throughout the house. For all I knew, Roger was skilled with a crop and as avid a trainer as most men in these parts. I didn't want him getting any ideas – or permission from his master to come in – for I needed no instruction about how to get the most out of the animal I controlled.

And I did control Pearce, because I refused to let him inside me. Rocking, rocking, I sat astraddle, feeling the base of his shaft and the light fur of his balls rubbing my open slit. I was still aroused from my downstairs encounter, despite the way I'd spent myself in Desiree's face. Perhaps it was just this sort of shaft I needed to drive me into a deep sleep, after all I'd seen and done today.

I caught Pearce's eye and imitated the look he usually gave me, that relentless, unblinking gaze of passion and promise that told who belonged to whom. He stared back, holding absolutely still, for fear the bed would creak if he started a counter-rhythm. His jaw clenched with the effort, sharpening his expression with heightened desire.

Leaning back, I widened my thighs so I could rub my nub against his shaft. The tip of it glowed a brilliant pink in the lamplight, and the veins on its underside coursed with his powerful current. When I shifted my grip up its length and then down again, time after time, he closed his eyes. He was getting fuller, harder ... I could feel the vibrations from deep within him, predicting an eruption like he'd seen in the cellar. I wondered how he'd gotten down there, and where he'd hidden himself so I hadn't sensed his presence. But that was part of the mystery that made Pearce Truman so enticing.

For the moment, I was just delighted to be with him again, our confidence restored as we pleasured each other. I gripped and let go, rocking and shifting my weight against his balls, savouring the sensations that travelled into my inner core through a very wet cleft. The moisture made a sucking sound as I moved, as it seeped out of me on to Pearce, and he became that much more excited.

'Ride me,' he commanded hoarsely. 'God, Vanita, jump on me and *take* it!'

'No!' I leaned back farther, shimmying my lace-covered breasts. From his angle, I imagined them resembling flesh-coloured melons suspended in stretchy net baskets. 'You're going to pay for the way you stranded me at Aunt Lill's, and the way you've been hiding here, like a thief in the night.'

'You know you want me.'

'Oh?' I opened one eye, arching my brow. 'Maybe I'm all fucked out. The victim of overstimulation.'

'When hell freezes over.'

I tried to ignore the quiverings in my slit, still tender from all the times the poor thing had been worked over today. 'Or perhaps, after seeing the Hartes for the perverse lot they are, I never want another lover. I might just get me to a nunnery –'

'And I'll be your priest, Sister. We wouldn't last two minutes under a vow of chastity, and you know it.'

I had to swallow a laugh. His face was growing downright desperate and he was thrusting upwards against me, in spite of his efforts to remain still. But it was the sudden tensing of his jaw, the thinning of those lush lips against a wave of need that sent the same desire shooting through me. If I'd learned anything during today's misadventures, it was about myself – how much I craved sensual attention, and how badly I wanted what this mysterious magician and his magic wand could do for me.

With a quick up and down, I impaled myself. My hips took on their own purpose: I'd never sat a saddle with so much frenzied energy. With Pearce buried deep inside me, I rode hard and hellbent, falling forwards on to my hands for balance. Levered this way, I thrust faster, until his hot, bulbous head butted my womb – bearing down, so each forward and backward motion pressed high into my slit and then against my clit. The black doily fell across his face then, adding an even more roguish appeal to the man beneath me. Bad to the bone, he looked, and the devilish mesh stretched with his grin when my breasts slapped rapidly against my ribcage.

My juices ran between us, kicking up the heady scent of our unleashed passion while making a wet, sucking sound each time our bodies came together. The man beneath me had lost all sense of telling me what to do. He was gripping the spindled headboard for dear life, driving upwards inside me until I rose up from the mattress.

I fell forwards into a savage kiss, feeling the scrape

of his crisp beard and the edges of his teeth. Pearce wiggled furiously beneath me, as though caught in the spasms of a seizure.

'Take it, Vanita,' he rasped. 'Take me over that line with all you've got.'

Clenching my eyes shut, I drove myself against him, battering my hips into his. The air hissed between his gritted teeth and he convulsed, grabbing my backside with a slap of his hands to pump his seed inside me. We thrashed together, first with his climax and then with mine, a series of controlled explosions that set the mattress aquiver without making the bed dance.

I collapsed against him, panting. He wrapped me in his arms, his breath rushing rapidly past my ear. It took several moments for the room to stop revolving, and then I slipped off sideways to lie along his length.

'Did I take you?' I teased.

'Every last inch of me. Every last drop,' he wheezed. Then he opened one teasing eye to catch my reaction. 'But it was only because I allowed you to. Gave you the illusion of control, just to see where it would lead.'

He was probably right. I doubted I would ever overpower him in any real sense. Yet, as I sank into a dreamlike state beside him, I also realised that I liked his invincible attitude, his insistence on coming out on top every time, even when he appeared to be ridden rather than riding.

'Good night, Pearce,' I whispered against his softly furred chest. 'See you in the morning.'

But of course, that's not how it happened at all.

12 My Proposition Backfires

'You're late for breakfast, Vanita. Daddy sent me to fetch you.'

I refused to acknowledge the too-cheerful voice that bullied me from my bedside, and only after Desiree had hopped on to the bed, straddled my quilt-covered form and begun to rock wildly did I open one eye. Every limp limb of my exhausted body told me it couldn't be morning yet. But then, in this house, it was difficult to tell day from night because they never opened those funereal velvet draperies.

The young woman trouncing me appeared opalescent and fresh, nattily dressed in a navy shirtwaist with a collar trimmed in red braid. Her hair was snowy white, pulled up into an elaborate knot at the crown with teasing tendrils bouncing at each temple.

'Stop it!' I snarled, resenting her effervescence. 'I'm not leaving this room until you find me some clothes. I refuse to sit at that table wearing a dog harness, or anything else your father cares to humiliate me with today.'

Desiree chuckled. 'Ah, so he's gotten your goat. That's the whole secret to Daddy, you know. Once you act as though you *like* what he's doing to you, he loses interest.'

She got off me, leaving me to think about that tidbit. When she returned, I was sitting on the side of the bed, pulling the crumpled crimson dressing gown around me, feeling decidedly rumpled myself. 'Is there water in my pitcher?'

'Yes, your majesty, I saw to that hours ago,' she replied, and then mocked me with a bow. 'You'll have to be satisfied with this old thing. Pity your dear aunt hasn't sent your clothing over.'

Desiree was humming as she left my room, and when I held up the dress she'd tossed at me, I knew why. The damn thing was *hers*, which meant I'd be lucky to squeeze into it; I'd look just as ludicrous as I had in that belled harness and horse blanket. I knew better than to keep Franklin Harte waiting, however. It gave him more time to conjure up my punishments.

A quick washing-off brought to mind the various ways I'd been pleasured last night, for my poor slit was aching from all those activities. While I hadn't expected to find Pearce in my bed this morning, I was disappointed that he'd left without a word – again. The fiend had a knack of making my hopes soar and then letting them shatter. My only consolation was his renewed commitment to keep my home out of the clutches of that greedy madman downstairs. I couldn't question his methods, for Pearce seemed to appear wherever I needed him, at the moment all other hope had failed me. But it would be nice to be treated as his equal – his partner – in this venture that literally meant my life or death ... by gradual insanity, if nothing else.

My reflection did nothing to boost my spirits. The peasant-style dress Desiree loaned me flounced nicely enough over my hips and legs, but the fitted black bodice, which laced and tied, was far too snug. My breasts strained against its front panels, peeping between the lacings while mounding up over the top of the low neckline. With my hair straggling down and my bare feet and legs, I looked less reputable than a gypsy whore out to solicit business. As bedraggled as Cinderella at the mercy of her wicked step-sisters.

When I padded down the grand stairway and into

the dining room, all at the table ceased their secretive talk. Desiree smirked, elbowing her twin, while Damon smiled as though ready for another round of raucous play downstairs. Franklin, however, rose from his chair with a foxlike grin. 'Well, if a lady must be late, she should make an entrance. And that you have, Vanita. Good morning at last, my dear.'

'Good morning,' I muttered, taking the chair he pulled out beside his own.

'Good morning, *what*?'

Considering what his daughter had imparted moments ago, I put on my sweetest smile. 'Good morning, Daddy. Sleep well?'

He stood ogling the cleavage that bulged above my bodice, wearing the nasty little grin I'd come to despise. 'Sleep is the farthest thing from my mind with *you* under my roof, Miss Wells. I can't help thinking of your lovely mother ... all the ways she surrendered herself to keep Wellspring in the family. For *you*.'

Heat prickled in my cheeks, for this was a new story – and not one I wanted to hear. I let it pass for the moment, because who could prove it true or false? Whom could I trust to tell me what actually happened?

I heard the cranking of a key in the kitchen, followed by a rumbling from a track in the floor I hadn't noticed at dinner. Instead of Roger serving us this morning, Magnolia was sending out Frankie, the clockwork who so closely resembled my captor. Like the flesh-and-blood Harte beside me, he wore a fresh suit of white linen with a crisp cravat at his collar, along with that permanent leer Damon had rendered so accurately in iron. As he clacked along the side of the table towards the twins, he carried a tray of coddled eggs, a platter of bacon, a bowl of sausage gravy and a basket of steaming biscuits. Nothing resembled last night's mystery meat, or could be construed as Pegasus. My stomach growled like a ravenous bear.

I watched Desiree and Damon take their portions with apparent confidence. Once again it gave me pause, when they thanked the mechanical man as though he'd stopped between them by choice ... as though he were an old and trusted servant. Frankie then ambled stiffly over to the man in white, and it seemed to me his painted smile diminished somewhat – further sign that this dungeon of a house and its inhabitants were affecting my mental state already. I wondered if Franklin or his son might be flipping a switch from under the table, for how else would the clockwork servant know when to stop and then start again?

After taking three eggs and a forkful of bacon, Franklin spooned steaming gravy over two opened biscuits on his plate. He then twisted the key in the mechanical man's back and sent him towards me. Why didn't these people just pass the food to each other, like a normal family when the help was away? I didn't dare ask. At least Harte wasn't deriding Damon's creation and making us all squirm and grovel today.

As Frankie approached, however, his iron-eyed gaze seemed to lock on to my bosom and he stopped too fast. The rest of the eggs, slick with butter and bacon grease, slid off the platter to land with a *splat* on my exposed breasts, followed by a large splash of gravy – much to the delight of all three Hartes.

'Don't just sit there, boy!' Franklin crowed. 'Here's your breakfast, served up in fine style! And we all want to watch you eat it!'

I'd instinctively sprung up to swat the slippery eggs on to my plate, but a cane suddenly crossed my collarbone.

'You'd better sit pretty, Vanita. Stick out your chest to keep those eggs from sliding off, until we decide who gets to devour them.'

A sick feeling replaced my hunger. Grease and gravy were dribbling between my breasts and down their sides, seeping out the front of the dress between the lacings, while three pale yellow eyeballs leered up at me. Frankie's gruesome grin never wavered, and I felt like knocking the damn platter from his hands so it would strike Franklin Harte in the teeth. My host, so impeccable in his white linen suit, kept watching for me to do that very thing, still holding his cane against my chest with a hand encased in kid.

'It would be cruel of us, after last night's dinner initiation, to gobble your breakfast – enticing as it would be, served on such fine china,' he added with a wicked grin. 'I see you haven't yet got my son eating out of your hand – or eating you anywhere else – so you might as well claim those eggs now. Put them on your plate like a good girl, Vanita, and we'll get on with our meal.'

How dare he insinuate I'd kept them from their breakfast! Once again I was the object of the lewdest observation, for I had to support my breasts with one hand while gingerly picking up the soft eggs with the other – and of course they broke open. Warm yellow goo then oozed over my skin, and I scooted back so furiously I knocked the platter from Frankie's hands.

'You're not excused, young lady,' Harte muttered. 'If you're not going to eat, and you can't behave – after all those years of finishing school, no less! – then we'd best get on with the morning's conversation. I'd hoped for more congenial circumstances to announce my decision, but once again you've spoiled things. What would your mother say?'

Glaring at him, I sat back down. The quiver in that

cane was warning me that Franklin's anger – or arousal – would soon get the best of him. I just wanted him to make his damned announcement so this fiasco of a meal could be over. With quick fingers, I picked what food I could from my chest and flicked it on to my plate.

Glancing at the twins, who were sedately eating their bacon and biscuits, Franklin cleared his throat ceremoniously. 'After reconsidering what you said last night – because I'm not a total tyrant and I do listen to you, Vanita – I've decided that we should indeed host a wedding. A lavish, magnificent affair like Harte's Haven hasn't seen since I took Alice as my bride.'

The matched pair across from me looked as stunned as I did. 'But, Daddy –'

'Hush, daughter! We should give Vanita the chance to express her joy and gratitude.' He gazed at me expectantly, puffing out his chest with the pride of broadsiding my emotions once again.

'I – you needn't go to the trouble,' I stammered. I looked to the twins for support, thinking Damon might repeat his speech about never wanting to mate, or that his sister might protest for her own envious reasons. But they stared silently at the table.

'No, of all the young ladies I've brought here, you deserve proper nuptials – your dream of a beautiful ceremony come true,' he continued gallantly. 'It will show the world you're truly one of us – that you're *family*, which is a concept close to my heart. And I don't want my friends thinking I'm cheap and shoddy, depriving you of a proper wedding because your Aunt Lillian bankrupted you. No, Vanita, Franklin Harte won't be known as a penny-pincher! Although these pennies just beg for it.'

With that, he gripped my nearest nipple between his thumb and forefinger, cackling like a jackal when I winced and pulled away. As he licked the egg yolk from his finger, I got the distinct impression he was hungry for more.

He was right, of course: a ceremony, with guests and a dinner served by white-coated servants on the lawn, would indeed make me a permanent resident. I would be the mistress of Harte's Haven ... whether or not the groom consummated our relationship. I would be trapped there forever, the constant victim of this relentless humiliation, unless I disappeared as mysteriously as Alice had all those years ago. It seemed Aunt Lillian had once again betrayed me without even being present, because her illustrious plans had backfired.

The pair across from me sat in silence, utterly stunned. The only sign I saw of their chagrin was the dimple flickering in Damon's cheek as he worked his jaw.

I desperately wished Pearce would appear. Had he heard this latest assault on my sanity? Or was he off somewhere, working to get me back to Wellspring as soon as possible? I glanced towards the doorway of this dark, overfurnished room, wishing for a ray of his fiendish hope, but my wishful thinking was childish, at best. And Franklin read me as quickly as he perused the betting sheets at the race track.

'Why are you such a fool for that prick Pearce Truman?' he demanded, instantly bringing his children to attention. 'Surely your daddy taught you that such a man can't be trusted. And why would an otherwise bright young woman like yourself believe a word he says – especially about reclaiming Wellspring? He's working for your Aunt Lillian, and he's her lover, as well. Everyone knows that, Vanita.'

I pressed my lips in a tight line to keep from crying. Uncanny, how this cad had not only guessed my thoughts but knew exactly what he was talking about.

He must have eavesdropped while Pearce and I were in Daddy's study, for we'd been absolutely quiet in my room last night. Not a word above a whisper nor a creak of the bed.

Franklin raised a bushy eyebrow. 'Be sure he never comes here – certainly not to your room – again, Miss Wells. Your behaviour last night was on the level of a guttersnipe's, and I won't tolerate that in my house. Not with my son's future bride!'

He turned to his twins then, the righteousness of an Old Testament patriarch shining in his eyes. 'And you two – if you see any sign of Mr Truman, you're to alert me. Or, given the chance to dispatch him, you have my permission and encouragement. We can't allow him to contaminate our honourable intentions.'

I would have choked on that, but Damon and Desiree straightened in their chairs, as though they'd been deputised and granted the rights of a bounty hunter. The gravy and egg yolk were now congealing on my breasts, giving my chest a chunky, ochre crust, but that was nothing compared to the jelling of the blood in my veins. If Pearce got caught – probably because we couldn't keep our hands off each other – Franklin's Southern gentility would disappear along with my lover. My only hope out of here would die, and I'd be worse off than dead if I were caught with him. My soul whimpered like a little lost pup. It seemed that no matter what I did in this place, things took the wrong turn.

'Well, now that we've discussed these matters, I'll see to the business of the day,' my host said crisply. 'I'll be inspecting the tobacco crop in the west forty, and will go from there to Devil's Dungeon. Seems we're having trouble with contrary workers again.'

He turned to me then, a pointed expression sharpening his beefy features. 'Some of those workers, sentenced to a life in my mines, started out exactly where you are – brides-to-be. But they couldn't make my son love them. Take heed, my Vanita. You look much lovelier with that cold, greasy food on your breasts than you would with black grime smeared on your face and caked into every crevice of your bare body. They never got their clothes, either, you see.'

With that he rose, glittering with his own sense of importance. And why wouldn't he? He'd cowed his children into a speculative silence once again, and he'd stolen my secret thunder. Effortlessly. As though he saw all and knew all, without revealing how. He was king, and he didn't need a reason for anything he did.

As Franklin passed through the doorway, I sprang from my chair to follow him. My mother *would* be mortified at this morning's crude activities, and Daddy *had* honed my instincts about whom to trust. My best bet was still on Pearce Truman, and I had to cling to that hope until I escaped from this onerous household.

'Franklin – Daddy – please! May I have a word with you?'

He stopped beside the bottom of the stairway, gripping that gold-headed cane in his gloved hands, and then turned with an imperious air. 'And why do you deserve it, after the way you've tested my patience two meals in a row?'

I crossed my arms beneath my bosom to distract him. 'Because I'm here through no fault of my own! And because – because I have a better idea!' I hedged boldly. 'A way to see that Damon becomes a man without your hosting an expensive wedding, just for show. Your friends will see right through that, you know. They've known him as long as I have.'

That got his attention. Now I had to follow up with something so irresistible he couldn't turn me down. Why I'd scurried out there on such a wild hair, I wasn't sure – except I couldn't just sit there with egg on me, appearing gulled and helpless. If I didn't save Wellspring and myself, who would?

'If you're wasting my time on another of your foolish fantasies, you'll be sorry.'

Daddy had taught me that the best bargains were struck when one party offered the other something he'd profit from – something that might even put him ahead of the man making the proposal. At this point, I had absolutely nothing to lose by promising Harte the moon. If it was a son who got into my pants – even if the real manhood affirmed would be Franklin's – then that's what I'd have to deliver. Even if I didn't have the faintest idea how.

'You want me to prove Damon's a man – one who lusts after women, as you do,' I began, hoping I sounded more confident than I felt. 'I can do that. But in return, you'll cancel the wedding – that was Aunt Lillian's idea, anyway. I want Wellspring, free and clear. And I want to go home as soon as I've seduced your son.'

The man in the immaculate white suit eyed me warily. 'What makes you think I'll fall for this? What makes *you* any more enticing to my candy-assed boy than the others?'

I shrugged so provocatively my gravy-caked breasts overflowed the laced-up dress. 'I'm saving you the expense of a lavish wedding – and the embarrassment of your friends knowing it's a sham. As a woman who understands what excites Damon, I know precisely how to put his cock where you want it.'

For emphasis, I rubbed the top of my thigh, watching his reaction as he considered my proposal – and watching the bared breasts lolling above their black laces. I didn't like the way his mouth quirked, but I had no room to quibble: I'd made an outlandish proposition, and if Harte called my bluff I'd have to follow through.

With a sinister grin, the man in white leaned so close that his breath warmed my egg-smeared cleavage. 'All right, Vanita, here's our deal – I'll proceed with plans for a June sixth wedding, for appearance's sake – and because that's the twins' birthday. But if Damon screws you before the ceremony, you may return to Wellspring and it'll be yours, free and clear.

'*If*, however, you fail to make him a man by then, you'll not only go through with the ceremony, you'll become *my* possession. My love slave,' Harte breathed, arching his dark brows. 'Failure to comply with my every wish will land you at Devil's Dungeon, where those other poor girls work eighteen-hour days, naked, and never see the sun. Never hear a kind word.'

His eyes glittered only inches from mine, and I dared not drop my gaze. I wasn't surprised by his demands – after all, this man had a carriage fitted with satin manacles. But the images they conjured up were indeed incentive to seduce Damon Harte beyond a shadow of anyone's doubt. Which meant I'd break my vow to Pearce.

But betraying a demon's dare seemed inconsequential, considering the deal I'd just made with this devil in white: I would truly lose my self, heart and soul, as well as my parents' legacy, if I didn't meet Franklin's demands. Solemnly I extended my hand to shake on our deal, just as Daddy would have.

Harte used the hand clasp to pull me against him, where I could smell breakfast on his fetid breath. 'I can't wait to claim you, sweet Vanita,' he whispered moistly against my ear. 'For the next two weeks I'll live in a state of high anticipation . . . and arousal. You have no idea how badly I want you, nor how I intend to sate my desires. But you're about to find out.'

With a laugh that chilled me, he wetly kissed my cheek and then shoved me away. As he swaggered out the front door, I realised I'd just opened myself to far more anguish than he'd proposed by staging a wedding.

Or had I? I wasn't the most experienced of women, but intuition told me this so-called gentleman had considered me part of his deal with Lillian Gilding long ago. I'd simply made it easier for him to claim his prize.

I sagged against a newel post, at a loss. The scum-green walls of the vestibule closed in around me, enfolding me in their musty gloom while erasing all hope from my heart. No matter what I did here among the Hartes, I got sucked deeper into the quagmire of their malicious intent.

'Well, you've got balls. I'll grant you that.' Desiree's voice came from behind me. 'Hasn't been a man – certainly not a woman – to challenge Daddy that way since Mama tried it.'

I turned to see her in the dining-room doorway, spectral in the dimness. 'And what happened to your mother, Desiree? I never heard.'

'She's gone to a better place. We were only twelve when we lost her, and you can see what's happened to this family since then.'

I nodded, for I knew her emptiness well. 'I'm sorry. I was eleven when my parents were struck by lightning. That *is* how they died, you know.'

For a moment we stood in silence. Then I realised my rare opportunity, while she seemed vaguely sympathetic to my plight. 'Will you help me, Dez? I can't do this alone.'

Her crystalline eyes shone in a face of alabaster, and I had to admit that when Desiree Harte wasn't kicking up wickedness, she was beautiful in a truly luminous way – a shining light in this house of dust and dusk.

'Damon and I have decided to host a betrothal ball, because we're long overdue for some fun around here – and to make Daddy think we're co-operating with him,' she added in a conspiratorial tone. 'I doubt my dear brother will become your lover, Vanita – you'll probably meet the same end Mama did. But I suppose there are worse fates.'

13 Dressed To Kill

It was a welcome diversion when Mrs Marley, the seamstress, came a few days later to outfit me for the wedding. I played the part of the excited bride, of course, because I couldn't let on about my plans to be gone before I married into this nefarious family. And no one was happier than I that this stout little woman, with her hennaed hair done up in a bun like one of her pin cushions, demanded a workspace with some light.

'How *do* you people *see*?' she twittered at Franklin. 'I must work in natural lighting, to observe how my fabrics look against Miss Vanita's skin, and to ensure my measurements are correct.'

Franklin grinned like a fox with two chickens, escorting us to a courtyard at the back of the mansion. 'Will this suffice? It'll put Vanita in view of all the groundskeepers and stablehands, but I doubt that will bother her.'

Mrs Marley quirked an artful auburn brow at him. 'As I recall, poor Alice suffered the same affront,' she said stiffly. 'Do you intend to watch this time, as well?'

'Wouldn't miss it. Especially since I'm paying for all this.'

With that, he told Roger to direct the seamstress's driver to the rear of the house, and to have some stablehands unload her bolts of fabric. He chose a stone bench near a cluster of azaleas that bloomed in bright shades of pink – a welcome sight to eyes grown weary of deep greens and morose maroons flocked in black. Had I not known him for a tyrant of the highest order,

I'd have thought Franklin rather stately as he sat in his colourful garden, wearing a fresh white suit and a jaunty boater.

As we awaited the unloading, I felt a prickling on my neck and looked up. Desiree waved from her window, and I waved back. It was warm enough that she raised the sash, but – like her twin, who also peered out for a moment – she didn't linger in the sunlight.

'What a sad life,' Mrs Marley remarked as she readied her tape measure and tablet. 'Will the wedding be indoors, then?'

'Damon has requested a moonlight ceremony,' Franklin replied. 'We've set it for the first Saturday in June, here in the garden. Since Desiree will be Vanita's bridesmaid, you'll be outfitting her, as well. I want the girls wearing something that shimmers. Gowns that appear luminous in the light of the full moon.'

The wedding was only two weeks away! While I was more than ready to leave Harte's Haven, I had no idea if Pearce would assist me, or if I'd have to quickly convince Damon to co-operate. I was pulled from these thoughts by Franklin's grating voice.

'You must disrobe for Mrs Marley, Vanita. She'll need to take your full measure before we consider designs and fabrics.'

I glared at him, but it was useless to demand privacy. He sat with his legs parted, his gloved hands resting atop the gold-headed cane, as though he not only intended to watch but to direct the proceedings. To Mrs Marley's credit, she stood between us as she helped me out of another borrowed dress.

'I recall this gown from years ago,' she murmured, as though discreetly asking me why I was wearing it.

But Franklin heard every word. 'Yes, that belonged to Alice. She always admired your work, Mrs Marley.

And your ability to complete it quickly, with such discretion.'

The little woman scowled, scandalised that I'd been wearing clothes belonging to Harte's deceased wife. But she was no fool, so she laid the dress aside without comment. I stood before her dressed only in a corset, bloomers and silk stockings – which I assumed were Alice's, too.

'Seems this process would be more efficient if I assisted,' Harte suggested slyly. 'Here – I'll take her measurements while you write them down.'

Before the seamstress could protest, Franklin snatched the cloth tape from her fingers and looked me over furtively. One glance quelled the remark Mrs Marley was about to make, about his lewd behaviour as well as the stablehands who were gathering around. Pleased to be the centre of attention, and once again in control, Harte snapped the tape imperiously.

'It's the least I can do for my future daughter-in-law,' he remarked, as though reminding me what a favour he was granting me. 'Shall we begin at the top, with her lovely neck?'

Franklin looped the tape over my head and then tugged on it, grinning as he noted the numbers for the seamstress. 'Perhaps a necklace of the finest pearls would suit as a wedding gift,' he murmured. 'Something in several strands ... a choker, with an H made of rubies in the front. Would you enjoy that, Vanita?'

His flared nostrils prompted my reply. 'Yes, Daddy,' I rasped.

'Then you shall have it. And as we measure above your bosom, I would suggest a full complement of silk underthings, appropriate for a new bride.' His hands moulded themselves over my breasts, squeezing until I sucked in air. 'White would befit the occasion, I suppose, but I – er, Damon – has a marked preference for black. Flimsy little camisoles in French lace, with black garters and stockings. For the honeymoon, of course.'

I knew better than to think Damon and I would leave the estate – if indeed I couldn't escape before this travesty of a wedding. Harte then tightened the tape under my arms for a reading, and around the fullest point of my bosom, and then directly beneath them, his breathing growing more pronounced. 'Turn around,' he rasped. 'Take in a truly beautiful sight.'

Indeed, as he pivoted me to face away from the house, I sighed in wonderment. The lush, rolling pastureland shone in a springtime green, dotted with fine thoroughbreds like I hadn't seen since we'd raised them at Wellspring. White plank fences separated the training areas from where these graceful animals grazed, and beyond them I saw endless acres of little green tobacco plants, rising as though to worship the sun. Small cottages sat in a row to the west, whitewashed and adorned with golden forsythia and lilacs bursting into shades of lavender. I could smell their sweet perfume and I longed to pick some, to walk beneath this bluebell sky with the cool grass tickling my bare toes.

'You'll soon be mistress of all you survey,' Franklin announced with a grandiose sweep of his hand. 'A fitting gift for the woman who'll carry on the high tradition of the Harte family.'

Never mind that this contradicted his earlier disinterest in heirs. A snicker caught my attention, and then I noticed our audience. The groundskeepers and stablehands.

'She can be *my* mistress, for sure!' one of the nearest men proclaimed. 'Show us some more of that titty, boss!'

Franklin chortled, again covering my breasts with

his gloved hands. 'You, Felton, can have Miss Vanita the moment you catch her! I've brought her here for my son, and if she's stupid enough to attempt escape, you're all charged with the responsibility of returning her – to me, personally. And if you catch a dark-haired bastard with the Devil's own beard sneaking around the grounds, you're to shoot him on sight. Or better yet, truss him up and let *me* dispatch him. Are we clear on this?'

This was met with a raucous murmuring and the nodding of heads. I saw at least a dozen hands in the grass now, paying closer attention when they learned they had a stake in my future. As hard as I'd tried not to respond to Franklin's handling, a ripple went through me when I realised so many sets of eyes were fastened on his hands as he massaged my bosom.

I cried out when he slipped his fingers inside my corset to pinch my nipples, twisting them between his gloved thumb and forefinger. Chuckling, he continued this stimulation until I was wiggling in spite of my best intentions. When I bent forwards, a reflexive action to such intense stimulation, he popped my breasts free of the constricting undergarment and offered them up to his men.

Applause and whistles rang out. Franklin got behind me then, buckling my knees with his as he rocked against my bottom like a rutting dog. The cheering grew louder, and I squeezed my eyes shut to escape their eager stares ... but also to conceal my arousal. Through the layers of his suit and my bloomers, a randy shaft prodded me, and his heaving chest signalled a stud ready for conquest ... ready to make me his slave, in front of witnesses.

Was this why my aunt had loved acting? Playing to admirers as she provoked them with her scanty costumes? Mama hadn't said it in so many indelicate words, but I'd had the impression Aunt Lill didn't perform in legitimate theatres where the audience arrived in evening apparel. As a child, I'd sensed my mother's lesson about the shame of such women, yet here I was performing in much the same way – simply allowing Franklin's antics to cover my own enjoyment of being bared. I was shocked at my reaction, but too brazen to stop.

'Mr Harte! If you *please*!' came the seamstress's indignant warning.

'Oh, I please, all right,' he replied, egged on by his men's approving murmurs. 'And if you think my treatment of Miss Wells is lewd and detestable, just wait until it's your turn!'

Mrs Marley turned triple shades of crimson and then went to study her bolts of fabric. Meanwhile, Franklin's hands had slithered along my sides and now spanned my waist as he continued his parody of humping me from behind. The men's eyes glittered as they watched my breasts bob. The corset was now bunched around my waist, revealing the upper half of my flushed body. With a quick jerk on my bloomers, Harte bared my legs as well.

'A fine filly, indeed!' someone called out.

'Just wait till I catch her! She'll know she's been ridden then!'

'Oh, Felton, you're not half the man I am! Miss Vanita deserves *me*!'

With one arm Harte held me against his heaving body, while his other hand slipped between my legs. Below the white corset, my exposed thatch was teased by the breeze – and then by a single gloved finger, which instinctively slid between my pouting, hot lips to that little nub that craved such attention. Again I wondered why Franklin always covered his hands ... what misdeeds he'd been caught at that warranted constant concealment. The wickedness of this notion made me writhe against him.

'That's right, sweet Vanita,' he crooned so all could hear, 'show us your true nature. Show us what pleasures await the man who sinks his shaft inside your hot little twat. They can smell your honey now, and they all want a taste of it.'

A cry escaped me and I arched backwards, reacting to the bold strokes of that kid glove against my sensitive tissues. He was circling my clitoris, panting against my ear as though at any moment he planned to drop his pants and complete the deed. Around and around went his finger, spreading the slickness that leaked between my legs as he clutched me against himself. My head dropped back as the spasms inside me tightened like the coils of a clock being wound with a key ... a key that kept rubbing my nub with its thumb while two fingers slipped into my slit.

My mouth fell open with a groan. My body shook, poised for that leap towards the sunburst that would free me from these pent-up sensations, when footsteps rushed up behind us.

'Father, for God's sake, that's enough! Vanita's done nothing to deserve this!'

Franklin snorted, wheeling us around to face his son, who glared from beneath a hooded cloak of black velvet. 'Unless I'm losing my touch, she's enjoying it even more than the rest of us. But then, how would *you* know that?'

'She's mine! You gave her to me!' Damon cried, wrenching me from his father's grasp. '*Must* you prove, again and again, what a greedy beast you are?'

The crowd's murmurs went higher in pitch, mocking him as a prissy sort. Franklin shot him a speculative gaze, drinking in every move as Damon tugged my corset up into place. Never had I been caught in such an awkward position: my body cried out for release, while my mind felt truly grateful that I wasn't to become any more of a public spectacle. I rested against the luxurious velvet cape, catching my breath, wondering what would come of this dramatic rescue attempt.

'You men! You have your work, so get on with it!' the younger Harte ordered, waving them away with a sleeved arm that rippled richly, revealing black leather gloves. 'And now, Mrs Marley, shall we cover my fiancée and continue this session inside? I've opened the front parlour draperies, and I'm sure you'll find the light there acceptable.'

'Yes, Mr Harte,' she said with a relieved curtsy. 'Thank you so very much, sir.'

I detected a vengeful edge to Franklin's swarthy features as he watched his son escort me into the house, but he joined the workers returning to their tasks. He'd triumphed for the moment, and he'd try for me again when the opportunity presented itself. In such a shrouded house, full of nooks and crannies, he could choose a time and place at his leisure.

'Thank you,' I murmured as we stepped inside, for I realised what might happen if the hands thought they, too, could take liberties to keep me captive. I stopped to adjust my underthings, but Damon steered me into the nearest room and shut the door. He dragged a black leather finger up the inside of my thigh. Then he inhaled the wet scent he'd caught, chuckling. 'You made an enticing sight out there, Vanita. I sense I arrived *just* in the nick of time.'

I sucked in my breath when his hand returned to its purpose, and I had to grab his shoulders to keep from falling. This knave in ebony velvet was parting my legs, tickling my still-swollen clit with a fingertip of softest kid leather, until my eyes widened and I had to nip my lip against a scream. Instantly my need was rekindled, all the more blatant here in the summer parlour, where a platinum man in the boldest of black capes was bringing me off with his finger.

'Damon, I –'

'It's so cruel to leave a lover on the verge,' he whispered, his eyes becoming translucent pools of pink. 'Lest you believe me totally immune to a woman's charms, let me satisfy a little more than your curiosity.'

Before I could reply, two fingers teased at my opening while his thumb pressed against my clit. I sucked air and clung to him, my body tensing with this unexpected pleasure. On the other side of the wall, Mrs Marley was telling Felton where to carry her yard goods, and at the moment I stiffened for my climax, Damon plunged double fingers inside me. I wheezed, muffling my cries against his shoulder. Deeper he probed, twisting and prodding, kicking up a scent of leather mingled with my musk. I convulsed against him, my hips thrusting uncontrollably as he continued his attentions.

When I collapsed, panting, I felt his chuckle. He helped me stand upright again, straightening my crumpled underthings, and then offered me his handkerchief. 'Now, go in there and demand five of everything, fashioned from Mrs Marley's most expensive fabrics. Have her design you a wedding gown like no other woman's ever worn, with seed pearls and miles of lace. Desiree will help, if you like. She's got a knack for dress design – and for spending Daddy's money.'

My mind was still spinning from my climax as I wiped myself. I spoke in a rapid whisper, desperate for this man's understanding.

'But don't you see?' I pleaded. 'You're helping him dress me like – like a lamb for the slaughter! A vestal virgin destined for sacrifice! You know damn well your father's planning to claim me for himself, unless I beat him to the punch – with your help!'

His pale eyes widened, and he shook off the hood so his cream-coloured hair shone as the only light in the room. 'What are you getting at?'

'Take me, dammit! End this farce before it goes any farther – and steal your daddy's thunder once and for all!' I whispered frantically.

His expression waxed wistful. 'I'm sorry, but it's not that simple, Vanita. I'd like to help you – truly I would. But if I give my father control over who I love or who I marry, what do I have left for myself?'

I could only stare at him, wondering whether to burst into tears or slap him.

'Go on, now. Play along, like my sister and I have done all our lives,' he replied quietly. 'You'll be a fool if you try to escape. The last young lady who did that was handed over to the stablehands so they could all have a go at her while Daddy cheered them on. Bide your time, and we'll see what we can do.'

Bide my time? As though I had months before the wedding! As though I could leave without Franklin being aware of it! I clenched my fists, but I didn't hit him – I was too angry and disappointed. Damon was willing to sate my body, to make me dance in frenzied splendour, yet he was still forfeiting control to his father.

I stalked down the hall to the front parlour. Mrs Marley and Desiree looked up from a length of something that shimmered like silk between them, yet had the sheen of pearlescent satin ... so gossamer the light from the window passed through it as though it were only a dream.

'Oh my,' I breathed, thinking it would split like the threads of a spider's web if I dared touch it.

An albino spider's web, came my next thought, because Desiree's expression told me she already had plans for this exquisite fabric. And it would suit her like a second skin; make her every bit as beautiful as a bride while rendering her wicked beyond belief.

'Make *my* gown from that!' I declared. 'Damon wants me dressed in a splendour like you've sewn for no one else, with yards of lace and seed pearls to make me shine. And he's the groom, after all.'

I sensed, from his sister's scowl, that I'd regret my impulsive decision. But if I was to be paraded before guests in a farcical ceremony, supposedly to wed a man who was long on show but short on backbone, by God I would indeed indulge myself!

As Damon had suggested, I then ordered an entire trousseau of fine lingerie and hosiery, evening gowns in peacock and crimson and rich Paisley silk, and dresses suitable for daytime as well. After all, I'd been forced to wear the outmoded clothes of a dead woman, as though I were damn lucky to have them tossed at me.

By the time I'd satisfied my whims with the dress-maker, I was feeling much more buoyant. In control. Like I *mattered* again, and could have a hand in a destiny that did *not* include these conniving white twins and their lecherous father.

I had Magnolia bring in some tea and cakes, and enjoyed watching Desiree choose fabrics for new day dresses, as well as a splendid white satin to wear at the wedding. She had a fine sense of style, and chose colours to complement her ghostly complexion – although she'd closed the draperies long before Mrs Marley finished scribbling her requests. Her final choice was a gown of watered silk in the palest of blues, like her eyes.

'We'll be hosting a betrothal ball next Saturday,' she

remarked as she put on her regular clothing. 'Please have Vanita's gowns and this blue one ready to hem by the week's end.'

'I'll hire more ladies and be back on Friday,' the seamstress agreed. It was no wonder she whistled under her breath as she strode towards her carriage. Figures hadn't been discussed, but I was estimating a total of several thousand dollars – and grinning at the thought that somehow I'd be long gone before Franklin could leer down the low-cut front of that wedding dress.

Desiree slammed the front door and turned to me, her features sharply feline. 'I saw that shameless display in the garden, and heard every word dear old Daddy said to you,' she spat. She came to stand directly in front of me, her nose only inches from mine as her icy eyes shot sparks. 'Do you really think I'll let you become mistress of all you survey, Vanita? Harte's Haven is *mine*! God knows I've earned it!'

14 Moonlit Madness

I didn't see the twins for the rest of the day. Franklin had also made himself scarce, so I wandered the tomb-like halls of Harte's Haven, pondering the home and possessions of a family who'd lived in Kentucky as long as my own had. It was snooping, yes – but since I was to become a part of this odd clan, I considered it research. I hoped to stumble upon something that would inspire my escape.

The furnishings were expensive, if neglected. Had the walls been painted with brighter colours, the place would be a showcase, compared to most plantation homes ravaged in the War Between the States. I suspected Franklin Harte had preserved his mansion by playing both sides of the fence – supporting Confederate generals with generous contributions, while wooing Union powers to prevent the pillage they'd wrought upon so many of the South's estates. The crystal, silver service and china still graced the cabinets of the butler's pantry. Upstairs, in what had been Alice's room, her finery still filled the armoires, and jewellery I knew to be genuine lay shimmering in her vanity drawers. Most families had lost such heirlooms and luxuries, and couldn't replace them: farming crop lands without their slave labour came before such frills as formal wear.

What set the spacious, musty rooms apart from other homes, however, was the conglomeration of clocks, and the wind-up oddities to be found atop tables and credenzas. Damon had poured years of his life into making these trifles of wood and iron and coils – but then, what else could a man of his nature do? The timepieces and gewgaws paid tribute to a spirit confined by skin too easily burned; translucent eyes envisioned a life of leisurely wealth supported by his father's crops and horses and coal. He had no need – nor inclination – to concern himself with the realities of adulthood, so he made things to amuse himself and his sister.

One such toy was a wind-up dog, of ivory and red-stained wood, fashioned like a spaniel. I wound the key in its back and gasped, startled at a tongue shaped like a man's shaft, and covered in soft leather . . . leather bearing stains from saturation, with the distinct scent of sex.

Another article was carved of wood, a trout so life-like I admired Damon's artistry and Desiree's skill with a paintbrush. After a few twists on this key, the fish opened its mouth to reveal a leather-lined throat that would accommodate a man's member. As the fish pulsed in my hand, I got the strangest feeling, imagining Damon pleasuring himself with it – indeed, when I examined its belly, I found the word 'blowfish'. Such a sense of humour seemed refreshing, considering the dreariness of the twins' environment and the man they'd answered to after losing their mother.

But I could not live like this. I couldn't tolerate a closed-in existence behind velvet draperies, shrouded in the funereal colours of these rooms. And the thought of Franklin Harte having me at his constant disposal was further incentive to get myself out of here. It seemed Pearce would be no immediate help, even though I trusted him to be working on my behalf to reclaim Wellspring.

I parted draperies of maroon velvet in the parlour, squinting as the sun blazed its way down the distant sky. Had the stablehands always been so evident? Or were they following Harte's orders to make sure I didn't escape? Until this morning when the dressmaker arrived, I'd been stashed in the mansion and hadn't considered the logistics of getting away. I'd be foolish to attempt it at this point, since I could easily get confused in the mazelike passageways between these rooms before I even reached the white-fenced pastureland. Except for a small wooded area south of the house, I'd be in plain sight if I tried to run.

The mansion seemed deathly quiet. I'd heard Franklin was going into Lexington – which could explain the show of 'guards' around the paddocks and garden – and I was guessing Damon and Desiree had found their own diversions. Probably comparing notes on Vanita Wells, that ungrateful, demanding little bitch whose presence put a kink in their existence. I wandered up the main staircase and into my room to pass the evening. After being humiliated in the garden, and spending a fortune on a wardrobe I didn't plan to wear, and then being told by both twins they wouldn't cooperate, I was ready for time alone. Time to contemplate my predicament, and my options.

I threw open the heavy draperies of my room to view the sunset. As I sat in the window seat, I looked in at my shadow, oversized and foreboding, projected against the ghastly flocked wallpaper that gave my silhouette the appearance of having smallpox. From this vantage point, I could also catch a glimpse of the early evening moon, a crescent fingernail clipping against the deepening azure sky.

In a matter of days I'd have to endure the betrothal ball, and a short time later, when the full moon marked Damon's birthday on June sixth, I'd be sealing my fate as his lawfully wedded wife. I shuddered at the thought.

I looked at my situation from different perspectives, yet found nothing to assist me. I'd been snatched away from Wellspring unawares, and I simply knew too little, too late, about the situation I'd been coming home to. Being the last to know about the dire condition of my finances had given everyone else the advantage all along.

Vanitaaaaaa ...

I stiffened, thinking a spirit hailed me. Then I recalled the whispering tubes and sighed. I was going to be the target of more ribald remarks.

Come outside and play with us ... dance naked in the moonlight ... naked and free with the ones who want you ...

Startled, I glanced out my window into the gloaming below. The trees now stood as dark skeletons against the night sky, and the rolling pastureland lay in velvet mounds as far as the eye could see. Peaceful and serene, with surprising light from so slender a moon.

Vanitaaaaahh ... let us fondle your fine skin ... let us take down your golden hair ... let us lose ourselves in your beauty ...

Was the voice male or female? Damon or Desiree? Or had Franklin come home to torment me? Despite my confrontations with them, gooseflesh was pimpling my skin as the low timbre of that voice slithered through the pipes and into my room.

And then I saw them – two lithe figures, identical except for Desiree's upswept hair and slightly rounded breasts. On impulse I raised the casement to immerse myself in the sounds of a spring evening ... to listen for whatever they might say. If I sat in the darkness, on the edge of the window seat, I wouldn't be noticed. Damon was setting a large box on the ground near the trees, and then he wound its handle.

As the tinkling notes of the music box spilled forth,

he led his sister into the moonlit clearing. It was sheer magic, as the slender siblings mirrored each other's steps, following the waltz with an eerie, ethereal grace. Their hair glimmered, opalescent, as the moon's light blessed them with the day's benediction. Here in the night they were truly free, creatures who endured the darkness of a lugubrious old house yet frolicked like faeries when sprinkled with stardust.

I sat entranced, filled with envy. They had invited me to join them ... should I? What if they were luring me into a trap set by the randy stablehands?

Vanitaaaahh ... dance with us ... feel our excitement washing over you ... come into our arms and free your shriveled spirit.

Again I stiffened, for the person I'd assumed was speaking now swooped in a tree swing, pushed by his sister. Their laughter taunted me – even though I realised now that Damon and Desiree were paying no attention to me whatsoever.

I fought the tightness in my throat, wondering if Franklin were trying to disorient me. Staring as hard as I could towards the stables, I saw no evidence of hands lurking in the shadows – in fact, the cottages at the edge of the property were picturesquely lit by lamps in their windows, suggesting the men were at home.

Vanitaaaaah ... lover, come to me now, while there's time. Meet me in the deepest shadows at the side of the house.

I jumped, driven by the sudden recognition of this different voice. My mind warned me that it could indeed be Franklin, making me hear what I wanted to, yet my heart pounded at the chance that it could be Pearce. If I cowered in the house, I might miss an opportunity to escape – or to glean information I could use against this family who held me captive.

Slipping off my shoes, I crept quietly across the

room. At the door I paused, listening intently above the beating of my frantic heart. The house resonated with the silence of a tomb, and I saw no light beneath the other bedroom doors. Down the hallway and to the stairs I padded, wishing I knew of a servant's stairway – a passage that didn't take me through the main rooms. I descended as quickly as I could into the high-ceilinged front hall. I didn't know where Magnolia and Roger were and at this point it was too late to wonder if they'd been instructed to watch me. I stepped out the front door and then sidled along the shadow of the front wall with my back against the cold white exterior.

I stopped at the edge of the wide front verandah, my pulse pounding. If it were Franklin who'd lured me here, I'd suffer the consequences of a soul that leaped before it looked. I'd barely slipped one foot off the porch's plank floor when two arms shot around to grab me. I swallowed my scream, greatly relieved to see a face outlined in dark, tousled curls and defined by that devilish beard.

'Took you long enough!' he rasped before clutching me into a kiss.

I kissed him back, laughing as our lips pressed together, hot and earnest. His body felt firm and virile against mine, not like Franklin's fleshy one – yet another reason to honour my vow to Pearce by getting away from Harte's Haven as soon as I could.

'I've missed you!' I breathed. 'But be careful, Pearce! Harte's told his hands to shoot you on sight, or take you to him, personally.'

'I've promised to restore your estate, and I'll deliver.' His obsidian eyes were shining into mine. Then he peered around the house, to be sure the twins still entertained each other. 'We've learned that Franklin all but stole Wellspring from your Aunt Lillian, during a series of strip-poker games he initiated. Seems no one's ever seen her at the race track, and we've spoken with a few locals who were in on the card games.'

'Then *grab* him! Call in the sheriff!'

Pearce smiled as though he wished it were that easy. 'We must proceed through the proper legal channels, love – convince the other men, who are Harte's influential friends, to testify before Judge Cavendish – or you won't get any of your money back. And without any money, or horses to generate income, Wellspring will be of little use to you.'

I revelled in the feel of his strong hands, wrapped around mine, as I gazed into his unwavering eyes. 'You're right,' I sighed. 'Sentiment alone can't bring back the Wells reputation. And what if Franklin's cronies say Aunt Lill enticed them into the games? From what I've seen, I couldn't refute them.'

'So you see what work lies ahead of me. And you'll understand if I can't be here to watch over you as often as I'd like.' He brushed his lips against my forehead, his sigh mingling with mine. 'Has it been horrible, Vanita? Have they backed you into too many corners?'

Now that he held me, and was doing his damnedest to win back my land, I didn't feel like recounting the gruesome details of my days here. It was enough to just breathe with him, and feel the warmth of his body ... and the prominent ridge now rubbing against my front.

'The wedding's set for the full moon, on June sixth. Damon's supposedly requested an outdoor ceremony.'

Pearce scowled. 'But he's claimed he'll never marry.'

'They're playing along, appeasing their daddy. Suggesting strongly that I do the same – although it's an onerous task. What a pig Franklin is!'

He laid a warning finger along my lips, his smile bronzed by the moonlight. 'You're a crafty sort with plenty of horse sense, Vanita. You'll find a way to stay ahead of him!'

I nodded, wanting to believe in myself the way he did. 'The betrothal party's next weekend – another idea Desiree claims will keep the game afoot, although I haven't a clue who's invited. The only friends I've seen are ones of Damon's creation.'

Pearce's grin recalled what he'd seen in Damon's workshop. 'Is it a clockwork ball?'

'I think not, silly. Desiree and I ordered gowns and ... wedding dresses this morning.' I paused, bitter-sweet. 'It used to give me such pleasure, being fitted for new clothes. But I hope I won't be around here to wear these.'

'Pay attention to who's here that night. You might find an ally, in case I can't make an appearance myself.'

'But if Franklin spots you in the –'

'He won't.'

It was a sly reply, rendering his face foxlike as he considered a plan. But he didn't share it – perhaps so I couldn't betray him unawares. Then he scowled, looking towards the trees. 'Shhh ... The music's stopped.'

I held my breath, realising that even the cicadas had stopped chirping. Silently, drawing me with him, Pearce crept along the house's shadow, peering over to where the twins had been dancing. 'They're gone,' he whispered. 'Odd, that. We would've heard their footsteps if they went inside.'

More boldly now, I leaned away from the house to see if I could spot their shimmering bodies in the moonlight, out by the pasture or heading towards the cottages. But the swing floated empty on the breeze, and the music box sat silent where Damon had placed it.

'I don't like this. I'd better go back upstairs,' I said, wishing more than anything we could strip off our clothes and enjoy the moonbeams in the nude. Damon and his sister had made it look so inviting. So free.

'I'll take you myself. To be sure they're not waiting to –'

'You're returning to Wellspring,' I insisted, tapping his chest with my finger. 'If you keep getting distracted, wanting between my legs, I'll *never* get my home back!'

'Turn around.'

The timbre of his voice sent lightning up my spine. Gone was the easy teasing, and in its place came that mysterious black magic he had a way of holding me hostage with. Pearce's eyes riveted mine, shining in the moonlight like beacons down the primrose path, and the little currents that always tickled my veins when he was near now raced through me.

Without waiting for me to comply, he swung me around in front of himself, facing away, and pawed at the back of my dress. I clutched the side of the house for balance and then sucked in my breath: the twins were slipping back from the woods, hand in hand, as though returning from some covert mission. Damon hopped into the swing again and his sister stepped on behind him, standing astraddle, with her feet on either side of his hips.

'Have you ever seen such a pair?' I whispered, shimmying to help my bloomers fall.

'Oh, I prefer *this* pair.' He cupped my breasts with warm, eager hands. 'If you move just so . . . and promise not to scream . . . I'm betting we'll see quite a show.'

Indeed, Desiree was pumping in earnest, bending at the knees while her twin stretched his long legs towards heaven. The muscles of his backside flexed after each fall backwards, to propel them higher. Their skin seemed to radiate its own light, and the grace of their movements suggested they played together this way every chance they got.

'Hold your skirts for me, love. Lean forwards.'

How was I already wet and ready for him? Was it the sight of that luminous twosome swooping through the air, or the fact that we were out here where any of the hands – or Franklin – might spot us? 'This might not be such a good idea, if –'

'I want you, Vanita,' he rasped against the tender shell of my ear. 'And there's not a man alive who can keep me out of your hot little hole.'

With that, his fingers found the wet flesh already pulsing for him, wanting him to fill it, and he began the hypnotic circling of my clit. Tickling, teasing it with just a fingertip, he pushed me beyond control until I almost cried out. Slipping his other hand gently over my mouth, he then shoved his thumb high inside me. I bucked, trying to be silent while he tortured me this way until my juice dripped out from insides screaming for release.

'Now?'

I nodded feverishly, my eyes nearly popping as he slid his shaft in from behind. At this angle, because he was taller than I, I had the sensation of being lifted off the ground with each of his thrusts ... which he matched to the swooping up and falling back of the swing in the moonlight. I wiggled against him, wanting it faster, but he chuckled low in his throat.

'Patience, my sweet. I've waited a long while for this and I don't want to rush a single moment ... a single stroke. Oh, God, would you look what he's doing to her now?'

I'd already seen it, the way Damon arched backwards and was now extending his tongue up towards his sister's slit. They didn't miss a beat – swooping up, falling back – as she parted her thighs farther for him. Desiree moaned with his first contact, her legs quivering as she gripped the ropes.

Swooping up ... falling back ... and behind me, Pearce grunted at the display before us. He was rubbing my clit harder now, pumping himself against me in a faster rhythm, which made his excitement contagious. 'My God, he's got to be ten inches long!' he breathed.

And yes, I couldn't help but notice the erection jutting up from Damon's lap like a pillar of white fire. On he pumped, sucking his sister's cunt as she tried to maintain the force of her own thrusts to keep them going. Her head fell back and her hair came loose, swinging like a curtain of crumpled white satin in the night.

I exhaled hard against Pearce's hand, my thighs straining around his shifting knees. White-hot inside me, the spirallings began and I pressed myself against his other fingers, filled nearly to bursting with the pressure of our clandestine coupling.

'Hold it ... hold it, love. He's going to shoot like a geyser any moment now. And so will I.'

The man in the swing gave a final pump with his outstretched legs, burying his mouth between Desiree's thighs, and then a stream of liquid crystal rose in the moonlight, sparkling like champagne from a fountain. Desiree shrieked and rocked in place, and I came right along with her, clenching my eyes shut with a silent scream. Behind me, Pearce rutted like a crazed stud and then bit my shoulder as he shot me full of hot seed. For several moments we couldn't stop thrusting to fuel each other's climax, drawing out the ecstasy for as long as we dared. From the woods, and from behind the stables, several male moans echoed in the quiet of the night.

Clutching me, my lover struggled to catch his breath. 'If I weren't so concerned about your welfare, it'd be worth your staying at Harte's Haven just to watch those wicked twins go at each other.'

'Don't get any ideas!' I teased, gasping for air. 'Now put my dress down and get out of here. Seems we weren't the only ones watching. And why do I have the feeling you arranged this whole thing as a diversion? How do you *do* that?'

Pearce smiled against the side of my face. 'A man makes his own best luck, Vanita. And when you gamble on randy hands taking a peek, when the boss is gone, you can't lose.'

His chuckle sounded so cosy as he kissed me, as though we were old friends turned lovers with all the time in the world to savour that relationship. 'But don't think you'll have your way with me so easily, next time I see you.'

'And when will that be?' I asked, already missing his sanity and solidity in a world that seemed totally askew.

'You'll be the first to know. The only one to know.' He kissed me then, fondly cupping my breasts. 'Watch your back, sweetheart. The twins are realising what a fine diversion you are – a familiarity that won't bode well, come time to convict Franklin of stealing your estate.'

With a final, driving kiss he left me, disappearing into the shadows at the front of the house. I watched him, trying to figure out how he came and went, but I couldn't linger. It was safest to be in my room, with the chair propped under the doorknob.

The next morning, after a breakfast made bearable by Franklin's absence, I found Desiree seated at a walnut secretary, writing out invitations to the ball. She wore a pale shade of pink that rendered her fresh and delicate, looking every bit the lady of the manor, while I felt hopelessly gauche in her mother's cast-away clothing.

But Cinderella would go to the ball, I told myself. And perhaps the handsome prince would appear to whisk her away, to that happily-ever-after I'd demanded of him. In a week, I'd find out.

Those days passed slowly, although the twins tried to alleviate my anxiousness. After all, who did I know on the guest list? What if I were afloat in a sea of strange faces, washed along towards that inevitable wedding, once my betrothal to Damon Harte became official? Desiree quietly insisted *she* would be the hostess, and would therefore make all the major decisions, while the bride-to-be obeyed her wishes. This left me with little to do but wonder: would I escape Harte's Haven before I became permanently ensnared?

Franklin arrived home on Wednesday, his nose red with whisky and his air more furtive than before. When I caught a whiff of perfume that smelled all too familiar, I blurted, 'How is my dear Aunt Lill? And what did you screw her out of this time?'

It was the wrong thing to say, but I stood with my fists on my hips, forcing him to answer before leaving the pea-green vestibule.

'Such cynicism doesn't become you,' he muttered, smoothing his pomaded hair back as though his latest escapades at Wellspring had left him exhausted. 'I merely invited your aunt to our betrothal ball, and of course to the wedding, now that we've set the date. Seems the proper thing to do, don't you agree?'

'And she's coming?'

'Every time I reach for her,' he said with a sneer. 'And yes, to the festivities, as well. Too bad your parents aren't alive to witness such a momentous occasion. The joining of two of Lexington's oldest, proudest families – which marks the *end* of the Wells line, of course.'

Blood rushed to my face with my effort not to slap

him, full force. 'Too bad that'll never happen. Too bad you'll lose your bet, Mr Harte.'

'How so?' His gaze remained steady, yet I noted a tic in his cheek.

'Damon's coming around. Now that he's convinced you to invest so much in this wedding, he'll fuck me just to spite you.' I kept my eyes wide and triumphant. This toady in white had cheated me of my dignity, but, as Pearce had pointed out, we make our own best luck and it was time I fired back.

Franklin leaned forwards, his grin growing wicked. 'Your mama wasn't much good at calling my bluff either, Vanita. When she first came sniffing around here, on the pretence of telling me Alice was leading your daddy astray, I didn't fall for it. But her legs were spread, so I took what she was offering me – already knowing the venerable Jared Wells was in hock to his eyeballs, ploughing Alice's furrow so she'd cover his bad track bets behind my back.'

'That's not so!' I blurted. 'My father's ledgers prove beyond a doubt that –'

'He wrote down any damn numbers he pleased, just like the rest of us,' Harte hissed. He was leaning so close to me now, the soured whisky on his breath made me grimace. 'He was in so deep – at the race track, and with Alice – that even if that lightning hadn't struck your parents down before their time, they could never have repaid their debts to me.

'Better think about that before you try to buffalo me again, Vanita. I've little patience for women who think they're smarter – or more socially acceptable – than I am. The way I see it, I should've claimed you a long time ago, as my payment for debts covered and services rendered.'

With a malignant grin, he ran a kid-gloved finger down the side of my face and neck until it stopped between my breasts. I again wondered why he kept his hands covered – did it have some connection to those past scandals? – until he shoved me away with the force of that one finger. Caught off guard, I landed hard against the wall. My face flamed, and my heart was pounding so fiercely I couldn't breathe, much less reply to his allegations. His nasty laugh echoed in the vestibule, leaving me in a quivering, sickened heap on the floor.

What was I to believe? Had Daddy been a gambling man, desperate to hide his debts from Mama – and me? Had Mama known it, and gotten caught in Franklin's fiendish web? As proper parents, they'd never discussed such issues in front of me. Nor had Lorena, or my Aunt Lillian, hinted at any dissolution, even when I was old enough to better understand such matters.

Once again I wished for Pearce's unflinching confidence: he *would* restore my legacy to me, and I *would* escape this plantation to claim it. No matter what Harte told me, I had to *believe* I could triumph over his cruelty, because believing was seeing.

For if I didn't believe that, the future I saw was bleak indeed.

I pondered these things, keeping to myself as much as possible for the next few days. I trusted no one in the Harte household to answer my questions, nor could I ask Mrs Marley about this matter when she came on Friday for our fitting. The henna-haired seamstress seemed sympathetic to my situation, but we didn't talk about it in front of Desiree. I could only feign my delight at becoming a bride, pretending to revel in the fit of my shimmering, translucent gown and the other dresses she'd made me.

I could only hope that at the betrothal ball, I'd learn something – or meet someone – to get me out of this horrible house.

15 The Charade and Its Players

My heart thudded as I descended the staircase, clad in a gown of shimmering crimson accented in black. Its high waistline emphasised my breasts, left bare beneath a bodice of black lace that didn't conceal the nipples pressing into its mesh. Desiree had insisted I was to be the evening's centrepiece, and Mrs Marley had outdone herself: one side of the gown was slit high up my thigh, to reveal black garters and stockings that would show with every step. Ebony mink formed a ruching around the gown's hem, at the waist, and down the deep neckline. I felt bawdy and brazen – not a bad thing, considering my mission to seduce Damon Harte. This half-moon evening marked mere days before the wedding I didn't plan to attend.

The crowd caught sight of me and sucked in its collective breath, as the heir to Harte's Haven flashed me a dazzling grin. He looked stunning in a black dovetail coat and striped trousers, his button-front shirt stiff with starch ... stiff, like I hoped something else would become while we were among witnesses. It meant nothing, if we coupled and no one believed it.

He extended his arm, assisting me down the last few steps. 'Stunning. Absolutely stunning,' he murmured, bringing my lace-gloved hand to his lips. 'Scarlet and black bring out the vixen in you. And I do so love a willing, wanton vixen.'

Those around us twittered their approval – a garish crowd for a summer ball. I'd expected ladies in lavender and yellow, but saw a sea of suggestive jewel-toned dresses trimmed in black, every bit as jaded as my own.

Desiree strolled up to us, flushed and girlish in her pale-blue brocade. Indeed, she stood out in this crowd as a paragon of innocence among the damned. I realised then that she'd chosen her fabric with this in mind, so she could be the belle of my ball.

But the way Damon was gazing at me – at my bobbing breasts with their distended nipples – I didn't care. Desiree had insisted this crimson favoured my dark blonde hair, and hope quivered through my body: coupling with her brother finally seemed feasible. He took my arm, pulling me possessively against his side, and introduced me to the friends he and his sister had invited.

I nodded at a Harolyn Pricket, whose eyes and brows were drawn with dramatic lines of kohl – and who fluttered her lashes at me from behind her black fan. She was considerably younger and taller than her escort, Glenn Morell, whose sleek suit of deep green emphasised a barrel-chested figure with swaggering hips. As he drew my hand to his lips, he grinned.

'What a pleasure at last, Miss Wells,' he crooned. 'I've just come from London to oversee my firm's investment in thoroughbreds – hoping to do business with your stables, of course. Breeding has international appeal, you know.'

Those around him chuckled as though keeping a delicious secret, and I soon lost track of names in the crush of guests wishing to meet me. Never had I attended a gathering of such *intensity*, of style and manner and colour. These women plied their paints and flaunted their assets, many of them ready to split their seams and spill out of their fitted bodices. Even the men seemed overdrawn, like caricatures of continental gentility, and the way they all wanted to touch me, beyond the polite handshake, set me on edge.

Yet Damon and his sister chatted easily with them, the friends they'd somehow met in spite of being held hostage by this house and their pale skin. It gave me a new admiration for their social skills; for the life they'd cultivated while appearing to stay under their daddy's thumb.

And Franklin ... Franklin strutted through the double front doors as though he'd chosen the moment for his entrance, with Aunt Lillian coyly clinging to him. I'd never before seen him in black, a suit more severe than his son's that rendered him truly villainous as he smiled across the parlour at me.

'So you've met our bride?' he called out over the chattering crowd. 'And isn't she the most splendid filly you've ever beheld? No one's happier than I that Damon has finally found a woman who arouses his ... soul.'

The laughter was polite – even from Aunt Lill, decked out in a frothy confection of a dress men would've described as 'titty pink'. It was designed to show quite a lot of that asset as she bobbed and nodded acknowledgement, while Franklin led her among their friends. When she came close to me, she favoured me with a pointed smile.

'This monied company becomes you,' she murmured, fingering the mink edging of my dress. 'It's all on your shoulders, Vanita. After seeing you spread for Pearce, Franklin intends to witness your tryst with Damon, as well. I tried to convince him to go easier on you, since we all know it's a lost cause. But he's an insistent man. Very, very insistent.'

I noted a large hickey near her ear; teeth marks that surely belonged to Franklin. And she bore them so proudly! The thought of how she'd forfeited herself – and Wellspring – during strip-poker hands she probably lost to seduce him, sickened me. But I had to play the blushing bride, or at least a woman eager to marry into this noxious man's family. Most of these guests probably knew of the wager Franklin and I had made, so I had to behave as though I'd already won it. It was my way of staying sane.

It also kept me from peering too anxiously among the crowd for Pearce. One look at him and I'd give myself away – not to mention exposing his presence – so I half hoped he wouldn't show. Roger ushered in more guests, and Desiree guided them towards the tables laden with food while Damon encouraged the drinking of Magnolia's renowned rum punch. The downstairs rooms were becoming crowded with a more staid circle Franklin had invited, many of them from other venerable families who'd bred Kentucky's finest racehorses since the sport had begun.

I was relieved when Damon escorted me to the staircase. 'Our musicians await you in the ballroom,' he announced from the first landing. 'Please join us, and accept our thanks for celebrating this momentous occasion with us tonight.'

His words rang out confidently, but when he turned me to proceed up the stairs, he was hailed by his raucous father. As Franklin hurried up to the landing, clutching his cane in one hand and a tumbler of bourbon in the other, I anticipated remarks I'd rather miss.

'Although our plantations and horse farms cover vast acres that keep us miles apart,' he began ceremoniously, 'I'm sure rumours of this fine-looking couple's circumstances have reached your ears – rumours that Vanita is seeking to save her inheritance, while my son is proving himself a *man*, worthy of all I've acquired. Let me assure you those rumours are true, because I started them myself!'

My heart shrivelled. After a brief pause came polite, awkward laughter, which spurred Franklin on. He teetered against his cane, swilling his bourbon – and Aunt Lill was egging him on with winks and the wiggling of her hips. I wanted to vanish into thin air, and Damon's sympathetic squeeze of my arm was small consolation. Perhaps if his father thoroughly scandalised and embarrassed me, he'd feel compelled to couple with me before this wedding from hell could take place.

'I must say that – to her credit – Miss Vanita is a sporting sort, and bearing up well,' the older Harte continued in a barely controlled bellow. 'Let us wish her our best. Her beauty and fortitude stand as examples to us all, and she would grace any family she chose to marry into. I'm just damn glad I got to her first!'

'Hear, hear!' an older gentleman near the buffet called out, a man I recognised as Rutherford Cavendish. My mouth went dry: if Pearce found enough evidence, this would be the judge hearing our case against Franklin Harte. He and the underhanded tobacco magnate were obviously old buddies.

It was a moment I badly wanted to see Pearce Truman. But Harte's leer told me he wasn't finished making me the evening's spectacle. He handed Damon his drink and then the guests gasped as he pulled a sparkling piece of jewellery from his pocket.

'No betrothal's official without a memento to mark the occasion,' he intoned, holding up a choker between his gloved hands. 'And I'm a man of my word. I deliver what I promise.'

Five strands of lustrous black pearls flanked a brooch that formed an H in blood-red rubies – a truly magnificent necklace, except I felt I was being scorched by the Devil's branding iron when he clasped it around my neck. Whisky fumes and the heat of my own fear made my head swim. Franklin stood so close, letting his hands linger on my shoulders, that there was nowhere to look but into his beastly black eyes, orbs that widened triumphantly as his nostrils flared with anticipation.

I began to tremble, from trepidation and the weight of Damon's stare.

'Lord love me, I've stunned her speechless!' Franklin crowed, playing to the murmuring crowd. 'And my pants are still fastened!'

'Too bad your mouth's not,' his son muttered, but it got lost in the guffaws of the old lechers below us. Damon thrust the tumbler at his father, sloshing liquor on his leather glove, and then turned me to go upstairs.

Once again I felt like the proverbial lamb being led to the slaughter ... a lamb at the mercy of a shepherd whose crook was a gold-capped cane, and whose friends circled like wolves awaiting my demise. The pearl and ruby choker rested heavily around my neck, more like that damned dog collar than a token of anything resembling love.

'Never mind him,' Damon muttered. 'He's already sauced, and we can only hope the bourbon – or your aunt – will take him out of circulation early. It's another of those nights I wish I weren't related to him.'

When the orchestra opened with a lilting rendition of 'The Blue Danube', however, I could almost forget the evening was a sham, and that the man waltzing me around the ballroom refused to make love to me. Indeed, Damon held me closer than was proper, pressing his long legs into mine to pivot me with a flair that made my gown flutter around my exposed thigh. We spun and swayed to the buoyant music until I was giddy. His smile told me he was enjoying this charade – making the most of a moment we'd neither one chosen, rather than simply enduring it to save face.

Once I saw the advantage of this attitude, I threw myself into the dance with abandon. It seemed the more I exaggerated the steps, posturing for him – just as we postured for the people who watched us with speculative expressions – the more Damon encouraged me with a smile like I'd never seen him display.

It was the look of a man impassioned. His hand brushed my breast and I sucked air.

My hopes rose like a phoenix from the earlier ashes of the week. Perhaps there was a chance ... perhaps, afloat on the evening's gaiety, he would grant me the favour that would set me free. Especially now that his father had humiliated us both with the choker. As the first dance came to an end, my partner bent me backwards into a daring dip, until I thought my breasts would spring out of my lace bodice. I raised my leg, displaying a length of black stocking and garters and bare thigh, and the crowd cheered wildly.

'Splendid. Absolutely splendid,' he breathed as he pulled me upright. 'If I had my way, you'd dance with no one else tonight.'

Another glance around the room had me hoping along these lines, for I didn't see that familiar dark mane and devilish beard. Pearce was either following leads on my behalf, or had actually heeded my warnings about staying away from Harte's Haven.

The orchestra burst forth with another showy waltz, and other couples joined us. This time I relaxed in Damon's embrace, appreciating the intimate candlelight from sconces on the wall, the mingling of expensive perfumes, the bright violins and rhythmic shuffling of kid slippers on the hardwood floor ... the taste of Damon's ravenous kiss, which took me by surprise.

When he released me, I blinked rapidly. 'If you're doing this for show, you're quite convincing,' I whispered, noting the furtive looks on the faces around us.

'Perhaps my earlier statement against lovemaking was ... hasty,' he said, his voice rising with emotion. 'I'm not making any promises – just as I know you don't want to go through with this wedding. But I admire the way you've borne up under such pressure, and I hope that when all's said and done we can be ... close friends, Vanita.'

'I'd like that,' I replied. Damon had always been the easier twin to deal with, so without missing a beat I kissed his cheek.

We whirled gracefully around the room, and I truly enjoyed being partnered by a man so sure of his steps. As we danced, I glanced at those around us, who tended to be the younger set Desiree had invited. One man in particular, dressed in a suit of peacock blue that defied all conventions of men's dress, stared openly at us. His dark brown waves fell away from a broad brow and full face, and he was guiding Desiree around the floor with a fluidity that showed her off to perfection. Quite a couple they made, peacock blue alongside robin's egg; darkly drawn facial detail contrasted with platinum. Desiree smiled smugly at me.

'If you'll excuse me, I do like to give Dez a dance at these events,' her brother whispered, and then he nibbled my ear. 'Daddy's in the corner with his cronies, taking bets on us, no doubt. You'll be safe for the next few minutes, anyway.'

I nodded, making myself as inconspicuous in the crowd as I could. Spotting a woman I hadn't met yet, I made my way to where she stood, near a cluster of brightly arrayed ladies gossiping in low voices. 'I don't believe I've had the pleasure,' I began, extending my hand.

Her grip felt surprisingly firm, considering her full-length magenta gloves trimmed with ivory lace. 'Pamela,' she said beneath the vibrant music. 'Pamela Tanner. A distant cousin of the Hartes.'

'So happy to meet you. I hope you're enjoying yourself?'

'Immeasurably. Does my heart good to see Franklin putting on the dog,' she went on with a flutter of her long lashes. 'You'll soon learn he has a ... stingy streak, when it comes to other people's enjoyment.'

Laughter bubbled up at her unexpected candour, from everyone around us. 'Perhaps, since Desiree made all the arrangements, he hasn't seen the bills yet,' I replied in a conspiratorial tone.

Pamela's green eyes sparkled, and the directness of her gaze caught me off guard. Here was an attractive woman, decked in bold magenta with navy and lace details, her sable hair pulled up into a ribbon to flow freely down her back. She studied me as though she were ... attracted, tracing the top row of the pearl choker with her satin fingertip. Since she was one of Desiree's friends, I didn't take offence. After what I'd experienced this week, I was finding the world of women and men a far different territory than I believed while I'd attended finishing school.

I excused myself after a few more polite comments. As I turned to mingle with the other guests, however, it was Franklin who planted himself in front of me. He smelled like a distillery and he had evil in his eyes. His hand found my waist and then wandered downwards.

'Such a beauty you are, Vanita,' he slurred, swaying slightly. 'The next dance is mine – especially since my boy is sniffing after his sister. He must be such a disappointment to you.'

I was slapping his hand away from the slit in my skirt, when the gentleman in the peacock suit stepped forwards. 'I say, old chap, you're a bit long in the tooth for this one,' he said pointedly. His English accent camouflaged a disgust I found heartening, and when he turned to me, he smiled brightly. 'Asa Haynes, at your service, Miss Vanita. I'd be so very pleased if you'd grant me the honour of this dance.'

He ushered me away from Franklin with such finesse I could only chuckle at the bewildered look on the lecher's face. 'You have my sincerest thanks, Mr Haynes –'

'That'll be Asa to you, darling.'

'– and I've been admiring your suit all evening. What a striking colour,' I continued, studying his bold features with a grin, 'and it takes a man with great panache to wear it!'

'To be sure, I've got plenty of that!'

Asa positioned us for a schottische, his chest puffed out as he swung me into the parade of dancers circling the floor to its happy rhythm. 'Have they told you what'll happen next, my dear? When the real party starts?'

'No. Why?' I glanced about, still hoping for Pearce, but instead saw Desiree smiling at another of her bold friends while her brother watched me from the punch bowl. 'Seems to me Franklin has already passed his prime, so –'

'Oh, he's never invited to this part! You'll see what I mean soon, so I won't spoil it.' His eyes wandered to my neck, lingering on the necklace that winked and glimmered with my slightest move. 'Too bad such a splendid array of rubies and pearls looks more like a noose than a necklace – which is precisely why that bastard knows nothing of our fun. But enough about him. You're in *our* company now, and you're going to love it!'

When Asa grinned, I again noted the overdrawn nature of his face; he seemed older than I'd first assumed, yet very much the gentleman as he guided me through the schottische steps. I sensed something keenly secretive about the guests Desiree had invited – how they all danced more provocatively than was polite, and how they exchanged furtive looks from across the crowded ballroom, especially with the twins.

I puzzled over this little mystery, pleased that it didn't include Franklin. He was now regaling a crowd of older gentlemen who stood around him like crows, bobbing and pecking at their drinks while he held court. Aunt Lill fanned herself in the corner, gazing at the men as though considering her next conquest.

Asa thanked me for the dance and passed me on to Damon, who pulled me close in the centre of the floor for another waltz. His friends pressed in around us as the music sent us sashaying around the dance floor, gliding and pivoting faster – as though even the musicians were in on the twins' secret and driving us to the evening's peak. My partner guided me expertly under his arm in a turn, his gaze afire with delight and something I'd not seen there before: unadulterated lust. Little flames licked at my insides and my hopes soared as he spun me around and caught me at the waist.

I laughed giddily, feeling weightless as my feet left the floor. As the song crescendoed into a grand finale, he leaned me back into another dizzying dip that sent my leg into the air. His kiss nearly consumed me, and I returned it with breathless abandon.

Then he pulled me up, still looking through me with those pellucid blue eyes. As the next song began, he ushered me off to the side. 'Don't ask questions, and don't look around,' he whispered, steering me to the door as though we were slipping off to a tryst. 'Dez and I have been anticipating this ever since you came, sweet Vanita. You've probably wondered how we survive the endless days in this vault of a house – and we're about to show you what none of Daddy's other marriage choices have been privy to. I think you'll enjoy it.'

Quickly we descended the stairs, our footsteps furtive. At the second-floor landing, he steered me down the hall towards the back of the mansion, and into a corridor descending through the centre of the house. I was about to remark about finally finding the servants' stairs, when he pulled me into another wicked kiss.

'Vanita ... Vanita,' he breathed. 'You were so beautiful in the ballroom, it's a pity to whisk you away from your admirers. But I want a moment alone with you ... to give the others a chance to slip away. We have another world out back of the house, by way of the caves that run beneath our pastureland – which eventually lead to the mines in one direction, and over to Wellspring in the other. Did you realise that?'

My dismay must've registered on my face, because he quickly kissed me. 'It's not what you're thinking, sweetheart. Nothing like catacombs, or dark, dank caverns full of bats. Come along and see!'

What could I do but go? If I refused him, I'd never win my wager with his father, for the dancing had heightened Damon's excitement and he was paying attention to me like a normal man! We continued down interior steps that took us near his workshop, and, grabbing my hand, he led me out into the night.

16 The Naked Truth

The sky formed a velvet dome, sprinkled with stars and a lustrous half-moon. We inhaled the refreshing air of the springtime night; the lilacs' subdued perfume and the smell of damp grasslands filled the air. Staying to the shadows, Damon urged me towards the swing and the thicket of trees beyond it. Once behind these bushes, invisible from the brightly lit ballroom on the third floor, he reached for me again.

I pressed my lace-encased breasts into the hands that caressed them, moaning with the overwhelming heat of his kiss. Undulating like braided snakes, Damon and I gasped for air while grasping every inch of flesh that would yield beneath our clothes before the others found us. Trying desperately to excite him beyond reason, I whispered, 'Please, Damon! *Take* me! Your friends will vouch for us, as proof to your father. You can go back to living the way you wish, and so can I!'

'I've addled you completely, sweetheart,' he teased, glancing towards the house. 'I'd like nothing better than to get between your legs. But after that, why would I want to let you go?'

This was an unexpected twist. I searched his face in the dimness, not wanting to blurt out anything that might hurt my chances of returning home. 'You know how it's got to be for us, Damon. Please don't confuse the issue by –'

'Shhh! Don't assume anything until you've seen what lies ahead. You might change your mind and never want to leave us.' He laid a gentle finger across my lips, his smile mysterious in the moonlight. 'Here come the others, Vanita. They're eager to share this adventure with you ... to get so much better acquainted with the woman who could bring new life to Harte's Haven.'

With that, he reached inside the knothole of a nearby tree. I heard something sliding ... an opening in the side of the small rise concealed by this patch of forest. Like a scene from *Ali Baba and the Forty Thieves*, the hillside moved to reveal a pathway leading beneath the earth. Damon took my hand and we entered the cave, just ahead of the voices behind us.

'This is some of your wizardry?' I asked, fascinated by the line of tiny lights just above the ground. The glow showed us the way down some rock stairs, where I heard water lapping.

'We discovered this cave when we were very young. It became our daytime hideaway, since we couldn't play outside,' he explained. 'And when Mama ... left us, it was our escape from that mournful house where Daddy never understood our needs or dreams. Watch your step. We're going to board that first gondola.'

I gazed in awe, for we stood on the shore of a waterway – a canal traversing the cave. The lights – little coloured lanterns, all connected by a pipeline – made the walls glisten with festive spring tints and revealed three sleek canoes tied to hitching posts. Damon stepped into the boat first, and then helped me aboard. Asa Haynes joined us, smiling at my amazement, and the other two gondolas quickly filled with the rest of the more colourful ball guests – including Pamela, the striking woman in magenta, and a woman referred to as Beatrice Carr, whom I'd watched but hadn't met. Desiree brought up the rear, seating herself beside Glenn and Harolyn.

Damon pushed us into the current with a pole,

where we floated gently along as though on a Sunday excursion. With the soft lanterns casting their beams up towards the ceiling and across the water's surface, the cave looked anything but spooky. The echoes of our breathing gave a sense of great anticipation as we glided along, around corners and beneath low-hanging stalactites glittering with crystals.

'This is a tributary of the Kentucky River, which feeds the underground spring at Harte's Haven – and at Wellspring, too,' Asa remarked. 'Truly a serene voyage, taking us away from a society ruled by politics and connivery, into our very own world where we can simply *be*, and enjoy ourselves. Just the way we are.'

Another interesting remark, but I was still gawking, dumbfounded by my surroundings. The air was surprisingly fresh, enveloping us in a warmth from the pastel lanterns, yet with a gentle breeze that kept the cavern from feeling stuffy. When we rounded another bend, taking the right fork rather than a left one that headed into darkness, the room was suddenly bathed in blue: the lights were now encased in underwater shields of cobalt, which made the river a shimmering aquamarine and dimmed the walls above us into a canopy like the night sky.

'Oh, my,' I breathed, gazing around me as I drank in the utter beauty of this underground canal. 'And I suppose all this is Damon's handiwork, as well?'

'We owe him much,' came a male voice in the boat behind us. 'His ingenuity has provided us a playground like no other, and we look forward to these events he and Desiree host. You'll see, Vanita. It's like a faeryland – like Alice visiting Wonderland, but without any imperious queens saying "Off with her head!"'

Laughter welled up around me. The gondola swayed with the current, picking up speed until a refreshing spray thickened into a mist, like a moonlit fog. Here,

Damon reached out and tied us to another hitching post. 'Come along, sweet Vanita. You've quite a night ahead of you.'

Into another room we went, and as we stepped out of the mist, I once again stood agape. 'These are natural caverns, but we've decorated them and adapted them to our use,' Damon explained. 'The striations of quartz and crystal caught our fancy when we were children, and over the years inspired us to design the soft lighting you see, and to invent entertainments we couldn't enjoy at the house. While you were studying sums and geometry and painting with your tutors at Wellspring, we were putting the same principles to work in a less conventional way.'

The walls glimmered with mineral deposits, in a vaulted room where our whisperings resonated as in an amphitheatre. Strategically placed sconces aimed light at formations of stalagmites, rising up from one end of the floor like majestic organ pipes, while other parts of the ceiling disappeared into a mystical vapour that drifted above us, to occasionally reveal clusters of minerals shining like stars.

'You learned your lessons well,' I murmured, allowing him to draw me farther into this room of seemingly endless proportions. We walked past pools of bubbling water where steam rose from their softly lit surfaces, and then into an area where tables welcomed us with platters of beautifully arranged fruits. It was beyond me how all of this could have been prepared, since Damon and Desiree had spent the day decorating for the ball, until a childlike young man approached us with a wide smile and a low bow.

'Vanita, this is Riki, our Polynesian houseboy. Simply ask, and he'll see to your every need.'

I leaned down, offering a smile of my own – and was taken aback by a beautiful face that was fully mature yet showed no sign of age or a beard. While Riki's body was splendidly proportioned, he stood only to my waist. He was sleek and muscled, wearing nothing but a colourful, cunningly wrapped loincloth. 'How do you do, Riki?'

'How do I do *what*, missy?' he replied with an impish grin. 'Master Damon and Miss Desiree, they say Franklin bring you here because you lose your home. They help me escape from a circus sideshow many years ago, and I am forever indebted. The friends, they like me, too! Is a good night to play naked, yes?'

I straightened, to keep from being bewitched by his sing-song accent. He did not look as if he had worked as a field hand or been made to do the other back-breaking manual work of slaves: his long, filed fingernails glistened pink like a seashell and his teeth, full and white, suggested perpetual laughter as he talked.

And as I glanced away from him, I saw that he'd accurately gauged the evening's activities: along a nearby wall hung pegs and wide, white shelves, where the other guests were already stepping out of their suits and gowns. They talked and chuckled among themselves quite comfortably, sending playful glances my way.

'I'm guessing you've never engaged in ... group play,' Damon murmured, kneading my shoulders. 'We like to relax this way, Vanita. We bathe, or have Riki massage us, and imbibe much better punch than you'll find at the house. It's a charade we've revelled in since we played dress-up with our parents' old clothes. We've just taken that game a few steps farther.'

The bodies I saw across the room, now illuminated with the cave's soft candlelight, shone with fascinating beauty as silks and serges were removed to reveal skin. All told, we were eight, and except for Damon, Desiree, Pamela and I, everyone was hanging up their clothing.

I recognised the first man – the Glenn Morell I'd met in the foyer, wearing the deep green suit – and wondered if he'd fallen from a horse and broken some ribs, to be wearing such a tightly wrapped band around his chest.

As though sensing my attention, he turned, unwinding the bandage with a daring grin beneath his thick moustache. The cloth gave way to a delicately curved chest and two breasts as full as my own, and when he pulled down his drawers it was a V of coarse, female curls I saw between his thighs. With a chuckle, he ripped off the moustache and bushy brows, and then off came the wig of dark waves. It was Mrs Marley, the henna-haired seamstress!

'You never had a hint of suspicion, did you, dearie?' she asked with a giggle. 'It's been my life's greatest pleasure, to bedeck you in this scarlet and black lace, and then to come tonight to admire you – and the rest of us – without Franklin ever guessing!'

My mouth fell open, but it made perfect sense: no ordinary tailor would have fashioned a suit that so perfectly camouflaged the female form beneath it, in a green most men wouldn't be seen in.

Then I noticed Asa Haynes, that gallant Englishman who'd led me away from Franklin and through a flawless schottische, peeling away his peacock suit to the same effect. This character, too, sported breasts any woman would envy and thighs curving up to a lush bottom, but now I realised that facial features I'd considered overdrawn were actually the artful application of theatrical make-up. This woman swayed towards me with her hand outstretched, smiling like a coquette long accustomed to bending her gender and fooling polite society with it.

'I see you're quite agog, Vanita,' she said, her English accent replaced by a fetching drawl. 'Didn't I hint that you were in for a real party? Without Franklin, we've all learned to truly enjoy ourselves at these affairs. I'm sure you don't remember me. It's been a very long time, and the rumours have served me well.'

I gawked into this woman's face, trying to discern her true features beneath the garish make-up. She was the oldest among us, yet that didn't diminish the bold, bare beauty I was trying hard not to stare at.

Damon patted my shoulder, his smile alight with pride. 'Vanita, may I present Alice Harte. My mother.'

My throat closed in total surprise. 'But you're – you supposedly –'

'Died?' she filled in, grasping my hands in hers. 'For all practical purposes, I was dead when Franklin became so obsessive and cruel I could rarely leave the house. It's a long story, best told another time, but let's just say the children helped me escape to this underground palace, and brought Riki to help me. I can't tell you what a supreme delight I get from dressing as Asa Haynes and attending balls right under Franklin's red, whiskied nose.'

'So you must *swear* never to tell him!' Damon insisted, probing my eyes with his orbs of crystal pink. 'You can understand now why none of Daddy's other bridal choices have joined us here. And why before, we never cared about hosting a betrothal ball.'

'And by God, if our secret gets out, you'll wish you'd never heard the name Harte!' It was Desiree aiming this statement at me, in a voice as steely as a dagger.

And with the two of them and their naked mother silently awaiting my response, I began to tremble as I looked from one to the other. 'I wouldn't dream of revealing your secrets – especially not your mother,' I breathed, placing a hand above my fluttering heart as a sign of my pledge. 'I certainly understand how living down here would be better than tolerating Franklin.'

Alice's gaze drifted up from my hand, to where the

pearl choker felt like lead around my neck. Recalling the same expression when Asa Haynes had expertly led me around the dance floor, I was struck by the magnitude of the lie Franklin Harte had so skilfully spun: he'd gone to great lengths to impress the guests with these black pearls and the rubies fashioned in an H – a necklace he'd mentioned earlier, to provoke me. I now realised he couldn't have commissioned such extravagant jewellery in the space of the past few days, and that he didn't need to.

'It's yours, isn't it?' I whispered, reaching up to release the clasp. 'I should've known –'

'Leave it on. For your own protection.' Alice enfolded my hands in hers, gazing at me with eyes that bespoke sorrow and terror I never wanted to comprehend. 'It's another one of his little power plays, to control you. Best to let him think he's succeeding, for now.'

My mouth went dry and my pulse raced into a full gallop, until I felt the veins of my neck throbbing against the wide choker and its blood-red brooch. If Franklin Harte had fooled me about this betrothal jewellery, and had led everyone to believe his wife was an adulteress – and dead – all to frighten me into submission, what other lies had he plied me with? What if his insinuations about Mama seducing him and Daddy's gambling debts weren't true after all?

What if Wellspring hadn't been bankrupted, and this whole tawdry affair was a scheme between Franklin and my aunt, to cheat me out of my inheritance?

For a moment, I felt distanced from the cave and those around me, ready to suffocate in my silent rage. My heart constricted at this unthinkable situation, until I nearly burst with the pent-up frustrations of the past week. I inhaled sharply, wondering how best to express the assumptions racing through my mind, for I *could not stay here*!

I unhooked the heavy choker, handing it to Alice. 'I can't wear this. I'll take my chances on Franklin's reaction.'

'Don't be a fool, Vanita. Once you leave, you can pawn that piece and begin restocking your stables.' The woman's expression remained as fixed as her gaze, her insistence accentuated by the paints she'd applied.

While hope flickered within me at her talk of my reviving Wellspring, I resolutely closed her two hands around the necklace. 'Horses paid for with Franklin's pearl noose will never grace my stables. They'd be constant reminders of how he betrayed us all.'

With a little sob, Alice embraced me, as though she'd found a lost child. The twins' platinum faces relaxed into pixie-like grins and their letting-out of breath came as the sign that they trusted me, too. I'd passed through another rite of passage, and was now a member of the secret society dedicated to the preservation of their fun – and their mother.

The lovely woman before me cleared her throat. 'The twins have told me of the predicament Franklin and your aunt have put you in, so perhaps I can help. But right now, Vanita, it's time to enjoy ourselves like never before. We've learned to seize the day, and we won't waste another moment of this night on the concerns above-ground. Promise?'

I blinked, still stunned by the revelation brought on by the choker, and my reaction to it. Yet now that soothing music filled the cave's chamber, and yes, Harolyn Pricket and that rather reserved Beatrice Carr had removed the elegant gowns from their very male bodies, I saw the advantage of relaxing and flowing with the moment ... for when had I ever known a moment in such a place as this, with such people as these? Never in my life would I have guessed that Harry Price, the county sheriff, and Beale Cornelius –

who managed the bank in Lexington, where Daddy had always done business – would pad themselves in strategic places, apply flawless cosmetics, and don ball-gowns suitable for a debutante's mama.

I didn't ask questions. I contented myself with assuming these two men – Harry with the reputation and the body of a stud mustang, and Beale a pillar of the Presbyterian church – bedecked themselves in such finery for the sheer joy of outwitting Franklin Harte while they socialised with the twins and his wife-in-hiding. So far, I knew every naked person in the room, and I was now far more familiar with the muscles and curves and privates beneath their everyday clothing.

Yet it seemed I didn't know these people at all, for when I saw Pamela dropping her gown and shucking her upswept wig, watching me with those deep green eyes to ascertain my reaction, I was further taken aback. Off came the stockings and bloomers to reveal powerful legs and a rampant erection like I hadn't seen since – since the *last* time Pearce had enticed me into the shadows.

But it couldn't be him! I would've known his grip when we met in the ballroom; would've recognised the heady, virile scent of him, and felt the fire that always flared between us with the first meeting of our glances! I *knew* of that man's presence before he even entered a room!

But indeed, when the magenta dress got hung on a peg, it was the intrepid Mr Truman turning to smile at me – but without his beard! I went at him with a cry of exasperation, grabbing his arms and shaking him. 'You should have *told* me! Should have *hinted* –'

'And spoil this surprise?' he replied in his normal low voice. He was shaking with laughter as he pulled me against his warm, naked body . . . and shaking with need, too. 'Didn't I tell you I'd find a way to outfox

Franklin? You just didn't realise cross-dressing and the bending of genders would be the order of the evening.'

My thoughts galloped wildly as I felt his fingers working the buttons of my dress. I caught knowing grins from Damon and Desiree, who chatted with their mother while helping her to punch, but I was having a hard time piecing this puzzle together. 'Does this mean the twins knew, and allowed you to come, then?' I asked quietly.

'When have I ever asked permission of anyone?' came his quick reply. 'When you mentioned a betrothal ball, I told Desiree I'd be coming as a precautionary measure.'

'And she agreed? Without telling her father you were on the premises?'

Pearce smiled richly, although without that devilish beard he looked paler than I preferred. 'Have I ever had trouble getting what I wanted from a woman, love? She thought it was a fine idea – again, because we're rubbing Franklin's nose in it.'

'But I thought ... I thought you were a *woman*,' I admitted in a very small voice. 'Do you know how stupid this makes me feel, Pearce?'

He lifted my chin to kiss me. 'Not stupid, Vanita. Never that. Simply engrossed in your own survival, as a stranger among stranger people than you've ever known. I have to admit a few of them had me fooled as well.'

His gaze wandered to the punch bowl, where the twins were helping their voluptuous mother to some punch. 'That Alice is a piece of work – and sure to be an ally, if we play our cards right,' he murmured. 'You and I need to compare notes about the past few days, and what we'll learn tonight. But right now, I've more important things to do.'

He kissed me again, more hungrily this time, and as

my clothes fell to the floor, Riki hung them up for me. 'You make pretty pair, pretty pair,' the houseboy commented with a wide, assessing grin. 'But keep the eyes open. You not seen everything the nights here reveal.'

17 I Take a Licking

With Pearce's strong, familiar hands massaging my body, I didn't care what else the night might reveal. I wanted to make love with a man I knew was every inch a male, and those steaming mineral pools appealed to me. We hadn't done it in water, and as I looked across the cavernous room, I saw that one of the bubbling baths was unoccupied. It seemed the perfect place to play, and to compare notes on what we'd each learned these past few days.

'This way, sailor,' I teased, slyly taking hold of his erection. 'This is an interesting crowd, but it's you I want to look at. And you I want looking back at me.'

'I'm your man,' he murmured, swelling within my grip. 'Heard more than one randy comment about the brazen blonde in the scandalous dress this evening, and I can't wait to fuck her.' He was walking closely behind me, his fingertips teasing at my bare backside as we passed the other bathers on the way to our own private pool.

But Damon had other ideas. Although his smile was wide, it had an edge I couldn't ignore. 'Come, come, you two – plenty of time for the usual nude frolic when you're alone. We've another contraption to show you. A delightful fountain like you've never seen, designed for all of us together.'

He extended his hand, and I was aware of something different, something more demanding than the Damon Harte I'd come to know. I glanced quizzically at Pearce, but sensed we'd best play by the house rules.

Our host led me towards a corner of the cavern I hadn't noticed, which he then illuminated by striking a match and making a succession of red gas lanterns burn around a circular pipeline. The crimson glow resembled embers from the Devil's own hearth and turned this area into a decadent arena where a fountain with eight fixtures around its outer rim suddenly spurted to life.

'Hop on!' he called to the others. 'Vanita loved the dancer platform, so we should show her the very best of what this carousel can do!'

Recalling that platform, where I'd cavorted with the oversized Hugo, made my body go taut, while my nipples popped out and my slit began to tingle. Pearce stood against me, nuzzling my thigh with his cock as the others approached the fountain with secretive glee, like children scurrying to mount a merry-go-round at the fair. I sensed I was in for another surprise at my own expense, yet I'd no doubt discover delights my previous life had never prepared me for.

As I looked at the eight fixtures, which were animal-shaped seats, I shivered with anticipation. Frogs and fishes shot streams of water from their mouths, while others resembled dragons and huge, slithery boa constrictors. They were constructed of iron and painted in jaded shades of red and black and deep green; colours from a nightmare gone awry, bathed in the scarlet glare of the lanterns. I swallowed hard, wondering what I was in for.

'Save a frog for Vanita!' Desiree called out, but the timbre of her voice made me look to where our hostess was slithering out of her ice-blue gown. Her fingers worked with the quick grace I'd seen while she wrote invitations for this gala, yet as the underthings fell away from her slender ivory curves I got a knot in my stomach.

Some twisted intuition made me pick up her clothing, nipping my lip as the milky-skinned twin turned towards me. With a grace born of total confidence, she raised her hands to remove the upswept platinum wig. And then I saw the same cropped, cottony hair as her brother's ... and the shaft that had shot like a geyser in the swing the other night, stiffening, only inches in front of my eyes.

With scalded cheeks I pivoted, feeling sick and betrayed and very much the fool again. I glared over at the man – or at least the *partner* – I'd danced so provocatively with ... and had kissed with such abandon ... and had propositioned with every intention of spreading my legs. I'd fallen for each sweet, seductive word this twin had led me on with, and my body had followed along.

'Desiree!' I hissed, clenching my jaw. 'You scheming little bitch! You let me believe you were – that I could coax you into –'

'Really had you going, didn't I, dear?'

With a husky chuckle, Desiree stripped off her black trousers and shirt, showing me what had been before my eyes all along, but I just hadn't seen it: except for their genitals, Damon and Desiree were damn near identical. The voices that were so alike, the physiques of the same proportions – the narrow hips and slender, long limbs, and the chests that meant this woman had no need of a bust band beneath her masculine black suit.

She stood before me naked, preening like a pearlescent cat, so very proud of herself for duping me. But for how long? How many times since I'd arrived at Harte's Haven had I thought I was talking to her, yet it was actually her brother? Recalling our waltzes, and those fiery kisses and inflammatory words, made me so angry I grabbed her shoulders before Pearce could catch me.

'I ought to just – By God, you deserve a –'

'Good, hard spanking?' she suggested, laughing as she shrugged out of my grasp. I'd never dreamed a woman so slight could be so strong, yet as I recalled her antics with Damon on the anniversary clock, and again on the swing, I realised she'd developed into a sexual acrobat from years of practice. How else did she amuse herself, after all?

'A spanking was always Daddy's solution, too – until the time he took his belt off for me, but it was Damon who aimed his cock and peed all over him. Nasty man!' she said with a shudder. 'It took us a while, but once we discovered we could keep Daddy off-balance by becoming interchangeable, he's kept his damn distance.'

I wanted to slap her insolent grin, yet who could fault her desperate measures? I struggled to compose myself, as shocked at my own reactions as I was by the sexual switching that inspired them. The charade had become second nature to these siblings: years ago they'd cut Desiree's hair and had a wig fashioned from it, and chose their clothing to camouflage their sexual attributes, and relied upon that colourless skin and hair to complete the ultimate twinship – appearances that fooled even their own father.

A firm grip on my shoulder brought me out of my wool-gathering. 'Shall we play along, Vanita?' Pearce whispered. 'You're upset, yes, but no one pulled this stunt to hurt *you*. They've simply fashioned their fun from a difficult situation, and got the best of old Harte in the bargain.'

Slowly I exhaled, recognising the voice of reason despite the way my senses and my captors had betrayed me again. It would be bad form to pout like a child, naked, in a group that included a sheriff and a banker – not to mention Alice Harte – whose support I might need to regain my freedom and my home. It seemed believing was indeed seeing: I had believed the character in the tuxedo to be Damon, and that's who I danced with and kissed and saw, until the truth was proven in the nude. A red flare went up in my mind: sometimes, even my own five senses didn't perceive reality accurately.

Pearce was watching my reaction as though our future success depended on it. His face, so cunningly redrawn with Pamela's cosmetics, was another reminder about how deceptive appearances could be; how, when I couldn't trust the people around me, or my own senses of sight and sound, intuition was my best bet. I ran my fingers along the slick skin of his jaw, where that dark, devious beard once grew. 'How long's it been since you shaved here?' I mused aloud.

'Years. Do you like it?'

'No! You look too tame,' I blurted. 'And you're a better-looking woman than I am. That's the worst part of it, you know.'

He chortled, steering me towards the frog Desiree was patting, wearing another of her wicked grins. 'I shaved so I could be with you, love,' he murmured. 'Right now, though, I want to see what sort of sport these people have devised for us. Might give us clues as to who we can count on later.'

His deep green gaze stopped my heart when we came to the carousel. 'You can do this, Vanita. Show these people what you're made of. I dare you.'

How could I back down when he put it that way? Pearce was once again making me rise to a challenge, and he would see me through it – no matter *how* smugly Desiree Harte was smiling at me.

I swung my leg over the green iron frog, whose backside was moulded like a saddle, so that my feet fit forwards on his front legs while I sat at a slightly backward angle. Pearce mounted one of the dragons, a Chinese red chimera that shot water from its nostrils, while Desiree and Damon took the seats resembling two serpents entwined, with their massive heads serving as armrests. Our host signalled to Riki, who cranked the handle that ran the fountain's carousel mechanism.

I sat spellbound, gripping the handles on my frog's head as we slowly circled the crimson-lit pool, with its jade-coloured waves lapping around us. As the wheel reached its full speed, I noted the others beginning to spin and gyrate in place.

'Crank your handles to wind the coils,' Damon called to me. The serpents he sat upon writhed as though charmed by the carousel's calliope music, while streams of water hissed out of them like forked tongues. His sister, enthroned between her two asps, shot an impudent stream at her mother's breasts. Alice shrieked, returning a volley through the mouth of her rainbow-striped fish, and the water fight was on.

Pearce grinned at me from his rocking dragon, firing at my backside. I swivelled to miss his onslaught, discovering that my frog would twist and turn as I did, and that pushing the handles into his head drew the water up from the pool and through his mouth. On impulse, I pushed and pivoted simultaneously, dousing everyone else in the moving, musical circle.

I laughed out loud, splashing my feet in the water! I hadn't ridden a merry-go-round since I was a child – and certainly never naked. Riki was now adding a thick liquid to the pool, and soon the heady scent of lemon rose from the water as it began to foam. 'A bubble bath!' I crowed.

'All for you, sweet Vanita,' Desiree replied slyly. Her serpents faced me, from perhaps twelve feet across the pool, so I could read her expression – and she had a definite plan as she sent her brother a knowing look.

'Activate the other gears, Riki,' Damon instructed, and Riki's grin grew wide. With the crank of a key nearly as tall as he was, the Polynesian filled the cave with the sound of tightening coils. My frog began to vibrate as we spun in place. When I saw the others leaning into their beasts, I realised the potential for some profound stimulation and pressed my wet sex lips against the seat. Growing up on horseback had taught me a similar tactic, but it hadn't prepared me for *this*!

The warmed iron pulsed against me, and as I spun and rocked, the sensations multiplied. I was suddenly far more interested in discovering just how erotic this private massage could become, but a stream of lemony water splattered my back. I swivelled to return fire, cutting loose with a volley that caught Alice between her bouncing breasts.

'Do that again and you'll pay, little girl!' she teased.

Giggling, I pumped the handles of my frog and doused her, riding higher on the beast's neck as the pulsations rioted against my privates. My clit was throbbing, coaxing me to rock against the frog even as Pearce and I exchanged shots of water. His dark, enlarged eyes told me his dragon was giving him the same sort of attention, and that he was straining to control himself.

Indeed, all the riders in this erotic circle were panting now, their cries more strident as they rocked and shot off water. We were children again, but on a naughtier level, which made the game fiercely competitive as we splattered one another's breasts and erections. The centre of the pool foamed a devilish red, lending a decadence to our play and driving us on. The vibrations had claimed my body now, making me one with my mount as I neared the point of no return.

'Now, Riki!' Desiree called out.

Suddenly, my frog split down the middle, splaying my legs as it locked into place facing the others. Before I could scramble off, Damon dismounted and splashed up behind me, wrapping his wet thighs and arms around mine so I couldn't possibly move.

'You're going to love this, Vanita,' he panted against my ear, and his rock-solid erection prodded my spine. 'Open up, vixen. Show us that sweet little cunny, and scream with an ecstasy like you've never known. It'll come to that, I promise you.'

I was about to demand that he let me go when a stream of warm water splashed my slit. It was Desiree, positioning the heads of her snakes to shoot one and then the other. Again and again the warm, lemony water splattered against my open folds, stimulating my clit with dead-on precision until I fell back against her brother, panting.

'Let go,' he whispered. 'Open yourself . . . let the pulse of the water drive you wild, sweet lady.' He clutched more tightly with his thighs, wedging his pecker into the crack of my arse. Stroking me with his wet finger-tips, Damon ran agile hands up my thighs and stomach until he was cupping my breasts in time to the music and the strikes of water.

I felt utterly helpless – and utterly enthralled by the sensations coursing through my body. The water became more insistent against my clit as the others aimed their streams with Desiree's, keeping a beat that had overtaken my entire body. I squirmed to escape such rapid-fire, overwhelming pleasure for fear of bursting with it, yet I began to wiggle so I wouldn't miss a single hit. Faster it came, that erotic water, until I was shaking with the need for release.

'Oh God . . . Oh God, please – please –'

Harder the streams struck, pelting my sensitive tis-sues until my insides clenched and I threw my head back. Then the water went hot, and I became one gaping, greedy hole seeking release. I let out a scream that sounded downright insane.

The room echoed with my wild cries as the pulsing water continued its relentless attack, until I fell back into utter mindlessness and Damon's embrace. He was rubbing against me with a frenzy I knew well, and with a deep, drawn-out grunt he shot his warm seed up my spine. I longed to lie there limp against him, recovering from a climax that had sapped my strength and sucked all rational thought from my mind.

But Desiree wasn't finished with me. She and her friends had dismounted and were wading naked through the pool, their eyes on my prize as I sat captive on my iron frog, spread shamelessly before them.

'I believe I'm next on the lady's dance card,' came a low voice, and when I opened my bleary eyes, Pearce was standing alongside me. Damon obliged him, and Truman slid behind me on the frog, pulling me close against his wet, furred chest.

'My God, Vanita,' he rasped, nuzzling the damp skin beneath my ear, 'I knew you were beautiful, but watching you from that angle as you bucked and writhed, well, it's left me quite –'

'Needful,' I breathed, rubbing my butt against his stiffened cock. 'But if *I* must endure the torture of these twins, you should, too.'

'It's the price I have to pay,' he teased. He cupped warm water over my swollen breasts, gazing raptly as my nipples poked out in response.

'And pay you will,' Desiree said with a snicker. 'You're going to hold our princess hostage while we all give tribute. Then, if you've got any left, you can take your turn.'

'You can count on it.' With his thighs around mine and his erection centred in the dip of my spine, I stretched languorously against him. I watched in utter fascination as a pale, wet Desiree leaned in between my legs, her tongue extended, to give me the licking she felt I deserved.

The first touch of her tongue against my inflamed tissues made me convulse. Pearce grunted in turn, moving us in a slow up-and-back rhythm dictated by Desiree's strokes. I felt oddly detached with her white hair shining between my thighs while the others looked on with envy, hungrily noting every nuance and quiver. With the tip of her tongue, she tickled my clit, giggling as my hips rose frantically – which in turn increased the sensations Pearce felt.

'Isn't she gorgeous?' Desiree asked them all, standing aside so they could watch while she opened my folds. 'Look how her curls cling so wetly to that carmine skin ... how inflamed she is, and how responsive.'

I groaned when two slender fingers slipped inside me to explore.

'So very slick and eager ... Can you smell her delicious heat? Can you see that pearly liquid pooling at the rim of her pretty little hole? Open for me, Vanita,' she commanded in a husky voice. 'Open wide and bear down. You know how badly I need to taste you.'

As though my sex were mesmerised by the power of her provocation – and by the watchful eyes of her friends – I opened myself to another stroke, and another, pressing into her fingers until, from deep within me, I felt a hot gushing.

'Push it out, Vanita. Pump it out, so I can watch it drench your hot skin and dribble on to Pearce's balls,' she murmured. 'God, what a sight the two of you make. I can't wait to lap you up and spread that honey over the base of that fine cock you're riding.'

Beneath me, Pearce groaned. He sat forwards, easing

me ahead of him to place my arms on either side of the frog's head. 'Damn you, Desiree, *take* it,' he muttered, 'because I'm certainly going to.'

He slid into my cunt so quickly I yelped. I now straddled the split green seat, my legs parted as far as they'd go, while Pearce pumped me from behind. Delighted at this new turn of events, Desiree knelt beneath us to catch my drippings, her hot tongue darting around my clit and then teasing at Pearce's shaft whenever he pulled out. Our audience moved in, whispering encouragement as she licked and nibbled us, rubbing his sac against me to increase the sensations.

I rose quickly into that inner frenzy again, my breasts slapping my wet chest as I struggled to hold on. Pearce was driving into me from one direction with strong, steady thrusts – a heady contrast to Desiree's butterfly flickerings from the front. My head began to spin and my body tensed in ecstatic agony.

When his gasp reached a point of imminent desperation, Desiree flattened her tongue against our throbbing, moving privates. With her upper lip against my clit, she rubbed until I convulsed, sending Pearce into a thrashing climax. Then she smacked my backside, making me jerk free – making our mingled, musky honey gush all over her upturned face. She licked and lapped and sucked us, purring like a contented cat over her cream.

When she finished, wiping her eyes, Desiree wore the most delighted smile I'd ever seen. 'God, Vanita,' she wheezed. 'You were never one to take orders, but you certainly come when you're called. You deserve a reward – a massage from all these friends who've come to love you.'

Her double meanings brought a detached smile to my face. I was aware of Pearce disengaging himself . . .

felt hands easing me from my split position on that iron ride ... was being gently turned over to lie in the warm water, now pungent with lemon and sex. I looked up to see Damon cradling my head and shoulders, smiling down at me as the water lapped at my sides. It was absolute heaven, and I wanted nothing more than to drift off to a sweet, sated sleep.

But Alice had other ideas. From my right side, she ran her soft hands over my shoulders and around the curve of my breast, while Desiree stood across from her and mimicked her motions on the left. When she drew my distended nipple into her mouth, I sucked air, on the verge of another climax. Through this fog of multiple sensations, I realised Mrs Marley was tonguing my stomach, teasing at my navel to make me giggle.

Pearce, meanwhile, had slipped his arms beneath my hips to hold me afloat, open and more accessible to the others. He watched with intense interest as Harry and Beale each took a foot, sucking my toes with a suction that made every hair on my body stand on end. I quivered with the overwhelming luxury of this group's groping, which became more intimate with each passing minute. Alice's tongue danced around my nipple, raising it to a straining little bead. I couldn't take my eyes off her euphoric expression as her hot, pink lips laved my lemon-scented breast.

Riki, who stood up to his neck in the water, had eased between my spread legs and was massaging the halves of my hips with firm, commanding strokes. 'Raise her higher,' he instructed in that exotic accent. And when Pearce complied, I felt inquisitive fingers exploring that puckery opening beneath the pool's surface.

Instinctively I tightened, and the little man chuckled. 'Relax, missy,' he crooned. 'My fingers are small ... very sensitive to your desires. Riki will show you how fine it feels to have both holes filled at once. Look at Desiree, how enraptured she is by your breast.'

Indeed, the white-haired vixen had latched on to me like a babe taking suck ... so smooth and pale her face was, with those long white lashes fluttering atop cheeks the faintest pink from her exertions. When she took a mouthful of my breast, I gasped with the intensity, thrusting myself towards her – and then towards Alice as well, while the two of them drove me to distraction. I was so overtaken by these sensations I didn't mind that Riki had set me up: at some silent signal, while I was distracted by the two female faces in my immediate field of vision, Harry Price had lifted Riki from behind, so he could drape his ebony legs over my thighs.

I felt a prodding below my slit, and then agile fingertips arousing me once again. Small but skilled fingers pressed on either side of my sensitive clitoris, until I groaned in spite of my trepidation. 'Please, Riki, I don't think I'll like –'

But he slid his little cock up my butt with an ecstatic moan and began to pump, with Harry's help. Meanwhile, he'd made an elongated fist, which he slipped into my slit, moving it at alternate beats to the music. Never had I been so utterly filled – so aware of the separate passageways in my nether region, separated by a mere membrane. I could feel his cock, as well as the fingers he was stroking it with while inside me. His face went tight, and he pushed back against Harry's chest. My honey was flowing and I began to quiver – but my breasts and my feet were also being stimulated at a quickening pace, until I wasn't sure where to let go first.

Suddenly it wasn't a choice. I screamed like a siren, cresting with the waves of my climax until my entire being was awash with an overwhelming surge, like a flare of lightning across the night sky, a tide of intense pleasure crashing against the shore.

And then I collapsed into velvety blackness.

18 My Last Chance Goes Bad

I awoke with a start, back in my bed but with my wrists and ankles bound to its iron rails by straps of black velvet. Desiree stood watching me, foxlike, wrapped in a filmy dressing gown, with her prodding, pink nipples clearly visible. She was a woman who knew her power; knew things she'd tell me only if I begged and did her bidding. I tensed, aware that someone had put me to bed naked – and that I didn't recall a thing about how this had happened.

'You're quite a piece of work, Vanita,' she said, and then ran a fingernail down my bare belly to make me squirm. 'Daddy couldn't be cockier, now that his cronies have seen that betrothal choker. And Mama – well, Mama is *quite* taken with you. Wants you to come for another visit, whenever we can slip into the cave again. You're now so much a part of the Harte family – so beloved and sought after – you can't possibly leave.'

My heart sank to an all-time low, and the seductive wraith beside me laughed at my anguish. What went wrong last night? Only bits and pieces, all of them associated with intense pleasure, came to me as I tried to recall what I'd said or done to further imprison myself. And what had happened to Pearce?

'Poor little thing,' Desiree mocked, rustling my pubic curls with her fingertip. She then twisted a clump of hair between her finger and thumb, and tugged. 'It seems your destiny is to surrender all that was to be yours, and become a slave in the enemy camp –

betrayed even by your own body. Your wicked, wayward . . . beautiful body.'

My slit throbbed despite the hatred that welled up inside me. How had I become so susceptible to the charms of a *woman*? A woman I couldn't trust for a moment, and who delighted in dominating me. She teased my clit with a fingernail until it jutted to aching attention, while she chuckled at my tortured scowl.

'Lucky for you, Damon has a softer heart than I,' she continued, removing her hand to watch my hips strain towards the touch she'd deprived me of. 'He's suggested that since you've been a good sport – a receptive victim, under the circumstances – you deserve our help. He still won't fuck you, of course.'

I had nothing to lose if I asked the most compelling question. 'You're letting me go back to Wellspring?'

'We've devised a way to deceive Daddy – again,' she said with a chuckle. 'You'll appear to win your wager, by the light of Friday's full moon. It'll cancel the grand wedding, but my brother and I are so pleased to have a sense of purpose – a new game afoot for a few days – we don't mind letting you go. Daddy will have to eat crow and pay for all the arrangements, which is the best part of it. And Pearce has agreed to help.'

I was fully awake now, my mind thrumming at these possibilities. Desiree's generosity would come with a price, of course, for she was a creature driven by her own desires – vindictive, but in ways that brought new peaks of pleasure into her limited life. 'What are you proposing?'

'You're to meet me at midnight on Friday, dressed in that diaphanous wedding gown Mrs Marley made you. I'll be in the swing, pretending I'm Damon – so very hard and ready for you, Daddy won't be able to keep his pants buttoned when he watches us.'

'But how –'

'You'll have to trust me, Vanita,' she whispered, leaning closer, so her sheer gown brushed my bare skin. 'We'll make a splendid sight as we pump and dip in the moonlight, don't you think?'

I quivered at the thought, appalled at my body's reaction while intrigued by Desiree's idea. She sprang lithely on to the bed to straddle my stretched-out form, wearing a look of catlike satisfaction. Then she let the dressing gown fall open, swaying backwards so it slithered off her shoulders and down her graceful arms, baring her pert little breasts and tight belly. The sight of her white pubic curls against my darker ones made me hold my breath.

'Of course, you owe me a favour before I make all these dreams come true,' she murmured, undulating slowly against my hips. 'I already know how very, very much I'll miss you, Vanita. I climaxed at least three times just from watching you explode when those streams of warm water splashed against your open pussy.'

My sex vividly recalled the delicious wet force, the avid expressions of the other admiring guests, the pleasure that was repeated in so many ways until I literally lost myself. 'What happened after I – ? I must've passed out.'

'Indeed you did,' she breathed, closing her eyes as she rocked. A trickle of her warm wetness slithered into my cleft, and my hips rose up of their own accord. 'We let you rest beside the pool until we were all sated. The other guests disappeared into the night, while Damon and I slipped up the cellar stairs with you. Daddy was drunk enough not to hear us, but he checked on you before he retired for the night.'

'Did he . . . do anything?'

Desiree chortled. 'Besides falling into his own bed with his clothes on?'

I grinned with relief. The thought of Franklin Harte fumbling for himself and rutting against me still ranked as the most onerous of notions. 'I suppose these velvet bindings were your idea. In case I tried to escape.'

A smile lit her ivory face as she walked forwards on her knees. 'I know what I want, and I go after it. And you're so grateful for my help – and for my brother's co-operation – that you'll repay me as only you can, Vanita. You're more attuned to my needs than you'll ever admit.'

With that, she eased herself over my outstretched arms, gripping two cherubs in the rails of the headboard, and spread her legs wide. Her pussy, rimmed in curls as white as her skin, pulsed visibly as she opened to me. She was hot and ready, her petals the irresistible pink of the azaleas in the courtyard, slick with pearly dew. Her thighs flexed as she positioned herself, and I lay fascinated beneath her, watching the subtle movements of her folds as she opened her hole. I stuck my tongue out to taste her, and she began to rock, right above my mouth.

'Oh God, Vanita . . . Vanita,' she murmured, writhing more quickly now. 'You've been a very good sport, and if you give it to me the way I want it – hot and hard and frantic – you'll be on your way home after our tryst Friday night.'

Her promise goaded me to do her bidding. Bound as I was to the bed's posters, I had no choice but to please her – I was at the mercy of her undulating hips and the cream-coated flesh she pressed to my face. With a gasp, I thrust my tongue inside her, probing the warm, slick folds to make her moan with unspeakable pleasure. When she was near the bursting point, I sucked her stiff little clit into my mouth, flattening my tongue against the underside of it.

Desiree screamed.

She smothered me then, writhing against my face and gushing with warm, buttery come. I struggled, making a choking sound in my throat, but Desiree was determined to take her full due. She kept pumping her honey, rubbing her wet sex over my nose and mouth. I felt last night's darkness stealing over me, and I wondered if this was the way I would die – if this alabaster woman would deprive me of Wellspring by drowning me during her climax. With my last conscious burst of inspiration, I closed my teeth around her clitoris.

Desiree squealed, laughing raucously. 'Did I scare you, Vanita?' she teased. She dismounted, and then slipped off the bed. 'You were every bit as wonderful as I'd hoped. So I'll see you at the swing, ready to fulfil my promise. You'd better make a good show of it.'

And with that she walked away. I gaped at her swaying backside as she passed through my bedroom door, leaving me tied to my bed, naked, with a sopping wet face and hair that was soaked with her come.

'Desiree, you –' I hollered. But I didn't dare offend her, now that my freedom was in sight.

An hour later, Franklin Harte entered the room, drinking in my predicament with a lascivious grin. 'My son says he's going to fuck you Friday night. Thinks I don't know him better than that, but I've seen him back out of this too many times. I can't resist watching him fail again, Vanita, so I'll take your aunt back to Wellspring and return for yet another fiasco. Aren't you glad you're beginning to fit right in, here at Harte's Haven?'

Without warning, he shoved a leather finger up me. I was still wetter than I wanted to be after Desiree left me dangling, but by God if everyone in this family could tell me one thing and then do another, I could behave as badly as they did! After some shudders and a loud cry, I convulsed, hoping I sounded convincing. It was the best way to be rid of this ogre who made the most of my enslaved state. To be fair, though, I had not yet spoken a word of refusal.

A few more thrusts, followed by another impassioned outburst on my part, satisfied him. To enrage me further, he tweaked my cheek with his damp fingers, like a father cosseting a favoured child. 'Clean yourself up, you little slut, and be ready for *me* to claim you after Damon falls short. That's the consequence of your misplaced wager, as you'll recall.'

With an unceremonious jerk, he loosened the strap around my right wrist. Then he, too, walked away – but in the doorway he turned with an imperious sneer. 'When I take you, I won't let you stop until you've satisfied me as thoroughly as you did my daughter. Better get your rest, little girl. Daddy can control himself for hours on end. And faking it again will be a big mistake!'

Before I could protest, Franklin yanked off his kidskin gloves. He came at me then, wiggling fingers that were red and misshapen with scars – gruesome wounds that made me squeal and clench my eyes shut, hoping to God he wouldn't touch me.

'Can't stand the naked truth, eh?' he taunted. 'Olivia tried to get rid of me by faking a climax, too. And when I came after her, your mother ducked my advances and shoved me towards a cauldron of boiling candle tallow, there in her kitchen. Yet another reason you owe me my revenge, Vanita.'

I turned away, shrivelling in horror, unable to breathe.

'You'd better find that pearl choker, little bitch. Nasty things could happen if you're not wearing it Friday night.'

Long after his footsteps faded down the hall, my

heart was pounding so loudly it drowned out the successive chimings of the clocks in my room and throughout the house – clocks that seemed to mark my demise.

I gave thanks for each day Franklin stayed away after that – even though he could've been scheming with Aunt Lillian at Wellspring – and passed my time trying to sort the truth from the lies, my friends from my enemies. A harrowing task, at best. Confusing, indeed.

As the moon rose golden and full in the lush night sky, terror warred with my eagerness for freedom. What if Desiree betrayed me? What if Franklin realised it wasn't Damon playing out this charade? I didn't trust any of these Hartes, and with the stablehands making themselves obvious around the grounds, I couldn't escape without dire consequences.

The thought of being had by Franklin Harte, with his oily grin and those scar-ravaged hands, drove me to distraction. I gazed sadly at the shimmering gown for tomorrow's wedding. The tables awaited their white linen cloths, beneath a large tented pavilion erected on the lawn. Vases of orange blossoms and pale-pink roses, imported from the coast at great expense, sat in the coolness of the cellar. The house smelled better than it had since my arrival, redolent with aromas of cake and fresh breads and roasting meats.

With what Franklin had spent on this lavish fiasco, I could have paid off my aunt's debts and reclaimed Wellspring – and he knew it. Damn bastard. How could any man take such delight in the failure of his son, and in watching a proud southern family's heritage go to ruin?

These thoughts enraged me, which was just the incentive I needed. As I slipped into the diaphanous dress, with its yards of delicate lace and the provocative beadwork on the bodice, I reminded myself that my own daddy was depending upon me to save a situation gone bad. He hadn't worked all his life for Mama's beloved Wellspring to be despoiled by the despot in the white linen suit, whom he'd always despised.

Pearce was right: believing was seeing. And I had to believe I could succeed on that swing; had to believe my display would be convincing, and that I could then prevail over whatever trickery Franklin Harte might have up his sleeve. Most of all, I had to believe I'd soon be walking through the doors of my home to reclaim it – no matter what Aunt Lillian or these insidious Hartes had in mind.

The lustrous, sheer silk clung to my bare skin. I stood in the moonlight's majesty and looked in the mirror, wishing it were Pearce I was so beautifully arrayed for, and Pearce I was to meet at the swing. My breasts rode lushly in the low-cut bodice, subtly shaped by the design of the seed-pearl flowers. From beneath them, the gown fell into a simple full-cut skirt. Even in the dim light, my feminine curls were visible beneath the translucent silk, and my skin shone a delicious pink. I left my hair flowing down my back, recalling how Pearce had wished to see it spread over his pillow . . . again wishing he hadn't disappeared to tend the business of reclaiming Wellspring on my behalf.

The clocks began to strike in succession, announcing the hour of my triumph – or tolling my doom. I refused to consider the consequences if the swing drifted empty, with everyone a witness to my betrayal. As the final strokes of midnight echoed in the gloomy rooms, I padded barefoot towards the back stairs. The future of Wellspring – my parents' dream for me – now depended on my performance and my pluck.

I paused at the back door, sensing the presence of others among the trees and watching from the barn's loft windows. The moon rode like a queen in all her glory, beaming down from a star-studded night alive with the singing of cicadas and the gentle swish of the breeze through the willows. The scent of lilacs and azaleas enveloped the courtyard, their heavy sweetness almost funereal. I swallowed the coppery tang of fear that filled my mouth.

The swing was empty.

My hand went to my chest. Should I wait? Or should I venture out, hoping I wouldn't be the target of mischief when Desiree didn't show up? Moments crept by on held breath, and the night sounds stilled until it was my own heartbeat filling my ears.

'Walk ahead of me. Unless you're backing out,' came a familiar whisper from the shadows behind me.

My pulse galloped and I sprang forwards at the bidding of impatient fingers. I still had no idea what this twin would do – how she could convince her father that Damon had taken a male interest in me. The grass whispered, cool and damp beneath my feet, a sharp contrast to the heat of Desiree's body and something prodding at my spine.

'I'm sitting on the bottom,' she breathed. 'Make a big show of stroking my monstrous cock and lifting your skirts, before you brace your feet on either side of me. Everyone has to believe you're getting the fucking of your life, Vanita.'

My gasp was quite sincere when the naked figure behind me slipped on to the swing, with an erection that jutted above moonlit thighs. For a moment I could believe it was Damon, and that he was so rock-hard he intended to pump and thrust for my benefit, as well as our audience's: the short, wavy hair glimmered silver, framing a face glazed with passion, the taut body flexed in anticipation as I gazed at fair skin and firm, slender arms reaching up the ropes. The splayed legs beckoned, and I reached out to touch a tall cock like I'd seen when Damon danced with this woman on his anniversary clock.

It was cool and smooth, pale wood carved and sanded to an eerily human gloss, with a bulbous head and a vein down its underside. The base of it disappeared into Desiree, and I realised this was another of their creations, designed for the mutual pleasure of those who rode it. She thrust her hips upwards, gripping the ropes and simulating male arousal – bidding me to impale myself on the magnificent dildo, which would provide the intimate contact she craved as well.

A muffled cough came from the direction of the house, goading me on. Gripping the appendage, I leaned towards that luminous face to make my show more convincing – and got drawn into a relentless kiss. Was this really Damon? Had he decided to make love to me, after years of eschewing women to spite his father?

I shook these misleading thoughts from my head, while her throaty laugh floated around us. No doubt in my mind – and in my hand – that this was Desiree luring me on, yet the whole situation had me so befuddled I realised what a fine line lay between fiction and fantasy . . . male and female in heat. Illusion and reality.

'Mount me, Vanita,' came the urgent whisper. 'Straddle me and crouch over my cock. As we pump and fall against each other, you're going to wish it could always be this good.'

Lured by the lusty undertones of a voice that could belong to either twin, I planted my feet on the sides of the swing. My partner raised my shimmering skirts – while I wiggled my hips suggestively in her face – and then I lowered myself until the wooden dildo rested against my sex.

Desiree pumped, lifting us into the air, and I moaned with the first penetrating thrust. I shoved my feet in the opposite direction, which pressed the cock more deeply inside my accomplice. She gritted her teeth with the pleasure of it, and then threw her hips and legs into another skyward shove.

The swooping sensation left my insides hanging suspended before I was filled again with the insistent pressure of the dildo. It was like flying, gliding through the moonlight anchored only by the pinion that connected me to another body as warm and pulsing as my own. My gown fluttered voluptuously around us, unfurling in a filmy trail of diamond-like silk when I pushed, and then hugging my bare backside with a sensuous caress as I rose backwards through the cool night air.

'You're incredible, Vanita ... all those little white pearls hugging your luscious breasts,' came her breathy declaration. 'I'm going to suck one into my mouth and make you scream with it, the way you did last night.'

Ravenous lips closed over my nipple, pressing the hard beads into my flesh. My breasts swelled, abraded by the fabric and the wet heat as Desiree sucked with long tugs of her tongue.

My head fell back and my cry echoed across the lawn as I shoved us into the air. I clenched my eyes with the ecstasy of it, and in my mind I could see the starlit vision we created, swinging higher, forwards and back, swathed in the sheer silk that clung to my body as though I were clothed in the moonbeams themselves. Never had I felt so adventurous. So free.

And when I forgot about the consequences of failing at this charade, my body responded by swinging against Desiree and her dildo with a rhythm that drove me against her to fill myself, to sate the fiery desire ignited by my imagination and her lust for a new erotic challenge.

The spasms coiled within me – flying high, hanging suspended – then falling fast and hard against Desiree. Our coarse curls rustled together and the shaft between us squelched wetly. She was lying back at full-length now as she drove us, her slender thighs spread so my bottom dangled between them. The moonlight showed me an expression of excruciating control and I felt a tell-tale shudder rack her frame. She leaned hard into the next thrust, and the base of the dildo rutted the opening of my pussy, as well as my clit. I screamed, lost in the convulsions of my climax, shooting out the slick juices from reservoirs deep inside me.

When I could breathe again, we were hovering just above the ground, our pumping and swooping coming to a halt. My thighs ached and the swing seat cut into the soles of my feet, but I didn't move. The young woman beneath me writhed and let out a keening, climactic cry – and around us, from the woods and the stables and the house, came muffled groans of release. Peeking between my slitted eyelids, I could see figures in the shadows, hunching and stroking their engorged members. Every male on the estate must have watched us – which filled me with a wicked sense of power.

'Get ready,' Desiree murmured. 'Once Daddy recovers, he'll have to make some sort of swaggering statement for the benefit of his men. We've got to move before they get close enough to see what you were really riding. Best to go our separate ways.'

I climbed down from the swing as quickly as my aching legs allowed, and could discern a white-suited figure at the corner of the house. He was fastening his pants. If Harte saw that my lover was still high and hard, there'd be hell to pay, so I let my skirts camouflage Desiree's secret weapon. She hopped to the ground, and slipped into the nearest thicket. The dildo made a slurping sound when it slipped out of her. She took a roundabout path of shadows towards the house, so I turned in a different direction – and came face to face with Franklin.

'So you did what no other woman could do!' Harte bellowed, still adjusting his white linen trousers. 'It would seem you've won the bet, Vanita – in front of all these witnesses. And just in time to call off the wedding!'

I glanced around, pretending to be shocked at discovering an audience, and then caught sight of a face in the moonlight – an angular, dusky smile surrounded by a mane of ebony, edged by new growth along his jaw. Pearce! He'd been here all along, waiting to escort me back when I won my bet!

I looked back at Franklin, ready to say that I had indeed prevailed, but I'd waited a second too long. The bear in front of me pivoted in the direction of my gaze, laughing maliciously. 'But you've disobeyed me, Vanita! I told you to break all ties with Truman, and here he is – just as though he knew about this little plot! After him, men! Somebody shoot the bastard before he gets away again!'

The wooded knoll came alive with hired hands whose whoops resounded like battle cries. In the time it had taken me to recognise him, Pearce was surrounded by Harte's workers. Still inspired by their voyeuristic activities, they spurred each other along.

'Hold him, Hank! My rifle's right here against this tree!'

'No, let Mr Harte do the honours!' came a voice I recognised. 'This fox has been in the hen house too long!'

'I got him!'

My heart sank and I clutched the folds of my dress to keep from crying. Pearce, too stoic to struggle, was now in the clutches of two burly stablehands. He would have been shot already, had Felton not deferred to their boss.

But as the rifle was passed to the man in white, a voice came out of the house. 'Don't you dare shoot him, Daddy! A peacock like Pearce would suffer a thousand deaths in Devil's Dungeon, don't you think?'

Desiree emerged, her vixen smile and swaying hips shimmering in the moonlight. She was still naked, but she'd donned her wig of upswept hair, which glimmered like ermine and left no doubt she was every inch a lady. The men halted with Pearce in tow, looking to Franklin.

'But it's best to get rid of him, once and for all!'

'Daddy, you're losing your touch!' his daughter insisted in an exaggerated drawl. 'And can't you just *once* give me what *I* want? You know how I love Vanita – how I've wanted her for myself all along. Send Pearce to the coal mines where he'll never see the sun – or be seen alive again! And maybe ... just maybe I'll share her with you, Daddy. Won't that be fun? You know Damon would never be so thoughtful.'

The knife of her duplicity twisted in my gut. She knew Harte's men would be out tonight, had told Pearce about her plan to mimic her twin, set the hook, so I had to appear or forfeit my estate – all within sight of the father she played like a violin. All to appease her lust and loneliness. Her feline smile confirmed these suspicions: I'd never really had a chance to leave Harte's Haven.

'You might just have something there, little girl,' Franklin said in a snakelike voice. 'It'd serve Truman right to break his back hauling loads of coal. The perfect punishment for ingratiating himself with Lillian, thinking he could undermine me!'

Harte stared at Pearce, caught between his two henchmen, and then smiled at me. 'All right, then – tie him up, boys! Toss him in the wagon and haul his sorry ass to the mines!'

The hands jostled Pearce between them as they ushered him towards the stables. I wanted to rush at them, crying out about this gross injustice, but I couldn't take on a dozen men – not while Franklin held that rifle. I wanted to knock Desiree to the ground and punch her pretty face for turning on me again. She'd never intended to set me free! I'd been a fool to believe her when she suggested our moonlight make-believe.

And I wanted to ram that rifle butt between Franklin Harte's fleshy legs, for all his slights against my parents, and for taking advantage of my wayward aunt – and for holding me responsible for all of it! For playing me as the last pawn in this insidious game of acquisition that spanned two generations.

But instead, I saw a split-second interval when Desiree was batting her lashes at her daddy, and the men were almost to the stables. So I ran for it.

19 Unexpected Guests

I made an easy mark, moving through the moonlight in a dress that shone like silver. As I struggled between bushes that tore at its fragile fabric, I only had a vague idea about escaping into the cave. Which tree had the magic knothole? How did I activate that hidden door? I'd gotten just far enough to make a fool of myself when Desiree sprinted through the thicket to grab me.

'We're not nearly through playing with you, Vanita,' she crooned, pivoting me. 'Did you really think we'd let you go, now that we've arranged your lovely wedding? Such ingratitude – and Daddy'll punish you for it! We intend to make you a full-fledged member of the Harte family forever, regardless of how Damon feels about you!'

My heart shrivelled. The undergrowth bruised my bare feet and my captor's hands cut like steely bands into my upper arms as she steered me back towards the house ... back towards Franklin, who watched us with a predatory expression. He, too, glowed in the moonlight, and the bulge in his white linen trousers looked like a pistol he was pointing from his pocket.

The thought of what he wanted to do to me had me jerking away from Desiree, slapping at her to free myself, but she was taller and far stronger than I. Laughing at my feeble attempt, she manhandled me to my room, shoved me on to my bed, and then hopped on top of me to bind my wrists and ankles with those velvet straps again.

'Surely your daddy won't want the ceremony to go

on, with his son's bride wearing rags,' I suggested, clutching at straws. My beautiful gown was tattered around the hem and sleeves, no longer suitable to be married in.

'Daddy wants to watch you walk to the altar naked,' Desiree replied with a laugh. 'Your comeuppance, for thinking you could outfox us. Your final degradation, after returning from that fancy girls' school to rule the estate your aunt gambled away! What an illustrious queen you are, Vanita!'

With that, she grabbed the flimsy silk and ripped my dress from the bodice downwards, sending seed pearls pinging across the floor with a glee that made me cry out. Mere minutes ago Desiree had been swinging me to unknown heights, delicious because they were illicit and forbidden. Now she mocked me.

And when Franklin joined us, my despair became complete. He entered languidly, lighting a lamp to cast more light upon my splayed features – to better witness my humiliation and the way the ruined silk curled around my bared breasts and thighs. As though to egg him on, Desiree slithered between my legs and tongued me relentlessly.

As Harte stood beside the bed, his breathing quickened. His cane hit the floor and he fumbled with his buttons, shucking the impeccable white jacket and tugging his shirt from his pants.

'I've waited a long time for this,' he rasped, his eyes fastened on my heaving breasts and the quivering muscles of my stomach. 'I thought my son might take an interest – sincerely intended to let him have you. But I've invested too much money and patience to let you escape. It's time to punish you for removing that choker, and for luring Truman here. Time to avenge your mother's cruel rejection, and the way she ruined me. You're excused, Desiree.'

The white blonde bobbing between my legs raised her face. 'But Daddy, I'm getting her ready! Letting you watch –'

'Get out. You've had your turn.' His pants puddled on the rug and he stood in his union suit, which sported a prodigious bulge above his thighs. 'You're greedy and presumptuous, like your mother, Desiree. I'm tired of you batting those white eyelashes – flitting around like a ghost in this house, reminding me with your colourless skin and eyes that you can't possibly be my child.'

The remark resounded like a slap, and the young woman recoiled as though he'd struck her. She slinked away, circling wide on the opposite side of the room to avoid him, her face grey with shock.

As she fled, Franklin turned to me again. In his haste, he popped the buttons from his underwear. 'You see, Vanita, I'm a man who tolerates betrayal and insubordination silently, letting the wounds fester and infect me until the poison simply has to spew out. You and I had an agreement, didn't we?'

My slit closed in upon itself at the sight of that big, blunt pecker poking up from his fist. I swallowed hard, focusing on his bearlike chest instead.

'You told me you'd make my son a man, in return for dismissing the debts against Wellspring. But it was Desiree you fucked in that swing,' he hissed. 'You, too, are every bit as duplicitous as your mother, and it's time for this to end. Time for me to collect my due, from women who slither like snakes and bite me in the backside.'

'I – I don't know what you're talking about!' I rasped, struggling against the ties at my wrists and ankles. Franklin was shoving the cotton undergarment below his torso, freeing an erection that swung like a club. 'I was only eleven when Mama and Daddy were struck by –'

'Lightning sent by God, to punish them for their sins,' he finished, tossing aside his union suit. 'What else could Lorena tell a little girl? That her mama was whoring at Harte's Haven? That her daddy drove over to confirm his suspicions, and found us in the carriage house, naked, with Olivia pumping Roger's big black dick while she sucked on mine?'

These images burned my brain, and with this beast approaching my bedside, I had no time to sift through all the stories he'd thrown at me this week. 'Mama would never have –'

'She was a woman, Vanita. She was a slut with come-on eyes and big tits – like yours – and she liked to shake them at me. Thought she could tease me without having to pay for it.'

He clambered over the foot of the bed, between my legs, his cock as ruddy and taut as his face. 'And once I fucked her, she couldn't get enough of it. Found excuses to come here and beg me for it – just like Lillian thought *she* could have me by playing silly games. You'll be begging me, too, Vanita. Just like you begged Truman to take you on your daddy's desk.'

The edge in his voice warned me that Franklin Harte was a man possessed, by misplaced passions and a vengeance that had poisoned him against everyone he knew. His dark hair writhed around his face as he knelt between my knees, stroking himself. In the moonlight spilling over the bed, his gloved hand fluttered up and down like a frenzied dove while his wild eyes were riveted on my breasts.

'I still have time,' I said. 'The tryst in the swing was Desiree's idea! You *know* how she works things so she'll have her own way! A gentleman of honour would allow me the full time before the wedding to win my wager.'

'Honour!' he grunted, grimacing with his excitement. 'As if honour would change Damon's taste in lovers! As if honour got me where I am today, or ever brought me what I really wanted!'

'I can give you what you really want, Franklin,' came a whisper through the tubes. The voice was breathy and seductive, distinctly feminine.

The man hunching between my legs clutched himself, searching the shadows. 'Who was that? Who's there?'

'It's Alice.'

My eyes widened and my heart pounded harder. Harte froze, his face a mask of disbelief. 'Desiree, you stop it this instant! I've had enough of your childish tricks!'

'Desiree's got nothing to do with it,' the phantom voice replied. *'It's Alice. I'm downstairs.'*

'If you think I'm falling for that one, you –'

'I've come for my son's wedding, Franklin. You can't keep me away.'

He reared back on to his heels, clenching his erection. 'Shut up! You can't fool me, bitch!'

'Say that to my face. I'm downstairs, in the kitchen.'

With great alarm, I watched the head of his engorged cock grow darker and more bulbous above his white-fingered grip. At any moment he might plunge into me, crazy with rage. And I was helpless against his attack.

'That's nonsense!' he cried, his knees quivering against my thighs. 'I left you for dead! Wrapped your body in a saddle blanket and had Felton bury you out behind –'

'Lucky for me he's a randy bastard who tried to fuck the boss's wife while she couldn't fight him,' came the acidic reply. *'I've been waiting for this moment, Frank-*

lin. I'm down here by the stove ... naked. Can you feel the heat from that sizzling griddle? I'm going to refry your –'

'Liar!' he cried in a strangled voice. 'Damn you, Desiree, when I get my –'

'– filthy hands,' the voice replied, only this time it didn't come through the tubes. Alice Harte stepped into the room's moonlight, nude, her glare like jagged glass. 'Those hands you can't keep off every woman you see, Franklin. The hands I pressed on to the hot griddle when you backed me against the stove to finish me off. Was I hot enough for you then, you bastard?'

His face went white, and at his first sign of movement Alice sprinted down the hallway, laughing. Franklin cursed and backed off the bed, clutching himself so he could run after her.

It was a monumental moment, seeing that he had no need for that gold-headed cane, while realising that every story he'd ever told me was probably a lie. Their footsteps and taunts – and the crashing of thrown objects – rang around the vestibule below, more savage than any quarrel I'd ever heard.

I pushed aside the grisly images of the past few moments, relieved that my tormentor had taken this bait. Why Alice Harte had brought herself out of hiding was beyond me. My gratitude did me little good, however, because even with Harte in hot pursuit of the wife who'd disfigured him, I was still bound to the bed. I worked my wrists feverishly against their velvet bindings, until another movement at the door made me freeze.

A wraithlike figure, wearing a shapeless white nightshirt, entered on silent feet. Once more I feared myself the victim of misspent revenge. Had Desiree removed her wig to fool me again? Her daddy's accusations had pierced her like an arrow, poisoned with her mother's apparent indiscretions and doubts about who fathered her. She'd fight like a wounded animal now, lashing out against whoever came into view. My body stiffened, bracing for more torment.

But when she reached to untie the binding around my ankles, I saw a distinctly male member bobbing beneath the nightshirt. 'Damon?'

He put his finger to his lips, his gaze intense. 'If Daddy hears you through the tubes, he'll know I'm helping you,' he whispered. 'Come on, Vanita. Mama's risking her life and we're the only ones who can help her out of here.'

No time to question him or to ponder the predicament Alice Harte had placed herself in. 'Slide down the bannister,' he instructed earnestly. 'We'll go down the back way, into that room where we rode the dancer platform. From there, we can get you out undetected.'

I could only nod and hurry ahead of him as he urged me from the room. As a child, I'd been too strictly disciplined to slide down railings, so sailing along the Harte's curving staircase in a wedding dress made me want to cry out with a gleeful fear. My gown fluttered about my body on the descent, and Damon caught me before I rammed backwards into the newel post. We padded down the hallway to the small door the servants used.

But it was open, and voices raged below us.

'Did you really think you were rid of me?' Alice taunted. 'Even if I were dead, I'd come back to haunt you, Franklin Harte!'

'Stop running so we can talk!' came his winded reply. We heard a loud crash, and Damon grabbed my hand.

'Be careful, Vanita,' he whispered. 'He's like a blind

bull down there. I'm going to light a lamp, but stay in the shadows. Make your way towards the door in the back.'

Damon preceded me down a dark stairway that forced me to feel my way, sliding my bare feet along one step at a time. A pale glimmer lit the bottom after a few moments, and the ruckus continued as Franklin searched for his fugitive wife.

'You had *years* to talk!' Alice's retort came from the far shadows. 'But instead you held me hostage in my own home, telling our friends I was possessed, and that you'd put me in an asylum for the sake of the children!'

'If you hadn't spread your legs for every –'

'That's all in your head!' Alice cried. 'How was I to know you couldn't get aroused unless you had a *victim*? Even if it was only in your sick imagination!'

I gripped the railing at the bottom of the stairs, not daring to enter the shadows. A chill enveloped me, until gooseflesh covered me and my knees shook. To the left the lamp wick sputtered, and just ahead, by the oversized anniversary clock where Damon and his twin had seduced each other, I saw the slender blond beckoning me with a silent wave.

My inclination was to bolt back upstairs, but the man with the translucent eyes feared for his mother's safety – and I'd be less than thankless if I didn't assist her. If nothing else, I could follow Damon's lead until we reached that far door. Perhaps we could smuggle Alice out with us when we got there.

I panicked when I lost sight of him, as he rushed easily between those clockwork wonders of his own creation. Something fell hard to the floor and Franklin cursed, sounding exhausted. Was that the cranking of a key? The spitting of a match made a feeble glare, and suddenly, the lifelike forms on the dancer platform loomed before me. Damon lit the lamp as the circular plane began to revolve slowly; the calliope wheezed through a series of crazed pitches before reaching full speed.

I saw Alice then, hugging the wooden Hilda for balance.

Franklin saw her too, and stepped alongside the revolving carousel with halting steps. 'Damn you, stop this thing!'

'I don't know how!' she cried triumphantly. 'Even a child can ride a merry-go-round, Franklin. Why can't you?'

Realising he might wait in place, to grab her when she came around, I decided to create a diversion. 'Have you never seen your son's genius at work, *Daddy*?' I taunted. 'He gave me the ride of my life on this little toy! Wouldn't you love to watch?'

I leapt nimbly on to the carousel, waving as I went by him. It was like flaunting the red flag before the bull, however, and Harte took the jump. He landed beside Hugo, whose glossy wooden body was just gyrating to life as Damon cranked the mechanisms at the control panel. When a jointed arm knocked Franklin on the shoulder, he staggered sideways and clawed at the air for something to grab on to.

Alice laughed, bolder now. 'Just can't stand it, when another man's shaft is bigger than yours! Look at that thing, Franklin! Now *that* could make a woman scream for more!'

'You're right, Alice! I've ridden it,' I called above the music. I carefully circled the inner edge of the platform, so I could draw Harte's gaze to myself; divert his attention so Damon could board and overpower him.

'That's Hugo, and he loves to caress his partner!' I cupped my breasts with exaggerated motions, bringing the shreds of silk over my nipples to make them glisten in the lamplight. 'It's quite an uplifting experience, to have Hugo pick you up and spread your legs!'

I mimicked this, too, my heart pounding as Franklin staggered in front of the jointed statue to watch me stroke myself. Fear tightened his face, yet the platform's movement was mesmerising him with the same fascination I'd felt during my first ride aboard this toy.

'And then he penetrates you with that hot, pulsing shaft,' I continued, thrusting my hips forwards and back, 'and he pushes it faster and harder, holding you prisoner, vibrating inside you until you *explode*! I screamed with him, Daddy! I rocked against him and took him deep inside me until I was shooting out so much juice –'

As Franklin leaned forwards, following the details of my story, Damon engaged the final mechanisms. Hugo's wooden arms closed around Harte's naked body and lifted him effortlessly, while the painted, moustachioed face leered with perpetual glee. The huge wooden cock – sheathed in leather like Franklin's hands – was greased up and ready to prod, making the man in its grasp cry out with fear and fresh rage.

Spinning hypnotically in place now, the wooden dancer lifted his powerless partner again and this time Hugo guided Franklin's backside unerringly on to his quivering spindle. The timbre of Harte's cries rose from rage to pain – but the rest of us knew not to dawdle. As Damon locked the mechanisms into place to keep the platform spinning, Alice and I hopped off. We three hurried out the back exit into the night, with Franklin's frenzied cries echoing behind us.

20 My Past Falls Into Place

Once again as I entered the hidden passageway to the cave, I felt awestruck. Alice held one hand while her son grasped my other, and we descended the softly lit stairs towards the underground river. It lapped serenely around the waiting gondolas, as though none of the startling events of this evening had occurred. Riki was there, his grin a slash of white in his dark face as he helped us into a boat. He poled with quiet efficiency, allowing us to settle ourselves for the ride.

How could I describe my feelings? In a very few hours I'd gone from a tryst in a swing with a woman who promised my freedom, to being bound in my bed again, almost attacked by Franklin Harte – and then discovering his insanity, and the nasty secret hidden inside his kidskin gloves. Sensing my inner turmoil, Alice pulled me close against her soft body.

'Life gets confusing,' she murmured. 'I'm sorry you've been dragged into such a mess, Vanita. It's not at all what your parents envisioned for you.'

My parents. From deep down and long ago, I conjured up their faces, painted with the innocent strokes of the little girl who'd been orphaned by a storm: lightning struck their carriage on the ride home from Lexington, where they'd settled some estate business. Or I'd believed that story, anyway. I vividly recalled the hands coming to the house, and their hushed conference with Lorena as I eavesdropped from the upstairs landing, picking up on their fear and confusion.

And when Mama's housekeeper pulled me into her

arms to break the news, I hadn't had an inkling that she might be lying to protect my innocence; to preserve the memories a young woman ought to have if she couldn't grow up with her mother and father. Time had stretched endlessly in those days, and the months had meandered even after Aunt Lillian sent me to Miss Purvey's school. Yet in the last few days, my entire past had been called into question.

'Tell me what really happened to them,' I breathed. I closed my eyes, to let the rocking of the gondola lull me into a sense of security – even if that, too, was a lie. 'I don't know what to believe, after Desiree and Franklin told me so many conflicting stories.'

'That's how he keeps his conquests off-balance. I was among the trees watching you and Desiree in that swing, hoping such excruciating loveliness could somehow continue – if you couldn't go home, that is.'

She sighed, shaking her head. 'Poor Desiree can't see the needs of others. Has no sense of how she hurts them, manipulating them into the physical contact she craves.'

I didn't answer. Resting against her, I watched Damon's face from across the gondola. I sensed he wasn't any more aware of his paternity than Desiree had been: the tension gnawing at his jaw told me he'd overheard Franklin's accusation, and had as much at stake in this conversation as I did.

'Desiree was shocked to learn she wasn't Franklin's child,' I ventured quietly. 'At least that's what he told her, to get rid of her.'

Alice sighed disgustedly. 'He conveniently forgets to mention that his poor mama was an albino, too. Learning to play against her weaknesses, as a child, made him the monster who'd say such awful things today.

'But your mama – Olivia was a fine woman, Vanita.

She was very happy with your daddy and led a full, productive life at Wellspring,' Alice continued quietly. 'It was Franklin who couldn't keep his pants fastened, and he pursued her to aggravate your father. I suspect a lot of his trips to Devil's Dungeon and his other tobacco land actually took him to Wellspring and neighbouring estates, where women might fall prey to his charms. Or that's what *he* considered them, anyway. It was his domineering lies and cruelty that drove me away.'

I considered these things carefully before daring to probe further. 'So he thought he'd killed you? After he backed you against the stove, and you scorched his hands?'

'Yes. When I saw young Damon over his shoulder, I found the strength to fight back for once – hoping my child wouldn't witness my murder,' she explained with a sad smile for her son. 'I then feigned unconsciousness so convincingly that Franklin took me for dead. Wrapped me in a blanket and had Felton haul me off.'

I admired her a great deal for rising above the doormat status ingrained in southern women – and for hiding herself on the plantation, and attending dances disguised as one of Damon and Desiree's male friends. Surely such a loving, protective mother wouldn't misdirect me about my own mama's fate. I didn't know what she'd say, but I had to trust somebody.

'So did Mama and Daddy really die in the carriage, struck by lightning?'

Alice cleared her throat, thinking back. 'If there were witnesses during that day's horrible storm, nobody came forward. Their bodies were retrieved from a charred, wrecked carriage and given a quick burial before the heat – and the rumour mill – made the catastrophe any more gruesome for you. Especially since your Aunt Lillian was the only blood relation anyone knew of, and she had to be traced to a stage in a California gold camp.

'But I wouldn't be surprised if Franklin had a hand in it,' she continued with a scowl. 'He was extremely jealous of your daddy's success with breeding thoroughbreds, and Jared had refused to cut him in as a partner a few weeks before the accident. We've had to draw our own clouded conclusions, I'm afraid.'

While this didn't solve the mystery, it cleared my mother of the indecency Franklin had attributed to her. I mused over other things he'd said, and decided it was best to dismiss them. If he had to render a woman helpless to become aroused, it made sense that he'd intimidate me with his nasty accusations when I lay bound and spread-eagled.

What a sorry coincidence that Pearce had shown himself at the wrong moments, and that I couldn't disguise my joy at seeing him – at believing I was finally free to leave Harte's Haven. By now, he'd be most of the way to those dreadful coal mines ... to toil in total darkness, probably forced to work harder than the others because Franklin demanded such relentless vengeance. I swallowed hard, blinking back tears. What if I never saw him again? What if he'd done his damnedest to reclaim Wellspring for me, and I'd unwittingly betrayed him?

'You have a lot to sort through,' Damon said softly. We were passing from the dreamlike blue-veiled passageway into the domed room with its striking formations of quartz stalactites. 'I think a hot soak would relax you, Vanita. Let us pamper you before we take you home.'

Home. It sounded lovely, but I'd been duped before. 'How do I know Desiree won't foil it all again? I can't afford any more false hopes while Wellspring remains in your father's clutches.'

'She's peeved at Daddy now, not you. When she hears him hollering, she'll no doubt go downstairs and make the most of his agony.'

'But what happens when he gets free and –'

'He'll be too sore to walk anywhere fast,' Alice said with a chuckle. 'And he has no idea about this underground hideaway. The children have kept my secret for their own safety, you know. And it's not in Felton's interest to reveal the truth, either. He rather likes the way I pay for his silence.'

They led me to one of the cavern's steaming pools while Riki fetched towels and some ruby-coloured punch. 'Sip this. It will help you to relax and dream pretty pictures,' the well-proportioned young servant said. 'Then I rub you all over with warm oil. Make you feel beautiful.'

Alice watched Riki's grin widen, and then turned her doelike eyes to mine. 'I'll massage you myself, Vanita. The water will feel heavenly after all we've been through tonight. And despite what he'd have you believe, I suspect my son can't wait to get his hands on you, either.'

She was peeling away the remains of my ruined gown, sliding the shredded fabric over my shoulders and breasts with warm, thorough hands. Damon stepped out of his nightshirt, watching his mother caress my dress down past my thighs. When he stepped behind me, pressing his erection against my back, it seemed to me I deserved whatever servicing mother and son lavished upon me. I closed my eyes as his hands came around to cup my breasts, while Alice lit little fires along my inner legs with her fingertips.

Yet as I stepped down the carved quartz stairs into

the warm water with them, I had one last doubt. 'What happens to Pearce, then? I've promised to be his, in return for restoring my estate. That's not going to happen if he's been hauled off to Devil's Dungeon.'

Alice smiled, framing my face with her warm hands as though I were her own beloved child. 'Have you ever known Pearce Truman to fail? Hasn't he always reappeared, just when you needed him most?'

Was this an intuitive observation? Or did the beautiful brunette before me know things she wasn't sharing? As I recalled the way Pearce had attended the ball, as artfully disguised as she, I decided not to answer that – or to question her. I eased further into the bubbling warm water, inhaling its refreshing lemon scent as Damon and his mother joined me.

The duet they played upon my body defied description. Resting my head on my arms, I floated face down at the edge of the pool, savouring the sensation of effortlessness and warmth. While Damon held me from underneath, his mother began to knead my neck and shoulders with slow, rhythmic strokes that relaxed the tightness from the night's misadventures. Desiree's turnabout faded away; Franklin's attempts at claiming me became like a bad dream I'd awakened from, safe. In Alice's able hands, I drifted into a deeply refreshed state resembling sleep, but which left my mind alert ... my body aware of every nuance and stroke and caress.

Such intimate attention from a female still took getting used to, and the closeness of Alice's bare body in the water was charged with a delicious electricity. Her hands concentrated on my shoulder blades, but slipped beneath the water now and then to fondle my breasts from the sides. With Damon's forearms near this area, I had the sensation of being caressed by two lovers at once – and when his mother moved farther down my back, the alabaster man beside me leaned closer to kiss my ears and neck.

'Do you like this, Vanita?'

'Very much,' I murmured. 'I could almost drift off to sleep, but I don't want to miss a single moment of such luscious attention.'

'Good. When we turn you over, it's my turn.'

I moaned softly, because his idea appealed – and because Alice's palms were making firm, circular patterns around my bottom, filling me with a yearning for more. Despite my highly relaxed state, I became aware of the pulse in my pussy, and the increasing warmth there. I secretly hoped someone's fingers would slip between my wet lower lips to massage that part of me as well.

Alice was a mind reader. With one hand still rubbing my bum, she slid the other one slowly between my thighs, chuckling quietly when my legs parted of their own accord. 'Ah, you're the sensual one, Vanita,' she said. 'Already slick and hot, a vessel wishing to be filled. Turn over, darling. I want to see how your dark blonde curls cling to your skin ... how the water runs in rivulets down your mound and around those rosy-red lips ... before I kiss them.'

With a languid sigh, I obeyed. It was enough to anticipate Alice's scrutiny, both with her eyes and her fingertips parting the wet curls for a closer look. But because I'd closed my eyes, I wasn't expecting to have my breast suckled while Damon rubbed his thumb around my other puckering nipple.

'God, you're perfect, Vanita,' Alice whispered. 'Like a dew-kissed rose with its petals opening to receive me. Such a tight little hole ... you're so aroused I can see your clit quivering with your pulse. Oh, my ...'

When her lips closed over my sex, her tongue massaged that nub that most wanted her, shooting a jolt of hot current through my body. Had Damon not been steadying me, my thrashings might have drowned us both, the need for release came on so fast. I spread my legs farther, thrusting towards the warm, rough tongue and the hard teeth she pressed carefully against me, compelled to do her bidding by the heat she created.

As I approached a peak, a tight coiling inside, she shifted. With my eyes still closed in anticipated ecstasy, I was aware that a harder body had replaced hers, and that Alice now cradled my head against her soft, wet breasts. My hips agitated the water and my impatient groans echoed in the domed cave.

'Please ... please fill me – finish me!' I pleaded, my eyes clenched with the utter pleasure of this experience.

Two strong hands found my hips as Damon stepped close enough to stroke me. Indeed, his cock felt long and hard as he rubbed the upper side of my cleft. His coiled hairs rustled wetly against mine and he angled himself so my most sensitive folds were pressed against the sturdy root of him. He thrust and let go, thrust and let go – to tease me until I could stand no more.

'Take me!' I demanded, insane with need.

'Are you sure? How badly do you want me, Vanita?'

He rubbed subtly against my aching clit and the spirals began a maddening ascent. It occurred to me that this went against my original bargain with Pearce – but then, how could I have known the realm of the pleasures offered me here, and how desperately I would want them? How could I have known Pearce would be hauled away, needing the same sort of help from me I'd depended upon from him? My devilish demon lover would never deny me the release I'd come to crave since I met him. He knew how much I needed it, because he'd taught me himself.

'Take me *now*,' I insisted. 'Ram it inside me! Fuck me! Fuck me *hard* – oh, God!'

With one fluid movement, he buried himself so deep that I curled upwards and my eyes flew open – to see Pearce Truman! As he drove himself inside me, his raven waves danced around his face, which was now sharply accented by dark stubble.

'Couldn't help myself,' he grunted, thrusting as though control would soon be forgotten. 'You were having too much fun with these other two, and I had to join you ... to join with *you* again. Get ready! I'm going to exploooode!'

Clutching my hips, he crushed himself against me, and the streams of warm semen sent me towards my own thrashing release. For several moments we hunched and thrust, grimacing with the power that passed between us. When I collapsed, Alice caught me and Pearce eased forwards to hold me close while we caught our breath.

'You've got some explaining to do!' I said between ragged breaths. I tousled his damp hair, revelling in the familiar, male scent of him. 'I pictured you slaving in the coal mines, doomed to die in Devil's Dungeon unless I could somehow get you out.'

Pearce brought me up out of the water, clutching me against his solid body. 'We have Alice to thank for this turn of events,' he breathed. 'Seems she trades favours with one of the stablehands who captured me, and he brought me here instead.'

I turned towards Alice, who was drying herself beside the pool now. 'Felton?'

'My connections come in handy,' she said with an alluring grin. 'But when you returned that pearl choker – the necklace Franklin gave to *me* before we wed – I was convinced you deserved my help. And your Pearce has definitely given me something to think about . . . a freedom I've never dared dream of, until now.'

She ran the towel teasingly between her legs, and then crouched on the edge of the pool where her coarse curls were level with our eyes. 'Did you mean it, when you said you could make Harte's Haven mine? Without interference from Franklin?'

I had to smile at the familiarity of her question. 'So this demon made you that dare as well? He must've compiled some very compelling evidence against your husband.'

'I have,' he replied, easing his palm against her privates. 'And as her part of the bargain, Alice has agreed to return us to Wellspring without Harte being any the wiser, so Clive and I can complete our case against him.'

My heart broke into a gallop at this thought. All these days and nights with my nemesis were about to end? I grabbed Pearce in a kiss that made him laugh and playfully slap my backside. 'You understand, of course, that I've had to show my appreciation as best I could. Alice drives a hard but . . . enticing bargain.'

With his middle finger slipping in and out of her slit, I didn't have to ask what he meant by that. It came as no surprise that Pearce had once again wagered with a lady, playing himself as part of the prize. And after all, when we'd first met, he was driving that paragon, Clara Purvey, to distraction with more than his wicked grin. He had the bargaining tool women found irresistible, and he knew how to use it. As I watched Alice grimace and tighten her thighs around his hand, I felt more aroused than jealous – a change from the way things would have been before I met him. But for men, having other partners was acceptable and even expected.

'What if I'd taken Damon as my lover? I came very,

very close, you know.' I glanced down at his muscled chest, until he lifted my chin.

'Those were the stakes all along, sweetheart,' he said, looking deeply into my soul with those serene green eyes. 'But you were mine from the moment I first saw you; from the time I claimed you on your daddy's desk, Vanita. You promised yourself to me, and I knew you'd come through. It's that simple.'

At that moment my life did indeed seem simple – as basic as breathing, now that we'd outfoxed Franklin Harte and were soon heading home. I let out a sigh I must've been holding since I'd been taken captive in his carriage, and let myself lean completely on the man who held me so tenderly yet so confidently.

'Don't get too comfy,' he murmured against my ear. 'We can't risk staying here for Desiree to find us, so we'll be travelling through the caves to Wellspring as soon as you can get ready. Then we'll have your Aunt Lillian to deal with.'

I blinked, for this reality was no small matter. 'Even as she was gambling my estate out from under me, I doubt she foresaw Wellspring without herself at its helm. She won't like being ousted from the house.'

'Those are the consequences of becoming queen, Vanita. I hope you're ready.'

21 His Willing Victim

As we settled into a gondola for the trip, it occurred to me again what sheer inner power Pearce Truman possessed. Without my knowing it – without making himself apparent to Franklin or Desiree Harte – this alluring man had been manipulating events and details in my favour. He'd negotiated with Alice to seal my release from Harte's Haven, and had made an ally in Damon as well: the albino had somehow secreted my new clothing into the caves and smoothed the path for my escape without letting his jealous, possessive twin interfere. And he'd gotten nothing, really, in the bargain.

So as I sat back against Pearce in the sleek little boat, while Riki took up his pole, I was elegantly attired in the peacock gown Mrs Marley had fashioned, and had a valise containing my new underthings. It gave me a great advantage, emotionally, to return home looking like an heiress rather than a ravaged hoyden in her rags. I'd bid Alice Harte a fond farewell with the promise we'd stay in touch after this whole sordid affair regarding Franklin and our finances was settled. It gave the feeling of a fresh start to this little journey; a solid sense of hope, after all the lies and betrayals I'd endured at Harte's Haven.

Riki untied the gondola and slid us smoothly away from the shore. Since we were leaving the part of the caves Damon and Desiree had furnished for their mother, we soon passed out of the beautiful blue-lit crystalline walls into a passageway fitted for safe, mundane travel. While torches flickered at intervals along the cave walls, they were only to light places where the underground river grew narrow or forked. Our miniature guide, his ebony body a handsome contrast to his white loincloth, seemed as much at home here as he did amidst his mistress's splendid domed rooms.

'Does Alice venture out often?' I mused aloud, letting my fingertips graze the cool water alongside the boat. 'She mentioned an outlet near Wellspring. I can imagine living under the earth becomes dreary, day after day.'

'Miss Vanita think I let her grow bored and stale?' he teased. 'Not so! You no doubt crave daylight hours in sunshine. We shall picnic in a grove overlooking fine Wells pastureland. I used to watch your new foals and fillies frolic, years ago.'

'We'll be watching them again – *soon*,' I said, my voice surprisingly tremulous. 'Thanks to Pearce, I'll be replacing my breeding stock, and refurbishing the stables and the house. It'll be lovely again, a true tribute to my parents' life work. I'll invite you over to see it.'

'Riki like that,' the little man replied. 'Missy must be careful, though. Franklin a crafty fox. He have many big friends, and finds ways to cheat and hurt everyone who crosses him.'

'So I've noticed,' Pearce remarked, yet he sounded utterly confident as he shifted me against the hardening bulge in his trousers. 'He'd have been trapped before Lillian Gilding lost everything to him, had I been called in sooner. But we do the best we can with what we have . . . eh, Vanita?'

Under cover of the cave's dimness, he'd manoeuvred the back of my dress around my hips, as a cover for what his inquisitive fingers were doing to me. I'd played along, of course, leaning back and raising myself to accommodate his furtive moves, until he had full access to my legs and what lay between them without Riki being any the wiser.

At the first touch of his fingertip, slipping between the open folds of my silken drawers, Pearce chuckled softly against my ear. 'I dare you to come without him knowing it, love. I want to titillate your slit ... tickle your little clit ... until you have to implode, without wiggling or thrashing or making a sound. Up for the dare?'

'What if I lose? What if he catches us?' I murmured back. I was already dripping wet, pulled into the mood by the element of surprise Pearce always seemed to have in his favour.

'I'll concoct some horribly degrading punishment ... strip you and command you to bring yourself off while Clive watches, perhaps,' he whispered in a mesmerising voice. 'But do you ever really lose with me, Vanita?'

I swallowed a gasp as he inserted his middle finger, slipping it in and out very quickly. The devil, he was holding me back against his chest, seemingly relaxed, until Riki turned to look down the channel again. Then Pearce pressed his thumb against the sensitive nub that most wanted him to – and brought his other hand around to join the one already reducing me to a quivering mass of raw nerve endings.

Our pilot turned again, his grin white in the light of a sconce. 'You make pretty pair. Look good among the uppity-ups at the race track, someday soon.'

'Thhhhank you,' I breathed, doing my damnedest not to thrash. Beneath my voluminous skirts, my legs were fully parted and two very busy fingers were plying my slick folds. In and out they alternated, creating a keen sense of rhythm with a back beat, brazenly begging my hips to dance.

'Shall I stop? Have I won already?' came the furtive murmur.

'No!' I rasped, and then smiled broadly at Riki's curious glance. 'Just adjusting myself on the seat,' I explained in anything but a normal voice. 'My poor backside's taken a beating of late, you see.'

'Missy like it? Desiree very good with riding crop.'

Just her name brought the memory of that young woman's pearly skin against mine as we pumped in the moonlit swing. I sucked in my breath, determined not to succumb – at least not so soon – to my own fantasies, and to the man who was driving me wild.

'Well, she won't be using it on *me*!' I replied a little too brightly. 'Once I discovered she was all take and no give, I resolved not to fall for her . . . charms.'

He'd turned to steer the gondola through a low opening in the earth, where we all had to duck to avoid cracking our heads. Pearce used the opportunity to crush me against his rock-solid erection while driving his fingers deeper inside me. I muffled my groan against my shoulder, wriggling my hips to torment him, as well as to release some of the energy building within me.

Never before had I accepted such intimate attention while trying to hide it from an unknowing observer, and every inch of my body quivered with the burgeoning need for release. My drawers were soaked, and when we sat upright again it was all I could do not to thrust madly against the hands that held my climax just beyond my reach.

Forwards we floated, through cooler, danker passageways where the darkness obscured all but the gentle lapping of the river's current. Like the water, my excitement was flowing throughout my body, directed by the wiles and power of my intimate magician. When he felt I was ready to implode, he quickly changed his stroke, or his timing, alternating between my inner slit and the clitoris which strained against the seam of my silk drawers. Once again I was held captive, this time by a man determined to possess me more completely than any of the Hartes: I was Pearce Truman's *willing* victim, and in that context lay an ecstasy beyond my imaginings.

'We be almost there,' Riki remarked. 'Here, in caves, time mean nothing. Trip taking hours pass in moments, it seem.'

How long had we been on the water? My befuddled brain had lost all sense of time and direction, and knowing we'd soon disembark near Wellspring sent me into a higher spin. My heart was fluttering like a caged bird about to fly free and my body quivered with my efforts to hold it still. I clenched my eyes shut. I put my teeth together with hard, steady pressure, while wrapping my arms around Pearce's vibrating thighs. Backwards I pressed, silently urging him to finish me, gripping his fingers with every throbbing, aching muscle of my slit. When I could stand no more, I rocked forwards, squirting little jets of juice as a *hissss* escaped from between my teeth.

'My God, we've been surrounded by water moccasins!' Pearce cried. 'Get us out of here!'

Alarmed, Riki poled the river bottom faster, intent on getting us safely to the mouth of the cave. In the darkness, I don't suppose he could tell where the nests of those supposed snakes might be, and once I climaxed with a series of rapid thrusts I collapsed against my lover. It was an effort not to laugh aloud, at the way Pearce covered for me, allowing me again to win the dare.

'You can repay the favour later,' he chuckled, hugging me close. 'You'll be so overcome with gratitude, once we've put Franklin and your aunt out of the picture, that you'll pleasure me for days on end. Perhaps forever.'

I turned to gaze at the dark face behind me, desperate to catch every nuance of his expression. 'Honestly? Do you mean –'

'I can't imagine finding another woman I enjoy more, with a . . . quim so suited to my whim.'

Suddenly we burst into sunshine, into a day filled with birdsong and a gentle spring breeze riffling the trees. When Riki looked back to check on us, he saw a grin as big as Wellspring all over my face.

'Happy to be home, yes?'

'Oh, you can't imagine *how* delighted I am!' I wheezed, for Pearce was still fondling my wet folds to play upon the little aftershocks he knew I enjoyed. The river widened, and as we floated towards a sand bar near the shore, I recognised the spot. 'Why, this is the far corner of our northern pasture! I used to ride here, as a child.'

From this angle, Wellspring appeared as verdant and lush as I remembered it, a far cry from the dismal interior of the house and grounds surrounding it. Riki poled the gondola up on to the sand bar and clambered out to assist me.

'Did you enjoy your ride, Miss Vanita?'

'Oh, you don't know much.'

I shaded my eyes with my hands. The rolling hills, like velvet, stretched towards the horizon in all directions, bounded only by a distant white fence. 'There was a time I'd have hopped bareback on to one of the horses and ridden up to the house. But I guess we'll be walking this time.'

'Soon you'll be riding however you want, whenever you want . . . whoever who want,' Pearce added under his breath. He turned to Riki with a nod and a smile. 'Thanks for your help, and give your mistress our fondest regards until we can deliver them in person.'

Riki bowed low and stepped back towards his boat.

'Miss Alice and Riki glad to see you then. Be safe now. Travel happy.'

We waited until he'd turned the gondola and poled himself back into the cave, waving until we could no longer see him. Then Pearce slipped his arm around my shoulders, gazing pensively towards the house we could barely make out in the distance. 'Let's keep them believing I'm a prisoner in Harte's coal mine. While you make your way to the house, I'll double back to the road. The help we need will arrive as soon as I can get them here.'

This meant I'd be facing Aunt Lillian alone – a daunting prospect, despite what I'd survived already. I couldn't whine, however. Pearce had kept his part of the bargain to bring me this far, and I could do no less than what he suggested. 'I'll bide my time. Maybe rest in the stable until dark, and take her by surprise. Will Clive still be there?'

'If we're lucky. Don't tell me you want to hear the creaking of those bedsprings again,' he teased, yet I detected the slightest hesitation in his voice. It occurred to me that this man in the roguish beard had managed to show up every time he was supposed to, at the moment I most needed him – ever since he'd fetched me at school. But did a magician's tricks never backfire?

I refused to think about it. Just as I didn't attribute the savage possessiveness of Pearce's kiss to any sense of doubt on his part. I had to *believe* we would win; had to trust that our good would triumph over the evils we'd survived in the name of my parents' estate.

So I put on my bravest face as I bid the mysterious Pearce Truman goodbye. And after he disappeared from my sight, between the green hills and scattered trees, I grabbed my valise and began my long walk to the house.

22 The Last Man Standing

Second-guessing Lillian Gilding was always a mistake, and I kicked myself for trying it alone the moment I entered the vestibule. She awaited me on the landing, illuminated in late-afternoon sunlight that set her red hair ablaze and shone through the stained-glass window behind her, turning her elegant ivory robe as colourful as Joseph's coat.

'You made a fetching sight, strolling through the pasture in your new gown this morning,' she mewed. 'The prodigal returns! Too bad your daddy wasn't here to welcome you. You would've had a horse to ride, and presents piling up in the parlour.'

'Too bad Daddy hasn't been here all along,' I retorted, gripping my hands into fists. 'I suppose you know Wellspring is mine now. You might as well pack.'

'Sending me packing?' she quipped archly. 'Without so much as a "Thank you, Aunt Lillian", or a fare-thee-well? What sort of manners did Miss Purvey teach you, anyway? I can see all that tuition money was wasted.'

'Your insults can't hurt me any more,' I said, stepping towards the stairway. 'Whatever guidance and guardianship you provided got gambled away. Not to mention my land and horses.'

'You'll be sorry you said that,' she spat, beginning her descent. 'Had you played the game my way and stayed home, you could've been mistress of Wellspring by now. But no! Miss Fancy Pants had to attend *finishing* school – and finish us! That's why I played the ponies, dear niece. Trying to win back what you threw away on a useless education.'

'I know the truth now, so you can stop covering for Franklin Harte at my expense.' I stepped forwards, nailing her with my gaze. 'Being called in as my guardian gave you a second chance to make something of yourself – but you've squandered your family's fortune and betrayed my parents and me! So let's just go up to your room and –'

'No, we'll begin in the study,' she said, blocking the stairs with her soft body and a hardened look. 'The ledgers are there – and so is someone you need to see. Someone who wants you very much, Vanita. Someone else you loved and trusted.'

Oh, God, has Pearce stabbed me in the back, too? While I detested having this thought, there was no persuading Aunt Lill to go upstairs and pack. Nor would I be able to move forwards with this mess until I knew who awaited me – probably with more evidence of my losses, and my misplaced trust. Lillian's face tightened with a catlike smile, that of a formidable woman who knows she's in control.

Pressing my lips grimly together, I preceded her down the hall. I tried to prepare myself for the leonine face edged in that raven beard; tried not to recall the tickle of his moustache when he kissed me ... wherever he kissed me. I hadn't trusted Pearce Truman when I first met him, and now I rued the changes in my attitude. My best judgment – my mental discipline and formal education – wafted away like smoke with a sweep of his sensual magic. Why hadn't I listened to intuition, all those times I'd suspected he was Aunt Lillian's shill?

I stepped into the study, with its heavy furniture and the lingering hint of Daddy's cigars, and stared.

Desiree Harte sat behind the massive desk, her hands folded over the open ledger.

'I'm *so* glad we had Mrs Marley make you that gown, Vanita,' she purred. 'It shows you off to great advantage. Makes you, my prize, all the more appealing.'

It took a moment to find my tongue, and then my anger flared up in one huge swoop. 'What the hell are *you* doing here? You've got no right to –'

'Did you really think I'd let you off the hook?' she jeered. 'It was one thing to fool Daddy in that swing, and then enlist Damon's help to snag him on the dancer platform. But when you turn on *me*, Vanita, you've got hell to pay!'

I didn't like the way her face went even paler with her rage – the way she stood up behind the desk, her pink gaze so heated she could've set my dress afire. 'I don't owe you a thing, Desiree,' I snapped. 'The original arrangement – one I never asked for or deserved – was between my aunt and your father. And it involved your brother and me.'

'But you didn't keep your deal! You never got Damon to fuck you!' she said in a voice approaching a shriek. She came around the desk, her upswept platinum hair quavering with her rage. 'And in the process, when my brother and I tried to help you – out of the kindness of our hearts! – you turned my mother against me, too! I wanted you for myself, Vanita, and Mama took *your* part! Helped you get away! Well, I won't stand for that!'

She was on me then, and when Aunt Lillian stepped behind me I realised I'd been played as a pawn once again. Would these people never stop scheming against me?

'I'll show you who you really are,' Desiree spat, grabbing the collar of my dress. With a sweep of her slender arm, she sent the ledger and the ink bottle flying from the desk. 'Underneath these pretty clothes – underneath these delusions of your superior status – you're just as greedy as the rest of us! Somebody touches you there, and you cave in! Slut!'

My aunt was laughing out loud, enjoying every moment as I got tossed upon the desk. She hooked her hands around my armpits, cradling me against her breasts to torment me more. 'You should've stayed at Harte's Haven,' she grunted as I struggled against her. 'You'd have lived in splendour there, with people who obviously can't get enough of you. Too bad you didn't see that I had your best interests in mind.'

I cried out as Desiree yanked my skirts up over my legs. I kicked at her, but with that phenomenal strength she'd displayed before, she placed a hand on each of my thighs to prise them open, and then rested her weight upon them.

'I smell your sex,' she rasped, becoming visibly aroused. 'You've spent yourself – your bloomers reek of it! Was it Pearce who brought you off? Or did Mama and her dwarf go at you? Either way, you know it was *I* who made you quiver and sing in that swing. It was *I* who licked you senseless on the carousel! And look at you!'

She tore my bloomers away at the split crotch, so caught up in her vengeance she didn't hear her father walk in behind her. 'You're soaked, Vanita! Squirming for it – oozing out honey so I'll lap at you like a hungry pup! God knows I've been sniffing at you since you came to us.'

She dipped her head to shove her tongue up me, nipping at my clit until I couldn't help but cry out. Franklin Harte watched smugly, tapping the gold head of his cane against his gloved palm: once his rabid daughter finished, he intended to take his turn. Aunt

Lill didn't seem a bit surprised about any of this, which told me these three had concocted another plot to keep me from reclaiming my home. I'd played myself into their hands by not waiting for Pearce to return.

Desiree danced around my clit with the tip of her tongue, reaching up to cup my breasts. Her breath fanned my sensitive flesh and she kept the edge of her teeth against my swollen folds, to remind me what havoc she could wreak if I protested. Pillowed against Aunt Lill's bosom, with my legs splayed on either side of a bobbing white topknot, I must've made an enticing sight for the man watching us. Franklin's face grew ruddier. As he fumbled with the fastenings on his pants, it was clear he was near the boiling point.

'Oh, God, would you look at it!' Aunt Lill said hoarsely.

How could I not? As his white trousers dropped, that plum-coloured shaft jutted towards me, veined and pulsing with an intent no woman could mistake. His kidskin fingers encircled it, squeezing and pumping, making his shirt-tails flutter like white flags. But a truce was the last thing on his mind.

'At last,' he murmured, stepping closer. 'You foiled me before, but this is an even more splendid opportunity! Claiming my prize – my due – on your daddy's desk, while my two favourite women look on. It's almost worth the trouble and expense you've caused me, Vanita.'

With that, he dropped his cane and shoved Desiree aside. His eyes glittered like black buckshot in a face the colour of raw meat. His daughter squealed, wiping her mouth with the back of her hand while sending him a murderous look, but he'd already stepped between my legs.

'Get alongside her, both of you!' he rasped, still fondling the shaft that was only inches from its target.

'Take an arm and a leg. We've got her where we want her now, powerless and spread before us for the taking.'

'But she's mine, Daddy!'

'Not until I've avenged the mockery she's made of our bargain. Vanita Wells is the *last* woman I'll allow to scandalise the Harte name by escaping, when she's betrothed to my son!' He paused to catch his breath, and to shove two gloved fingers inside me as I tried to wiggle away. 'She must learn to submit. She must know her place – beneath the man who will bend her will to his own!'

Was that horses' hooves I heard, or the pounding of my own pulse? Or the final countdown of my impending doom – as ominous as the bonging of all those clocks in the Harte mansion? Once again I was on my own, pitting my wits against those who should have loved or at least respected me, rather than rendering me helpless.

This thought inspired me, for it was a powerless victim Franklin Harte preferred. I calmed myself, hoping my ploy would at least buy me some time. From over Harte's white linen shoulder, Daddy's portrait looked straight at me, inspiring me to triumph over this madman and save the Wells reputation, along with the estate.

'Plunge it into me, *please*, oh please, Daddy!' I crooned in the most brazen voice I could muster. 'It's you I've been waiting for all along. *You* I want to feel gushing inside me.'

He sucked air, his gaze wavering. 'Liar. And a poor one, at that.'

'But no!' I continued, my confidence woven with the single thread of hope I had left. 'I loved it when you tied me, hand and foot, in your carriage! I revel in the power you've allowed me, the overwhelming power of my passion when I arouse you this way. You want me on top of you, pumping that mighty piston while you lose yourself in me. I want to suck you hard, Daddy. I want to swallow you whole, Da–'

With a disgusted grunt, he dropped his drooping cock. 'Damn you, Vanita, for –'

'That's my girl!' a familiar voice crowed from the hallway. 'Knows how to bring a man to his knees, for better or worse! You're finished, Harte. In every sense of the word.'

'You don't know a thing about it,' the tobacco baron snarled.

He instinctively made a swipe for his cane, but Pearce had rushed into the study and beat him to it. Dressed all in black, with his devilish beard regrown, he resembled a panther ready to pounce. 'Oh, but it's my job to know everything about you,' he said in a tight voice. 'Like how you embezzled Wellspring away from Lillian, piece by piece – placing huge bets at the race track, and then claiming her horses had lost, so you could pocket the winnings. Or selling her breeding stock at full value and then saying you only got half – or just pasturing them on your own land.'

'That's so ridiculous it doesn't deserve –'

'Or how about this one?' Truman demanded, his nose only inches from Harte's. 'Challenging her to strip poker, with some of your cronies in on the game, and not mentioning you played with a marked deck. Bamboozling thousands of dollars at a time!'

At my right, Aunt Lillian drew in a sharp breath. 'I *thought* something smelled fishy about those games! And now you're telling me –'

'That was the scent of your own wet pussy, Lillian,' Franklin said with a sneer. 'You loved every minute of flaunting your assets for us, and you know it!'

'But if the game was rigged –'

'And I have the marked deck that proves it was,' a sonorous voice chimed in. A stalwart man in a pin-striped suit came to stand beside Pearce, riffling a deck of cards between his thick fingers. Close behind the judge came another sombrely dressed professional I'd known for years.

'And we proffer our apologies, Miss Lillian,' the banker began, 'for taking part in what we assumed was all in fun, because Franklin said he returned your winnings in private.' Mr Cornelius scowled at the man in white, thoroughly disgusted at catching him with his trousers down. 'I never thought you'd sink so low, Harte. Or needed to.'

'Judge Cavendish,' my aunt breathed. She was gripping my arm so hard I could feel her pulse overriding mine. 'And Beale Cornelius. What do you mean, he *needed* to?'

'It's all clap-trap,' Franklin retorted, yanking up his pants. 'You knew the stakes when we began, Lillian. You asked me to place those bets at the track, and to invest some of your money in my mines to cover your spendthrift ways, and it didn't pan out.'

'But if you cheated me – if you intentionally –' Aunt Lillian turned me loose, her henna-red chignon aquiver with indignation. 'It was one thing to forfeit that money through my own foolishness. But to entrust you with it – and then learn you played me false on all counts –!'

'Save it, Lillian,' Franklin muttered. 'Don't be whining about what you so willingly turned over to me. You never cared about maintaining the stables, anyway.'

'But you kept baiting me, saying that *this* time, or *next* time, I could win it all back!' she cried. 'Had I known I was risking the deed on the turn of a marked card –'

'The Queen of diamonds, as I recall,' the judge remarked quietly.

'– I'd have turned you over to the sheriff!'

Harte shrugged, although his cockiness was fading. 'Harry Price would've sided with me, too, you know.'

'But that's all come to a halt,' another imperious voice announced, and Clive Reilly strode into the study with a sheaf of papers. He was fully dressed this time, as commanding a presence as when he'd managed the estate for Daddy.

I sat up on the desk, freeing myself from Desiree's grasp so I could smooth my skirts into place. Things were happening so fast that neither of us had commented; the young woman's expression withered as she looked from the judge to the banker to the lawyer, and then to her daddy. It was one thing to count Beale among her secret cross-dressing, father-crossing friends, but I doubt Miss Harte had considered the consequences of the banker taking him to task for his misdeeds against me.

'I have here the records from the race track, and sworn statements from others involved in your swindling,' Mr Reilly addressed Franklin, 'and on behalf of Miss Vanita, I'm demanding you turn over the deed to the estate, and make restitution for all breeding stock and loss of income over these past months you've been playing her guardian false.'

'That's the most ridiculous thing I ever heard!' Franklin guffawed, glancing at his cronies to rally their support. 'Lillian lost the estate by her own foolishness.'

'Perhaps. But since the property wasn't hers to gamble away in the first place, she, too, faces charges of mishandling the affairs of a minor dependant.' Clive's stern expression brooked no argument as he looked first at the red-haired siren shivering in her silky robe, and then back to Franklin. 'I'm suggesting you should be gentleman enough – honourable enough – to restore everything Vanita has lost, without a fight. If only to keep your ladyfriend out of jail.'

'Ladyfriend? Hell, Reilly, she's your whore, too!'

'Indeed!' my aunt clucked, crossing her arms beneath her cushiony bosom. 'I thought we had an arrangement, Clive. I thought –'

'I saw it as my duty to get more ... personally involved, when I suspected chicanery that would cost my client her intended inheritance.'

The attorney stood as tall as his diminutive frame allowed, refusing to back down despite the daggers shooting from Aunt Lillian's eyes. 'So please,' he commanded the tobacco baron. 'Let's settle this like civilised human beings. We can all get on with our lives – put this nasty business behind us – if you'll sign the deed back over, and also sign this document, which lists the articles and horses involved and their replacement values.'

As he extended the vellum pages towards Franklin Harte, the rest of us looked on in silence. We three women remained clustered near the desk, each of us pondering our personal stakes in this transaction, while Judge Cavendish and Mr Cornelius stood on either side of Pearce. The man in black gazed gravely at the plantation owner, his beard bristling when he clenched his teeth. The study resonated with an airless silence, as though time were holding its breath, awaiting this momentous decision.

Harte, however, began to shake with laughter. 'You can ask for whatever you want, for sweet little Vanita here, but you'll not be getting it. You see, I've *sold* Wellspring! So it's not mine to return!'

In the time it took my jaw to drop, Desiree sprang forwards. 'But Daddy, you said you'd give this place to *me*, because Damon was getting Vanita! You've lied to me again, you –'

She lunged at her father, but he caught her roughly against his side. 'We're all sick of your snivelling, little girl!' he snapped. 'I should've done more spanking and applied more discipline when you were a child.'

He glanced warily at us all, stepping purposefully towards the door with his struggling daughter in tow. 'I think we all know this drama's come to a close, and that I must get my recalcitrant child back home. You and your niece have a week to pack up and leave, Lillian.'

'It's not going to happen that way.'

Pearce's coiled voice silenced the room as he moved towards the door. 'Sheriff Price is waiting right outside, Harte. I'm sure he'd drop Desiree by the house on the way to town, where you'll either await your trial or settle up.'

'Trial, my ass! You've got nothing on me, Truman. You and this little pussy-whipped Reilly can take this matter to *my* attorney –'

'It's too late for that, Franklin.'

Rutherford Cavendish – one of Harte's good-old-boy cronies – stepped calmly to one side of the door while Beale assumed a position within grabbing distance as well. 'I warned you that your gambling habits would be your ruination, and your creditors have compiled an appalling list of unpaid debts, which your banker here confirms you can't cover. You should, of course, contact your attorney. But you don't have an ice chip's chance in hell of getting out of this.'

Harte's face darkened dangerously. He opened his mouth to protest, but Desiree beat him to it. 'Daddy, this doesn't mean – you can't tell me you've gambled away *our* home, too!' She began blubbering, the wild, uninhibited sobs of a spoilt child finally laid low.

'Stop your bawling before I give you something to bawl about!' her father muttered, and he shoved her into the hallway. With his banker and the old judge alongside him, and Desiree looking decidedly grim, the walk to the sheriff's waiting carriage resembled a funeral march. Recalling Beale and Harry in their female cosmetics and formal wear – was it only a week ago? – while the judge hollered out his lecherous support for Franklin, I sat astounded at the turnabout of my situation. What had come to a boil this past hour had obviously been on the burner longer than most of us knew, to be served up with such swift efficiency.

Clive Reilly watched the carriages leave, and then turned back to the three of us remaining in Daddy's sanctum.

'All's well that ends well,' he quipped, but his voice sounded thin – perhaps because Aunt Lillian stood with her fist planted on one hip, glaring at him. 'Shall we go, my dear? The sooner we tend to these other matters, the sooner –'

'And what other matters might those be?' she demanded. She towered over the man who'd once done her every bidding naked, and she intended to have her way with him again. 'If you're insinuating that I face charges of cheating my niece, then we need to *talk*, ducky! *You* were a willing accomplice at every turn! So willing, Mr Truman and Vanita would be shocked to learn how you begged and grovelled for my attentions!'

Reilly glanced nervously at me before responding. 'Be that as it may, princess, I was never involved in your dealings with Harte. In fact, I tried to dissuade you from keeping his company! You'll thank me for the way I recovered as much as I could these past months, depositing it in blind accounts so you couldn't lose it again.

'You see, I'm indeed a fool for you, Miss Lillian. In

more ways than you know,' he continued softly. 'I couldn't bear to see you homeless and disgraced.'

This heartfelt confession rendered the little attorney a curious shade of pink around his collar. His Adam's apple bobbed as he swallowed, looking up into the artfully drawn face inches above his own.

Lillian blinked. 'You're saying it wasn't all a farce, then? That those promises and love words you whispered with the tickling of my whip weren't just sweet nothings?'

'I'm a man of my word, Miss Lillian,' he insisted, his face aglow despite his more serious tone. 'I can't deny you face some serious charges – unless your niece sees fit to dismiss them ... or you allow me to set things right with the bank.'

'But you love me? Like you swore after I bound you to the bedpost?' She looked as befuddled as I'd ever seen her. I guess Aunt Lillian was amazed that a respected man like Mr Reilly was accepting her for the woman she was, willing to wipe her slate clean – but not *too* clean.

'I can't imagine living without you,' he breathed, again glancing nervously at me for understanding. 'You realise, of course, that my involvement in this whole affair began with my commitment to Miss Vanita, and to her daddy before her. I'm crazy for you, Lillian,' he repeated as he offered his bent arm, 'but my client comes first.'

'Words for any good watchdog of justice to live by,' Pearce intoned as we watched the oddly matched pair spar all the way to the Reilly's carriage. Then he raised an eyebrow in that devilish way of his. 'I certainly make it *my* practice for my clients to come first. Eh, love?'

23 My Real Heroes, Revealed

Something about the set of his bearded jaw told me the mystery of Pearce Truman was about to be solved: after these weeks of his vows and disappearings and dark, mystical gazes, as victory after little victory got snatched away from us, I now realised that this whole complicated affair had played out as though he'd written the script himself. Things had come together too smoothly, despite the unpredictable obstacles the Hartes threw in our path, to have been left to chance.

'Who *are* you, then?' I demanded, feeling a frustrated wonderment for the man who surveyed me so calmly. 'Dammit, Pearce, I've bared my heart and soul –'

'And your body. And I want them all, Vanita.'

'– and you've given me *nothing* to go on! Daddy would remind me of my manners – that I should thank you for all you've done to make Franklin and Aunt Lillian accountable for their misdeeds. But you've pushed me past my limits!' Crossing my arms, I forced his answer with my silence.

'Your face takes on a gorgeous glow when you're angry,' he whispered, his dark eyes focusing lower. 'And the way that stance brings your breasts to such a ... peak, why –'

'No changing the subject!' I cried. 'Who are you? And why are you here, really?'

'I knew you wouldn't let that go unanswered. You've got a mind like a steel trap – and I'm the poor sucker you've caught in it.' With a slight bow and a chuckle, he reached into his back pocket. 'Allow me to introduce myself, Miss Wells. Pearce Truman, Pinkerton operative, at your service. Hoping to service you many, many times in the years to come.'

I gripped his hand to steady the badge he proffered, to read the bold printing arranged around a human eye. '"Pinkerton National Detective Agency. We Never Sleep."'

'Rather appropriate, considering how you and I behave in each other's presence. With or without a bed,' he added, stepping close to enfold me in his arms. 'So you see, sweet Vanita, I've broken all the rules of my profession by allowing my heart to rule my head, and by getting involved with a client. You know, I hope, that this ceased to be a mere case assignment for me the moment I laid eyes on you.'

This took me back to what I'd seen through Miss Purvey's window ... to the way he'd backed me into my armoire, seducing me with his mystical words and obsidian eyes, daring me to believe in his powers. Indeed, as I looked up at him I saw the Devil's apprentice, a man with a demon's moustache who'd revealed more about me than I'd ever learned at the School for Young Ladies.

But as the realities of this past hour set in, I couldn't ignore the obvious.

'That's all well and good,' I replied sadly, running my finger along his dark, masculine jaw, 'but it doesn't get my land back, does it? If Harte has sold Wellspring, I'm no better off than when you fetched me home from school. Through no fault of yours, of course.'

His smile tore at me, because I so badly wanted to believe in it – so desperately needed to know he hadn't failed me, after all. Without even realising it, I'd come to trust this man, and although my faith in him had wavered a few times, I'd pulled through many a misadventure just to see if he'd make good on his promises.

'On the contrary, Vanita,' he breathed, this time reaching into the back of his pants, 'I have restored your estate, and arranged for several of your horses to be returned. Harte doesn't have the slightest idea, but it was I who bought Wellspring.'

Too surprised to speak, I snatched the document from his hand to stare at it. It was a crisp new deed, with a bill of sale displaying Pearce's showy signature. 'How'd you do this?' I cried. 'How'd you sneak this transaction past Franklin, and Aunt Lillian, too?'

'Smoke and mirrors? Black magic, perhaps?' Grinning, he underlined my name on the deed with his finger. 'Reilly and Cavendish collaborated on the set-up, when they realised how far along Harte's financial straits had progressed. We've been watching him for months now – mostly because Clara Purvey suspected your aunt's involvement in some sort of scheme, when Lillian insisted you not come home for the holidays.'

I considered this with a sigh. 'I've never cared much for Mama's sister, but I didn't think she'd sink so low as to gamble away my home.'

'And from all indications, at the track and during Clive's personal observations, we believe she fell in over her head. Thought she could recover her losses by plying her feminine wiles, but Harte was playing her fast and loose – and playing for keeps, so his own estate didn't get sucked under. High rollers out for revenge rarely make good, you know.'

It made sense: just as Franklin revelled in taking advantage of me because I was Jared and Olivia's daughter, he delighted in duping Aunt Lillian because she was so willing to be had. I firmly believed Mama never gave herself to him. And although I despised what my aunt had done in my absence, I realised she was more a victim of her own foolishness – and Harte's evil intent – than a criminal.

We still hadn't arrived at the bottom line, however. 'So you bought Wellspring outright?'

Pearce smiled with a gentility I hadn't noticed before. Indeed, he stood taller and took on a regal bearing. 'Best investment I ever made,' he boasted. 'My mother's family raised Lippizaners in Spain before she emigrated here with my father – an Englishman who recognised the opportunity for breeding fine horseflesh on Kentucky pastureland. So you see, it takes more than an ordinary filly to turn my head, sweetheart.'

Heat rose into my cheeks. Even though he was speaking with an openness he'd not shown before, the seductive press of his erection against my middle reminded me of his more carnal side ... the side I'd delighted in from the start. It was no time to get distracted by that, however.

'But how can I repay you?' I said softly. 'Even if my name's on this deed, I have no funds to cover your fee, Agent Truman. The idea was for Harte to return what he stole, not for you to pay my way home.'

He took my face between his supple hands, the answer to my plea shining with love – and obvious lust – in his bottomless green eyes. 'As I said, this began as a professional endeavour. But once I learned that Miss Purvey's pupil wasn't some homely wall-flower with a padlock on her chastity belt, I decided Wellspring would be the perfect gift to woo you with. To show you how much I admire your spirit, Vanita, because I hope we can keep on adventuring together.'

'But I can't let you just *give* it to me!'

'Why not?' He lowered his face so I stood in his seductive shadow, awaiting the kiss in his eyes. 'You made a deal with this devil, and you kept your part of the bargain. Just as I have.'

'But I didn't know –'

'Because I couldn't tell you. Couldn't risk revealing myself to anyone but Reilly, for fear the whole case against Harte would cave in.' Pearce grinned, undeniably proud of himself. 'And in the meantime, I've gotten that bastard out of Alice's hair, too. She's lost a few levels of luxury, but she can come out of that cave. Has a home and the tobacco fields and the mines – not to mention two devoted children. Or one is, anyway.'

I rolled my eyes, not allowing myself to think about how close I'd come to being held captive at Harte's Haven by Desiree's duplicity.

'I'm sure you could tell me horrible stories about that scheming feist,' he said, smoothing away the crease in my brow. 'But now that you're no longer trying for Damon, or at the mercy of that bastard Franklin, perhaps I can help you forget the nasty ways Desiree took out her frustrations. That's what it was, you know. The way she looked at you was a dead giveaway as far as her true feelings are concerned.'

There was a time such a statement would have sickened me. Pearce hadn't stated anything I didn't already know, however. I felt myself relaxing against him, against that randy ridge he was rubbing my stomach with. 'They lead a limited life, those twins,' I murmured, 'and while I'd dearly love to see that little bitch pay for the ways she played me false ... the worst revenge of all was built into her genes. Maybe she was relieved – overjoyed, even – when Franklin told her she couldn't be his child.'

Pearce kissed me gently, trying to distract me from such serious thoughts. 'She's a helluva hostess, though. I hope she'll keep us on her guest list.'

With a playful slap, I answered, 'Wouldn't be much of a party without Damon's toys, would it? Now *there's* a man with an imagination!'

'Oh, I don't know. There's something lacking in a man who can't set aside a few principles to love a fine filly like you, Vanita. Not that I mind being the only one.'

He kissed me insistently then, scattering my last bad thoughts about Harte's Haven and its unusual family. His beard rasped lightly against my skin as his passions rose; his hips wiggled a blatant invitation that made me realise how much more a woman I'd become since I met this wanton sorcerer. He'd seen me in my darkest hours and still wanted me for who I was, rather than what I could give him. I owed this man in black a lot more than whatever he'd paid for Wellspring – as Daddy's gaze from that portrait on the wall reminded me.

'Thank you,' I murmured. And because the expression on his dusky face drove away all rational thought, I could only say it again. 'Thank you, Pearce.'

'So you accept Wellspring as my gift?' Childlike delight shone in those green eyes, which gave him a whole new appearance. 'You're quite welcome, love.'

'No, I mean thank you . . . for teaching me to delve beneath the surface,' I said after a moment's thought, 'and for showing me how believing really is seeing – that what I believe is true, despite what others might try to mislead me with.'

When he held my hands against his chest, I could feel a halting in his heartbeat. 'And do you believe I love you, Vanita?' he breathed.

His words rang sweetly, the words every woman longs to see as a door opening to the rest of her life. I tried not to snicker: Pearce's cock was now quivering against me, insinuating its seductive heat through all the layers of our clothing – and every cell of my soul, as well.

'Yes, I believe you do,' I whispered, wiggling against

him, in spite of the moment's seriousness. 'And I believe I've fallen quite hard, quite deeply in love with you, as well.'

'Hard ... deeply. Words every man does his damnedest to bring together.' He kissed me again, his mouth working so urgently that our teeth collided. 'I've thought of a way you can repay me, Vanita. I know it's a matter of personal pride and integrity for you to do so, so I won't deny you.'

'You never were much for denying me, Pearce.'

'Nor shall I deny myself,' he replied, toying with the buttons of my gown. Then, as though suddenly recalling an urgent errand, he glanced towards the vestibule, which was growing dim in the shadow of late afternoon. 'We'll just pick up your valise, hop into my hired carriage, and get ourselves to St Louis. I dare you to go the whole way naked.'

I blinked, jarred by his sudden suggestion. 'St Louis? But we just got –'

'I have another promise to keep. For another woman.' He opened the bodice of my dress enough to slip his hand inside, to tease my nipple into an aching bud that rubbed against his palm of its own accord. 'Indulge me, Vanita. I won't hold back during the drive this time – and I certainly won't abandon you in our steamer cabin. You'll see Pearce Truman for the man he is. For the man he wants to be, with you.'

Stifling our giggles – for Pearce and I had laughed and made love the entire way from Kentucky – we slipped into Miss Purvey's office from the garden. Our aim was to surprise the headmistress not only with our unannounced arrival, but with an invitation to the wedding we'd planned for late summer. It seemed fitting to enter this sanctum through the window where I'd first seen Pearce in action, and he'd spotted me watching.

We made every effort not to give away our presence as we landed hard on her floor.

We needn't have worried, really: the punctual Miss Purvey wouldn't arrive until nine, and the sun was yawning at the far horizon. I stood for a moment, drinking in the familiar scent of lemon wax and the ticking of the clock – only one! – in the cool dimness of this room where I'd spent so many industrious hours. It seemed like a lifetime ago since I'd been a student at the School for Young Ladies, even though only a few weeks had passed.

The sparkle in Pearce's eye as he sank into the desk chair made my pulse trot. 'Here?' I breathed, as though the room had pulled me back into my former, modest self.

'Everywhere,' he replied, his whisper sibilant in the hushed room. 'You're mine and I never want to be without you, love. Never want to be more than a heartbeat away from penetrating your tight, hot pussy.'

'It's what you do best, right?'

'I've proven my point over and over, haven't I?'

Damn the man, he'd unfastened his pants and was waving a shaft that rose like a flagpole from his lap. Quite a point, indeed. I'd lost count of how many times and ways he'd taken me with it during our three-day journey.

'Suck me, Vanita. Then sit on me and pump until we have to muffle each other's screams,' he breathed in that sorcerer's voice. 'You're already wet for me. The honey's running down your thighs ... your bloomers would be soaked and smelling of sex for the rest of the day – if you had the decency to wear any.'

Yet again he pulled me over that edge, where I shucked propriety and allowed myself the ultimate pleasure of pleasing Pearce – and myself. With a final, hesitant glance at Clara Purvey's closed door, I knelt between his black-clad thighs. His sigh was its own reward as I slipped my wet lips over the hard, red head of his erection . . . so magnificent he was, pulsing at the touch of my tongue, all hot and slick and solid as I slid up and down the length of him. The hands framing my face tightened as he quivered.

'I want you . . . God, how I want you, Vanita . . . take me *now*.'

Could a woman resist such a plea, uttered with a desperate desire that never seemed to wane? The moment I rose, Pearce was lifting the skirt of my paisley-print gown, coaxing me on to his lap so my legs would wrap around him in the armless chair. He slid forwards beneath me, adjusting his angle so that with the first blissful plunge, he went right to that sweet spot we'd found high inside me . . . the place that sent me into immediate need, yet let me hover on the edge of ecstasy for a long, lovely time. I leaned forwards, shamelessly rubbing my clitoris in his coarse hair . . . hearing the music of our bodies in the rustle of this contact and the squelch of our wetness and our irregular breathing.

From deep inside me came the siren call of a climax, the kind that sent my head lolling back as I clenched my eyes and teeth in a silent scream. Pearce grabbed my backside and held me against his undulating hips, his own face tight with imminent release. He'd become so familiar with my body and its responses that he knew the exact moment to rivet our eyes – to run the tip of his pink tongue around lips set off by his thin, black moustache, and start into a low groan that spurred me on every time.

With a gasp, I cut loose. I kissed him hard, to keep my cries from carrying into the hallway – swallowing his outburst, as well. We shuddered together, soaring for several seconds, until we could finally catch our breath.

'You've learned a great deal since you left us, Miss Wells. I'm so pleased to see you're continuing your education.'

I froze with my face buried in Pearce's shoulder. There was no way to pretend the headmistress hadn't walked in, however: not only was it impolite, but Clara Purvey had always refused to be ignored. Slowly I opened one eye. Pearce's chuckle resonated in his chest as I gauged her reaction.

'Cat's got her tongue,' he teased, wrapping his arms around me.

'A black cat named Pearce. Lapping up cream as his reward for a successful mission, I take it.' Miss Purvey remained in the doorway, wearing a dove-grey dress I knew well, and yes – her topknot still sat askew in that endearing way I thought I'd never see again. 'Why am I not surprised to find you two here? And back so soon!'

'You assigned me a mission, you know. And Vanita made a fine, efficient accomplice – just as you said she would. Obviously inspired by the finest of teachers.'

'Thank you, Mr Truman,' the headmistress chirped. 'If you'll excuse me, I'll go fetch something I just put into the mail.'

As her sensible shoes clacked purposefully down the hall, I let out the breath I'd been holding. I clambered off his lap, unable to keep from laughing yet still mortified at being caught in the act. 'I'll get you for this!' I whispered, frantically smoothing my skirts into place.

'Funny, I could swear you've had me dozens of times.' He stood to retuck his shirt, casting me a curious glance. 'Why does this bother you, sweetheart? At

Harte's Haven you were naked to the point you *displayed* yourself as you came. And you know Clara's far from shy about spreading her legs.'

'But this is like fucking in front of my mother! Now hush – here she comes!' Smoothing my hair, I did my best to compose myself, suspecting that my lips looked overkissed and my dress was a mess, and the shine in my eyes gave away all I'd been doing these past several days.

Yet Miss Purvey, ever the epitome of decorum, graced me with a sweet smile and came straight at me for a hug. 'You look radiant, dear, and I'm so pleased to see it! We obviously have a lot to catch up on, but first –'

She handed me a large envelope, her eyes alight.

My hands shook as I tore the seal, for I'd expected to deliver news rather than receive it. And when I pulled out the stiff parchment, and saw my name written in elegant script beneath the school's arched heading, tears sprang to my eyes. 'My diploma! But I didn't –'

'The headmistress has the discretion of awarding degrees based upon academic performance and exemplary behaviour,' she intoned with a sly glance at Pearce. 'I was hoping it might lift your spirits as you dealt with a difficult situation. I can't tell you how glad I am to see you smiling, Vanita. You've apparently claimed much more than your beloved estate.'

I giggled nervously, launching into my announcement without regard for her instruction in declamation and decorum. 'Pearce and I are getting married next month! And of course, we want you to come!'

She clapped her hands together. 'I wouldn't miss it! How lovely for you both!'

'I have *you* to thank, Miss Purvey, for introducing us ... and for sensing all wasn't well at Wellspring,' I added humbly.

'Yes, well, after a thorough investigation on my part – and being just as deeply probed by Mr Truman – I surmised he was the man for the job,' she replied. And somehow, she kept a straight face when she said that. 'Since you have no mother, I've always felt responsible for your welfare, Vanita. But I'd be less than forthright if I took full credit.'

Miss Purvey arched a thin brow at Pearce, who was taking in our chatter with an indulgent smile. 'How much does she know?'

'Not this part. Had I not found numerous ways to . . . distract her, though, she might've figured it out.'

'Fine. I'll be right back.' With a smile almost as mysterious as Pearce's, she gripped my hand. 'There's someone waiting to see you, dear. I think you'll understand why we felt compelled to keep this secret – that it was by no means to hurt you.'

I stared after her, totally confused. What could possibly be left, now that I'd reclaimed my estate, and would even have horses grazing in my pastures when I got back? I gripped my diploma, gazing at my fiancé, and couldn't comprehend any sort of fulfillment I lacked. 'You're not going to tell me, are you?'

'Some things speak best for themselves, love. And sometimes, seeing is believing.'

There it was again, that mystical wisdom that set Pearce Truman several levels above anyone else I'd ever known. Understated; elegant in his simplicity – yet so emotionally complex I'd require a lifetime to truly figure him out. When I heard two sets of footsteps approaching, I managed to pull my enamoured gaze from his – and then let out a little cry.

'Lorena! My God – Lorena! It's really you!'

I ran to that old maid's embrace, and the fears and nastiness of the past few weeks fell away. Her body felt frail, and I didn't want to see the deeper lines around her eyes – the coffee-coloured face that bespoke trials I could never know, at the hands of Aunt Lillian. But at least she wasn't dead, as I'd feared.

'Lordy-Lord, child, but I'm sure glad to see my girl!' she said with a cackle. She pulled back for a look at me, her eyes narrowing in that knowing way I remembered from childhood. 'You've gone and grown up since I last seen you, Miss Vanita. Your mama and daddy would be mighty proud . . . even if you've been misbehavin' a mite.'

She turned then, to give Pearce a thorough looking over. 'You done good, though, honey. Got you a fine stallion that'll mount every time he gets a whiff. And that's the only kind worth keepin' around.'

'I – Lorena, I –'

She laughed at my tongue-tripping, yet sharing the intimate humour reserved for mature women made me feel I had indeed made a choice my parents would have approved.

'You understand, don'tcha, child?' she went on in a more serious voice. 'When that pea-brained aunt of yours lost all the stock to her foolishness, Will didn't have no job – and we could see the writin' on the wall. I tried to stick it out – to be there for you, when you come home from this fine school to take over and set things right – cos I owed it to your mama. But we took Pegasus and stole off like thieves in the night. Had to get, while the gettin' was good.'

The tears were streaming down my face, and even stalwart old Lorena was sniffling when I hugged her close. 'You'll never know how glad I am to hear this,' I whispered, snuffling into the shoulder of her faded cotton dress.

'You should know that it was Lorena who told me of the goings-on at Wellspring,' Miss Purvey said quietly. 'It took them several days to make their way here from

Lexington, but it was my greatest pleasure to meet her and her brother, and to have them here, safe, while you and Pearce got the situation settled. I never met your Aunt Lill, but I suspect she was ... less than charitable to your mother's faithful companion.'

I looked up through teary eyes, my smile wobbly. 'Thank you, Miss Purvey. I – I can't possibly thank you enough. Why, with Lorena and Will to help us get reestablished – and the dearest gelding a girl ever had, still alive,' I added to tease Pearce, 'I foresee a fine, bright future for Wellspring. Don't you, dear?'

That black moustache flickered wickedly. 'Aren't you forgetting something?'

As though on cue, the ridge in his pants wiggled, like a wink – but it was Pearce's face that held me spellbound. Framed in that black beard, with an untamed mane of raven waves, he radiated a masculine magic that made me powerless to refuse him.

Wildfire surged through my insides, a desire I couldn't deny. Like a green-eyed demon he seemed, this man who had possessed me. Yet he'd brought me through the valley of the shadow and back, intact. More a woman than I could ever hope to be without him.

I went to stand in front of him, gripping the width of the shaft that so brazenly beckoned me from inside his pants – propriety and present company be damned! 'How could I forget this?' I whispered. 'Or the man attached to it?'

Pearce swallowed so hard his throat clicked, aware of our two observers yet focusing solely on me. He didn't flinch as I ran my thumb and forefinger down the length of his erection. In fact, the secretive curling of his lips told me he was loving this new power I'd found – the passion that would propel us into a love like no other.

'It seems we've each kept our part of this bargain, and we've set a whole new life into motion,' I continued quietly. 'All that remains is to establish who will ride ... and who will be ridden. Come along and find out, Pearce. I dare you.'

LOOK OUT FOR THE ALL-NEW BLACK LACE BOOKS – AVAILABLE NOW!

All books priced £6.99 in the UK. Please note publication dates apply to the UK only. For other territories, please contact your retailer.

SWEET THING
Alison Tyler
ISBN 0 352 33682 X

Jessica Taylor is stunning. An LA girl into old movies, she plays X-rated games with hep guys who look like James Dean. What she wants most of all, though, is to be a big-time reporter. Jessica's editor, Dashiell Cooper, holds that key, but what he wants is *her*. No longer a believer in love, the cynical Cooper lives only for the thrill of the chase. He uses a whole repertoire of charmer's tricks to try and seduce Jessica . . . but she's not so easily trapped. What transpires is a game of S&M cat and mouse set in the hush-hush world of LA gossip columns and naked ambition. Another great LA novel from the author of *Strictly Confidential*.

ELENA'S CONQUEST
Lisette Allen
ISBN: 0 352 32950 5

On a summer's day in the year 1070, young Elena is gathering herbs in the garden of the convent where she leads a peaceful but uneventful life. Lately she's been yearning for something sinful: the intimate touch of the well-built Saxon who haunts her dreams. When Norman soldiers besiege the convent and take Elena captive, she is chosen by the dark and masterful Lord Aimery le Sabrenn to satisfy his savage desires. Captivated by his powerful masculinity, Elena is then horrified to discover she is not the only woman in his castle; the sinister Lady Isobel –

le Sabrenn's wife – is a cruel but beautiful rival and is out to destroy her. This classic Black Lace reprint is packed with brawny Saxons and cruel Normans. Travel back in time and witness sexual jealousy in the time of William the Conqueror.

Coming in April 2002

KING'S PAWN

Ruth Fox

ISBN 0 352 33684 6

Cassie is consumed by a need to explore the intriguing world of SM – a world of bondage, domination and her submission. She agrees to give herself to the inscrutable Mr King for a day, to sample the pleasures of his complete control over her. Cassie finds herself hooked on the curious games they play. Her lesbian lover, Becky, is shocked, but agrees to Cassie visiting Mr King once more. It is then that she is initiated into the debauched Chessmen Club, where she is expected to go much further than she thought. A refreshingly honest story of a woman's introduction to SM. Written by a genuine scene-player.

TIGER LILY

Kimberley Dean

ISBN 0 352 33685 4

When Federal Agent Shanna McKay – aka Tiger Lily – is assigned to a new case on a tough precinct, her shady past returns to haunt her. She has to bust drug lord Mañuel Santos, who caused her sister's disappearance years previously. The McKay sisters had been wild: Shanna became hooked on sex; her sister hooked on Santos and his drugs. Desperate to even the score, Shanna infiltrates the organisation by using her most powerful weapon – her sexuality. Hard-hitting erotica mixes with low-life gangsters in a tough American police precinct. Sizzling, sleazy action that will have you on the edge of your seat!

COOKING UP A STORM
Emma Holly
ISBN 0 352 33686 2

The Coates Inn Restaurant in Cape Cod is about to go belly up when its attractive owner, Abby, jumps at a stranger's offer to help her – both in her kitchen and her bed. The handsome chef claims to have an aphrodisiac menu that her patrons won't be able to resist. Can this playboy chef really save the day when Abby's body means more to him than her feelings? He has charmed the pants off her and she's now behaving like a wild woman. Can Abby tear herself away from her new lover for long enough to realise that he might be trying to steal the restaurant from under her nose? Beautifully written and evocative story of love, lust and haute cuisine.

Coming in May 2002

SLAVE TO SUCCESS
Kimberley Raines
ISBN 0 352 33687 0

Eugene, born poor but grown-up handsome, answers an ad to be a sex slave for a year. He assumes his role will be that of a gigolo, and thinks he will easily make the million dollars he needs to break into Hollywood. On arrival at a secret destination he discovers his tasks are somewhat more demanding. He will be a pleasure slave to the mistress Olanthé – a demanding woman with high expectations who will put Eugene through some exacting physical punishments and pleasures. He is in for the shock of his life. An exotic tale of female domination over a beautiful but arrogant young man.

FULL EXPOSURE
Robyn Russell
ISBN 0 352 33688 9

Attractive but stern Boston academic, Donatella di'Bianchi, is in Arezzo, Italy, to investigate the affairs of the *Collegio Toscana*, a school of visual arts. Donatella's probe is hampered by one man, the director, Stewart Temple-Clarke. She is also sexually attracted by an English artist on the faculty, the alluring but mysterious Ian Ramsey. In the course of her inquiry Donatella is attacked, but receives help from two new friends – Kiki Lee and Francesca Antinori. As the trio investigates the menacing mysteries surrounding the college, these two young women open Donatella's eyes to a world of sexual adventure with artists, students, and even the local *carabinieri*. A stylishly sensual erotic thriller set in the languid heat of an Italian summer.

STRIPPED TO THE BONE
Jasmine Stone
ISBN 0 352 33463 0

Annie has always been a rebel. While her sister settled down in Middle America, Annie blazed a trail of fast living on the West Coast, constantly seeking thrills. She is motivated by a hungry sexuality and a mission to keep changing her life. Her capacity for experimental sex games means she's never short of partners, and she keeps her lovers in a spin of erotic confusion. Every man she encounters is determined to discover what makes her tick, yet no one can get a hold of Annie long enough to find out. Maybe the Russian Ilmar can unlock the secret. However, by succumbing to his charms, is Annie stepping into territory too dangerous even for her? By popular demand, this is a special reprint of a free-wheeling story of lust and trouble in a fast world.

Black Lace Booklist

Information is correct at time of printing. To avoid disappointment check availability before ordering. Go to www.blacklace-books.co.uk. All books are priced £6.99 unless another price is given.

BLACK LACE BOOKS WITH A CONTEMPORARY SETTING

- ❑ THE TOP OF HER GAME Emma Holly ISBN 0 352 33337 5 £5.99
- ❑ IN THE FLESH Emma Holly ISBN 0 352 33498 3 £5.99
- ❑ A PRIVATE VIEW Crystalle Valentino ISBN 0 352 33308 1 £5.99
- ❑ SHAMELESS Stella Black ISBN 0 352 33485 1 £5.99
- ❑ INTENSE BLUE Lyn Wood ISBN 0 352 33496 7 £5.99
- ❑ THE NAKED TRUTH Natasha Rostova ISBN 0 352 33497 5 £5.99
- ❑ ANIMAL PASSIONS Martine Marquand ISBN 0 352 33499 1 £5.99
- ❑ A SPORTING CHANCE Susie Raymond ISBN 0 352 33501 7 £5.99
- ❑ TAKING LIBERTIES Susie Raymond ISBN 0 352 33357 X £5.99
- ❑ A SCANDALOUS AFFAIR Holly Graham ISBN 0 352 33523 8 £5.99
- ❑ THE NAKED FLAME Crystalle Valentino ISBN 0 352 33528 9 £5.99
- ❑ CRASH COURSE Juliet Hastings ISBN 0 352 33018 X £5.99
- ❑ ON THE EDGE Laura Hamilton ISBN 0 352 33534 3 £5.99
- ❑ LURED BY LUST Tania Picarda ISBN 0 352 33533 5 £5.99
- ❑ THE HOTTEST PLACE Tabitha Flyte ISBN 0 352 33536 X £5.99
- ❑ THE NINETY DAYS OF GENEVIEVE Lucinda Carrington ISBN 0 352 33070 8 £5.99
- ❑ EARTHY DELIGHTS Tesni Morgan ISBN 0 352 33548 3 £5.99
- ❑ MAN HUNT Cathleen Ross ISBN 0 352 33583 1
- ❑ MÉNAGE Emma Holly ISBN 0 352 33231 X
- ❑ DREAMING SPIRES Juliet Hastings ISBN 0 352 33584 X
- ❑ THE TRANSFORMATION Natasha Rostova ISBN 0 352 33311 1
- ❑ STELLA DOES HOLLYWOOD Stella Black ISBN 0 352 33588 2
- ❑ UP TO NO GOOD Karen S. Smith ISBN 0 352 33589 0
- ❑ SIN.NET Helena Ravenscroft ISBN 0 352 33598 X
- ❑ HOTBED Portia Da Costa ISBN 0 352 33614 5
- ❑ TWO WEEKS IN TANGIER Annabel Lee ISBN 0 352 33599 8

- ❑ HIGHLAND FLING Jane Justine ISBN 0 352 33616 1
- ❑ PLAYING HARD Tina Troy ISBN 0 352 33617 X
- ❑ SYMPHONY X Jasmine Stone ISBN 0 352 33629 3
- ❑ STRICTLY CONFIDENTIAL Alison Tyler ISBN 0 352 33624 2
- ❑ SUMMER FEVER Anna Ricci ISBN 0 352 33625 0
- ❑ CONTINUUM Portia Da Costa ISBN 0 352 33120 8
- ❑ OPENING ACTS Suki Cunningham ISBN 0 352 33630 7
- ❑ FULL STEAM AHEAD Tabitha Flyte ISBN 0 352 33637 4
- ❑ A SECRET PLACE Ella Broussard ISBN 0 352 33307 3
- ❑ GAME FOR ANYTHING Lyn Wood ISBN 0 352 33639 0
- ❑ FORBIDDEN FRUIT Susie Raymond ISBN 0 352 33306 5
- ❑ CHEAP TRICK Astrid Fox ISBN 0 352 33640 4
- ❑ THE ORDER Dee Kelly ISBN 0 352 33652 8
- ❑ ALL THE TRIMMINGS Tesni Morgan ISBN 0 352 33641 3
- ❑ PLAYING WITH STARS Jan Hunter ISBN 0 352 33653 6
- ❑ THE GIFT OF SHAME Sara Hope-Walker ISBN 0 352 32935 1
- ❑ COMING UP ROSES Crystalle Valentino ISBN 0 352 33658 7
- ❑ GOING TOO FAR Laura Hamilton ISBN 0 352 33657 9
- ❑ THE STALLION Georgina Brown ISBN 0 352 33005 8
- ❑ DOWN UNDER Juliet Hastings ISBN 0 352 33663 3
- ❑ THE BITCH AND THE BASTARD Wendy Harris ISBN 0 352 33664 1
- ❑ ODALISQUE Fleur Reynolds ISBN 0 352 32887 8
- ❑ RELEASE ME Suki Cunningham ISBN 0 352 33671 4
- ❑ GONE WILD Maria Eppie ISBN 0 352 33670 6
- ❑ SWEET THING Alison Tyler ISBN 0 352 33682 X

BLACK LACE BOOKS WITH AN HISTORICAL SETTING

- ❑ PRIMAL SKIN Leona Benkt Rhys ISBN 0 352 33500 9 £5.99
- ❑ DEVIL'S FIRE Melissa MacNeal ISBN 0 352 33527 0 £5.99
- ❑ WILD KINGDOM Deanna Ashford ISBN 0 352 33549 1 £5.99
- ❑ DARKER THAN LOVE Kristina Lloyd ISBN 0 352 33279 4
- ❑ STAND AND DELIVER Helena Ravenscroft ISBN 0 352 33340 5 £5.99
- ❑ THE CAPTIVATION Natasha Rostova ISBN 0 352 33234 4
- ❑ CIRCO EROTICA Mercedes Kelley ISBN 0 352 33257 3
- ❑ MINX Megan Blythe ISBN 0 352 33638 2
- ❑ PLEASURE'S DAUGHTER Sedalia Johnson ISBN 0 352 33237 9

❑ JULIET RISING Cleo Cordell ISBN 0 352 32938 6

❑ ELENA'S CONQUEST Lisette Allen ISBN 0 352 32950 5

BLACK LACE ANTHOLOGIES

❑ CRUEL ENCHANTMENT Erotic Fairy Stories Janine Ashbless ISBN 0 352 33483 5 £5.99

❑ MORE WICKED WORDS Various ISBN 0 352 33487 8 £5.99

❑ WICKED WORDS 4 Various ISBN 0 352 33603 X

❑ WICKED WORDS 5 Various ISBN 0 352 33642 0

BLACK LACE NON-FICTION

❑ THE BLACK LACE BOOK OF WOMEN'S SEXUAL FANTASIES Ed. Kerri Sharp ISBN 0 352 33346 4 £5.99

To find out the latest information about Black Lace titles, check out the website: www.blacklace-books.co.uk or send for a booklist with complete synopses by writing to:

Black Lace Booklist, Virgin Books Ltd
Thames Wharf Studios
Rainville Road
London W6 9HA

Please include an SAE of decent size. Please note only British stamps are valid.

Our privacy policy
We will not disclose information you supply us to any other parties. We will not disclose any information which identifies you personally to any person without your express consent.

From time to time we may send out information about Black Lace books and special offers. Please tick here if you do not wish to receive Black Lace information. ❑

Please send me the books I have ticked above.

Name ....

Address ....

....

....

....

Post Code ....

Send to: Cash Sales, Black Lace Books, Thames Wharf Studios, Rainville Road, London W6 9HA.

US customers: for prices and details of how to order books for delivery by mail, call 1-800-343-4499.

Please enclose a cheque or postal order, made payable to Virgin Books Ltd, to the value of the books you have ordered plus postage and packing costs as follows:

UK and BFPO – £1.00 for the first book, 50p for each subsequent book.

Overseas (including Republic of Ireland) – £2.00 for the first book, £1.00 for each subsequent book.

If you would prefer to pay by VISA, ACCESS/MASTERCARD, DINERS CLUB, AMEX or SWITCH, please write your card number and expiry date here:

....

Signature ....

Please allow up to 28 days for delivery.